A

1000

THE EMPIRE OF LIGHTS

THE EMPIRE OF LIGHTS

Robert Grossmith

HAMISH HAMILTON · LONDON

HAMISH HAMILTON LTD

Published by the Penguin Group
27 Wrights Lane, London W8 5TZ, England
Viking Penguin Inc., 375 Hudson Street, New York, New York 10014, USA
Penguin Books Australia Ltd, Ringwood, Victoria, Australia
Penguin Books Canada Ltd, 2801 John Street, Markham, Ontario, Canada L3R 1B4
Penguin Books (NZ) Ltd, 182–190 Wairau Road, Auckland 10, New Zealand

Penguin Books Ltd, Registered Offices: Harmondsworth, Middlesex, England

First published 1990

Copyright © Robert Grossmith, 1990

The moral right of the author has been asserted

Filmset in 11/13½pt Monophoto Baskerville
Printed in Great Britain by Butler & Tanner Ltd, Frome and London

A CIP catalogue record for this book is available from the British Library
ISBN 0–241–13035–2

Take this kiss upon the brow!
And, in parting from you now,
Thus much let me avow –
You are not wrong who deem
That my days have been a dream;
Yet if hope has flown away
In a night, or in a day,
In a vision, or in none,
Is it therefore the less *gone*?
All that we see or seem
Is but a dream within a dream.

Poe, *A Dream Within a Dream*

PART ONE

It shall be called Bottom's Dream,
because it hath no bottom.
Shakespeare, *A Midsummer Night's Dream*

I

Shaft of sunlight in a dusty corridor. Smell of the past: dinners and disinfectant. A curious quiet as if he is the only person alive or awake. Wandering through the cloakrooms where everything seems so small, duffel coats hanging by hoods from hooks, not touching the floor. Pausing before a classroom, its glass-panelled door disclosing rows of desks and boys in uniform, their gaze directed frontwards to where the teacher, serious, intent, explains the workings of some elaborate mechanical contrivance possibly representing the solar system or the molecular structure of carbon, all rods and spheres and wheels-within-wheels. At his back a blackboard daubed with half-obliterated symbols, algebraic, Aramaic. Through the classroom window a view of the pyramids and the sand sloping down to the deserted shoreline, gulls hovering, a child's abandoned sandcastle half-ruined by the incoming tide. He moves on, feet slapping cold against the damp cracked flagstones. Looking down, he notices he is barefoot and his feet need a wash, each toenail rimmed with a thin arc of black. Someone is calling his name – 'Daniel! Daniel!' – but there is no one to be seen. A door opens behind him, a hand reaches out for his collar –

He awoke with a gasp and a violent lurch of limbs, entangling himself in the bedclothes as he struggled to beat away the crab-like claw attaching itself to his shoulder.

'Rise and shine, sleepyhead.'

It took him several moments to compose himself. 'Don't ever ... wake me up ... like that again,' he managed to utter. 'Shout if you have to. Put the radio on. Bang a saucepan at my ear. Whatever. Only never grab hold of me like that, d'you hear?' He sat up and reached for a cigarette. 'What time is it anyway?'

'God, you're touchy this morning. Twenty to nine.'

'Twenty to nine! Christ, I've got a class at nine. Why didn't you wake me?'

He ignored the reply, if there was one, and threw himself out of bed, trying to dress as he hopped, stumbling, mumbling, legs in a tangle of trouser, to the bathroom. Minutes later he was grabbing his briefcase and slamming the front door behind him.

Outside it had been snowing and in the milder air of the morning the snow was beginning to melt, turning to a thick, soupy sludge. Walking was wet and treacherous. As he turned the corner he saw his bus pulling away from the shelter across the road, discharging a thick cloud of brown–grey fumes behind it. He started to run and for a moment thought he would make it. Then he lost his balance, his legs slid away in opposite directions, and even as he told himself, 'I'm going to fall, this is going to hurt,' he was up-ended, sprawling, on to his back, hitting the ground with a thud, and he woke up again.

The impact of this second awakening catapulted him upright in bed, where he froze, rigid, afraid to move, as if to do so would be to threaten disturbing some delicate equilibrium he had achieved and return him, helpless, to the dream. He cast a wary sidelong glance at the bleary red eyes of the clock-radio on the bedside cabinet, which blinked as their gazes locked. 6.20.

Jesus, the human mind.

Emmy stirred beside him with a groan. 'Whasmatter, whatimesit?'

'Nothing, go back to sleep, I'm getting up.'

He gathered his clothes in a bundle and padded down the upstairs landing to the bathroom to dress. Without her eight hours Emmy was impossible. A pale, luminous glow in the lower half of the frosted window-pane above the bath-tub told him it had been snowing overnight. This in itself was not remarkable – it was March after all – but it provoked in him nonetheless a curious shudder of disquiet, as if his dream had somehow foretold the change. Characteristically, his mind sought the rational explanation: perhaps his body had registered subliminally the drop in temperature (they always slept with a window open on account of Emmy's asthma), and this had translated itself in his dream-language into 'snow'. Stranger things happened at sea. Why did that phrase come into his head? It was a phrase his mother had always used.

Shaving absently, ploughing for a third time the already bare and reddened knoll of his chin, he tried to fix in his mind before it vanished, like a painter sketching a fading sunset, the fragile texture of his dream. Thinking back on it now in the cold daylight of reason, he could see that it was actually marred by a number of minor errors and inconsistencies. There was the dialogue, for example, whose obvious artificiality ought to have alerted him at once: he would never speak to Emmy like that, nor she to him – 'Rise and shine, sleepyhead'? Then there was the smoking; he hadn't smoked in years. And the briefcase he didn't possess, preferring a large leather holdall for his books and papers. Of course, in the dream none of this had struck him as unusual, everything had seemed perfectly ordinary and unquestionable, and it was this, he now realized, that accounted for the vague sense of unease he still wasn't able to shake off. Who was to say he wasn't continuing to dream at this very moment, the old Cartesian chestnut? We think of ourselves as sane rational beings, yet each night we return, tired and forgetful, to the same old house of horrors. Or is unreason perhaps our natural state and waking life a lunatic's dream of the real?

He prepared himself a light breakfast of cereals, toast and coffee, relishing the early morning stillness, broken only by the sound of the Reveley twins in the garden across the road, already up and building a snowman. Some sort of dispute had arisen between them and Daniel watched with interest to see how it would develop. It saddened him sometimes to think that he and Emmy would probably never have children of their own. The boys were great of course, but they would always be Emmy's, not his. It was odd to think that when they got married back in 1980 (Sean was four, Liam three), he'd been full of self-congratulation, smugness even, at having acquired with so little effort such an attractive and ready-made family. How smart of you, a voice within him would pipe, to have avoided all those early years of broken sleep and excrement and noise, all that thankless ministering to helpless homunculi, to have given birth instead by a sort of painless parthenogenesis to beings if not fully formed then at least capable of developing human and emotional, rather than purely physical, purely animal, attachments. How clever to have simply skipped that stage and started at the rewarding part. Who needed dirty nappies and constant bawling anyway? But recently, disturbingly, this voice had begun to be joined by another, no less persuasive voice which said something rather different. It pointed out how far Daniel's life was constrained by the responsibilities of parenthood and how little genuine affection the boys ever seemed to show him. It whispered maliciously in his ear. What a mug, it said. Already in your thirties and nothing to show for it but a pile of bills, a job you despise – come on, admit it, you do despise it, don't you? – and the burden of providing for another man's abandoned offspring. What a mug, what a sucker.

The sound of footsteps from above his head signalled that the objects of his reflection were rising. Reluctant to relinquish his solitude, he decided to walk to work. The fresh air, besides, would do him good, help dispel the last remnants of the clinging dream. He finished his breakfast, wrote a short note for Emmy on the back of an old phone bill, adding a PS asking her to buy some marmalade, and left.

The snow lay loose and powdery on the ground, not at all as in his dream, a fact that afforded him some small comfort,

6

reducing his sense of prescience. The normally drab street had taken on an unfamiliar, festive aspect in the snow: the trees had been transformed into complicated jigsaws of light and shade, the pillar-box on the corner had donned a skull-cap, the roof-racks of parked cars were piled high with fluffy white linen as if it was they that had brought the stuff in. He had a sense of having stepped back in time into a black and white world, an old movie, *circa* 1930, and indeed he now noticed with alarm that the street did appear to have been drained of colour: the house-fronts, the cars, even the pillar-box on the corner, all were merely varying shades of grey. Before he could develop the full implications of this discovery, however, a sudden whistling by his left ear caused him to turn his head and duck as a swift white blur flashed into his field of vision. Raising an arm too late to protect himself, he only succeeded in compounding the glancing blow delivered to his temple by the icy missile arcing at him from across the street, by striking himself with his own hand as he awoke.

This was no joke. This was serious. This was fucking serious.

Rubbing the tender spot on his temple where he had fallen against the edge of the bedside cabinet, he hesitated, blinking himself awake, before nervously surveying his surroundings. Everything was in its right place, everything was behaving as it should. He climbed out of bed – it was August, not March, what was he thinking of? – and cautiously parted the curtains. A low yellow sun was preparing to mount a cloudless blue sky. He checked the time – 8.10 – and tried to calculate whether the sun was the correct height in the sky for the hour of day, but gave it up, not knowing what time the sun rose or how fast it travelled. He walked to the dressing-table and confronted his unshaven reflection in the mirror. Paradoxically, it was the solidity of this spectre in the glass that seemed to him to furnish the most irrefutable proof of his identity. There he stood, that familiar, slightly stooped, round-shouldered figure with the gap between his two front teeth, the bald patch spreading inexorably across his crown, the compensatory growth of wiry black hair sprouting from nostrils and ears, the small red scar, vestige of an old shaving wound, in the cleft of his chin, the dull, watery eyes. No mistaking that mug. He touched himself in various sensitive parts of his body; he felt real enough.

Again there were those errors, those flaws: the note asking Emmy to buy marmalade, for example, which he never ate, indeed hated; the twins playing in the garden opposite, when the family had in fact sold up and moved several months previously; the pillar-box on the corner which didn't exist.

'Mmm-nn-make some tea if you're getting up, will you?'

Emmy lay all but buried beneath a swathe of blankets, her head of brown hair spread fan-wise on the pillow, like fronds on snow.

'Emmy, listen to me, I want you to do something.'

'If it means getting up, no.'

He yanked the blankets from the bed. 'Listen to me!'

'What is it, what's the matter?'

'Nothing, everything's all right, I'm sorry. It's just ... look, I've been having this really ... these really weird dreams ... I keep thinking I've woken up and then it turns out I haven't, I'm still asleep and ... look, just shake me, will you?'

'What?'

'Shake me.'

She responded obediently, taking him by the shoulders and shaking. 'Like this?'

'Harder.'

She shook him again, harder, and nothing happened again. The world stayed as it was.

'Thank God for that.'

He sank down on the edge of the bed and dropped his head in his hands. He closed his eyes. There was a sudden shrill ringing in his ears and he woke up.

2

For a long time he went to bed late. Once the pattern was established, once it became clear that the dreams had entered his life as a regular nightly visitation, he began inventing excuses to sit up alone, dosing himself with cup after cup of strong black coffee, hoping to delay the inevitable descent into the maelstrom of his unconscious. He said nothing about the dreams to Emmy. Why burden her with additional worries? She had enough to cope with at the moment, what with the problems they were having with Liam: the bed-wetting, the fear of the dark, the unruliness at school. Besides, she still hadn't fully recovered from the death of her father – does one ever really recover from that sort of thing? – at the nursing home the previous winter. Her father, senile, demented, wasted to a stick, no longer the man she knew and adored, the man whose awful jokes and groaning puns would send her into paroxysms of girlish giggles, but an alien who'd usurped his body, a man without memory, without humour, without a past. Poor old Sam. Poor Emmy.

'I'm going up then. Are you coming?'

'Think I'll just watch the end of this, love,' he said. A late-night Hammer horror film from the seventies. How dated they looked now. Had anyone ever really been frightened by these schlocky low-budget tales of anaemic vampires and moonstruck werewolves? If only his own nightmares were so conventional in their effects.

She got up from the chintz-covered sofa, stooped to pick up two of Daniel's coffee cups sprouting like mushrooms at his feet – 'Thanks, love' – moved towards the door. He saw her hesitate.

'Don't fall asleep in front of the TV, will you?'

'I won't.'

'Night, then.'

'Night, love.'

The door closed and he breathed a sigh of relief. No more dissembling. Now it was just him and the night. He could understand why Liam was so terrified of the dark. Who wouldn't be? Light was associated with everything we hold dear, everything good and clear and sane: to see the light, the light of reason, the light at the end of the tunnel. Where light exposed, darkness concealed. Darkness was the abode of vampires, werewolves, witches and things that go bump in the night. Darkness was the realm of lunacy and death, as sleep itself was a kind of death, a preparation for death, a rehearsal.

Even as these thoughts crossed and recrossed his befuddled brain, he felt his eyelids growing leaden and trying to close. For what seemed an interminable moment he struggled against the temptation to relax into that yawning abyss, to surrender to darkness and death, the TV voices receding in a confused rumble down the corridor of a party he went to long ago, where a woman with her hair in tresses and a sweet, unguarded smile stood beside him outside the bathroom. 'You're Daniel, aren't you – you teach at the uni? I'm Emmy, a friend of Gloria's. She tells me your lecture on Emily Dickinson's brilliant. I'd like to hear it sometime.'

A theatrical scream, finally, broke the spell, supplying him with the external stimulus he needed to drag himself free, a life-raft on which to clamber aboard from the swirling sea of voices, memories, bubbling in his brain. He forced himself to his feet, levering himself up against the arm of the sofa, still in a daze. Switched off the TV and stumbled to the door. What time was it? He glanced at the glass-domed clock with all its innards exposed, a wedding present from Emmy's parents, on the mantelpiece. Two a.m. What day was it tomorrow, today? Sunday, wasn't it? At least he could have a lie-in.

Crossing the upstairs landing on his way to the bathroom, he paused before Liam's half-open door. Perhaps he should just check to make sure he was asleep. He poked his head round the corner of the door and Liam looked up with a start. Curled on the edge of the bed, reading a comic in the dusty cone of light shed by the table-lamp. At the bottom of the bed his Thomas the Tank Engine duvet lay bunched in a heap where it had been kicked off.

'I can't sleep, it's too hot.' There was fatigue and petulance mixed with guilt in his voice, as if he thought Daniel might be about to scold him for still being awake.

'It's very late, Liam, have another try.' It occurred to Daniel that as tomorrow wasn't a school day it didn't really matter if he was up late or not. Still, it was a bad habit to let him fall into. 'Come on, put that comic down, I'll read you a story instead.'

He plucked a slender, brightly coloured book more or less at random from the bookshelf and brought it over to the bed.

'Not that one, I don't like that one.'

'Which one then?'

'I don't know, let me choose.' He made to get up from the bed but Daniel restrained him.

'Stay there. I'll read you a Pooh story, you like Winnie-the-Pooh.'

'All right, but not one with Tigger in it.'

'OK, not one with Tigger.' Good Christ, the boy was frightened of Tigger now.

He located a dog-eared copy of *Winnie-the-Pooh* on the bookshelf and selected the story where Piglet takes a balloon to Eeyore for his birthday and it bursts on the way. Surely that wouldn't scare him.

'Now, get under the duvet. I'll open the window if you're hot.' He did so, then returned to the bed and rested next to him on top of it. He stroked his hair and began to read. ' "Eeyore, the old grey Donkey, stood by the side of the stream, and looked at himself in the water." '

He recited mechanically, his thoughts elsewhere. He knew the story almost by heart anyway, having read it for the boys so many times before. Funny how kids never seemed to tire of hearing their favourite stories repeated. Familiarity seemed more satisfying than novelty.

Before the story was half-way over he noticed that Liam had dropped off to sleep, his body limp now and relaxed, mouth agape, thumb hooked in the corner of his lips. It must have been sheer nervous energy that had kept him awake, pure monster-breeding fear. But what were they to do? He was too old to sleep with Emmy and himself every night, though on odd occasions, when all else failed, they relented and allowed him to snuggle between them, much to his delight. Nor could he and Sean share a room, Sean being unable to sleep with the light on while Liam couldn't sleep with it off. It was a problem.

He rested the Pooh book on the duvet and closed his eyes briefly, summoning the strength to rise. It would be easier if we were like computers, he thought, if we were equipped with a simple switch that we could press to turn ourselves off, to put us into sleep mode. Machines didn't dream, machines weren't afraid of the dark, machines had it made.

There was a sudden scream and he sat up. The closing credits on the film began to roll. He was alone on the sofa in the lounge. The door opened. It was Liam.

'I can't sleep,' he said. 'I'm too hot.'

A perfectly articulated question framed itself within Daniel's mind, demanding to be answered. Am I asleep or am I awake? I don't know, he thought. I literally do not know.

3

What is it about me, she wondered, that leads me to get involved with Catholics with problems?

With Michael it had been the drink, now with Daniel it was dreams. Swapping one sort of demon for another. It wasn't as if she actively sought out men with problems, weak men, vulnerable men, the way some women did. Just the opposite. In her own youthful dreams and day-dreams she'd always imagined herself on the arm of a strong, silent, imperturbable type – Paul Newman, Robert Redford, Steve McQueen – someone assured and self-reliant, someone capable of shouldering her cares, not burdening her with their own. Had her motives in marrying Daniel been less than honest, then? Had she perhaps been attracted to him by his availability, his suitability as a father for her children? After all, she wasn't exactly young any more, there might not be many more chances. And whatever his failings, Daniel was a kind man, there was no disputing that. He would never raise his hand to the boys, hardly even raise his voice. So many horror stories these days about stepfathers abusing their stepchildren. Was it selfish of her to want a good father for her children?

But if only those dreams would stop. It was getting her down, disturbing her own sleep. Was that selfish of her too? But she had a job as well, she needed to be alert too. When was the last time she'd had a really good night's sleep, slept right through to the morning, instead of being woken by him traipsing in and out of the room, or standing at the window, or sitting hunched on the edge of the bed with his head in his hands, sighing? Sorry, love, did I wake you? As a matter of fact you did, yes. Of course, she tried to be sympathetic, but it wasn't easy. Still, at least he accepted he had a problem now, at least he'd agreed to see a doctor, though even then she'd had to talk him into it – what was the source of this irrational aversion of his to doctors? – she'd been the one who'd had to make the appointment. Sometimes it was like being married to a little boy. She'd wanted a husband, a man, an adult, an equal, not another child.

She turned off the shimmering road and into the gravel drive leading to the portico of the main school entrance. Thank Christ for her job, a bit of normality. The sun beat down on her back, warming her neck. How sensual sunshine was. Seemed a shame to be going back inside on a day like this, probably one of the last really warm days of autumn. Small price to pay, though. The memory of those years before the boys started school still hung fresh in her mind like a warning sign. Do not forget, it said. The washing, the shopping, the cooking, the cleaning, the settling of arguments, the sheer mind-numbing drudgery of it all. The conversations with other mothers in the park about breast-feeding and potty-training and figure-restoring exercises and the price of children's shoes. No, she was well out of that. Here she had something more to offer than mere maternal sustenance, here she was doing something useful, imparting practical skills, contributing to the breakdown of cultural and linguistic barriers. Well, perhaps not quite so grand as that, but it *was* rewarding. Not that bringing up children wasn't rewarding too, of course, but why did it have to be so tedious, why did one person have to sacrifice themselves so that others could grow?

Two of her students, Italian boys in expensive leather jackets, trotted up the steps in front of her, returning from the dining-room. One of them, Gianluca, the taller one with the incipient moustache, acne and lank greasy hair – to think! Sean and Liam would be teenagers one day, would they look like this? – paused at the top of the steps and bowed mock-ceremoniously as he opened the door for her. '*Signora*.' She returned his playful smile and gave her hips a slight wiggle as she entered. Probably just doing it so they can get a good look at my behind, she thought, and giggled to herself. Daniel was always telling her to wear more sensible clothes. 'Sensible' and 'modest', those were the words he used. They were the contraries, in his sartorial lexicon, of 'flimsy' and 'revealing'. 'Bit revealing, that dress, don't you think?' he'd say. 'Shouldn't you wear a bra? You realize you can see right through it when you stand against the light?' But for heaven's sake it was summer, the tail-end of it at least. Did he know how uncomfortable it was to wear a bra when it was hot? If he'd had his way, she'd have gone to work every day dressed all in black, like those women you see in Greece. Besides, she enjoyed the attention she received from her male students, it made her feel desirable and attractive, something Daniel was becoming increasingly incapable of, or uninterested in, doing.

'Oh Emily, I'd like you to meet Philip Rice. He'll be joining us next week. Philip's been teaching in Japan, before that he was in Sweden.' Marjorie Standish, the school's vice-principal, stood beaming beside her latest capture like a hostess at a cocktail party who's cornered the best guest.

'Quite a globetrotter,' Emmy said, looking between the two of them. Offered her hand and had it squeezed rather than shaken. Smiled. Actually he was rather cute. Those large, long-lashed hazel eyes, head of tight brown curls, that slightly quizzical, flickering half-smile as if he knew better than to take anything too seriously. Bet he's had lots of women. Sweden and Japan. How old was he? Twenty-five? Twenty-eight? Ten years younger than me and he's already done so much. Of course, it's easier for a man. God, he keeps looking down at my breasts, filthy sod, perhaps I should have worn a bra after all.

'I was thinking perhaps you'd like to show Philip around, Emily, before your lesson starts,' Marjorie was saying. 'I have a few things to do in town.' Didn't she always? 'Show him our resources room, the dining-room, the photocopier and so on. Sort of guided tour. Would you mind?'

'Of course,' Emmy said. 'It'll have to be a quick one, though.' She saw Philip smile and look at his shoes; what was he smirking at? 'I have a class in fifteen minutes.'

'Lead on, Macduff,' he said, misquoting, turning to shake hands with Marjorie and tell her how much he was looking forward to working at the school.

'Fifteen minutes should be long enough,' he said as they passed out of Marjorie's earshot along the corridor. 'For a quick one.'

She fixed him with what she hoped was a withering, but not altogether unfriendly, stare.

4

As the English department's only trained Americanist, Daniel felt himself in a somewhat egregious position, as if he fell between two stools, or rather two Chairs. Not only was he expected to run almost single-handedly the courses in Classic American Literature and Modern American Literature offered by the department, he was also expected to help out and fill in at short notice on virtually any other course, from Chaucer or the Metaphysical Poets to Contemporary Critical Theory, that happened to require extra teaching. It was too much. He'd been with the department nearly six years now, but because he was still officially the youngest and most recently appointed member of staff they seemed to think they could treat him like the new boy at school. Do my lines for me, will you, Daniel, write my essay for me. The beginning of a new academic year was a particularly hectic time, what with class lists to sort out, reading lists to compile, new lectures to write. What was he doing in this profession? He could be earning almost as much working as a milkman or dustman, without any of the hassle.

'I've had enough already and it's only the first week of term,' he said to Tod Finkel, one of his colleagues and few friends in the department, as they sat together in Daniel's room during a brief interval between two afternoon tutorials. Tod was their thirties man, solid, dependable, down to earth, rooted in quotidian reality, and a sort of wishy-washy pink with red blotches in both his physical and political complexion. 'Harry knows we're understaffed. Why doesn't he make a new appointment? Even a part-time one would help.'

'I'll bring it up at the next senate meeting if you like, but you know what their answer'll be. They'll say we're lucky not to be facing staff cuts. Anyway, more to the point, why doesn't Harry do more teaching himself? You know he's off again next week? Some conference in Frankfurt or somewhere.'

'Christ!' Daniel sighed. What a cushy number Thorncote had. Attending conferences, editing books, blathering on about the state of education and the arts on radio and TV, knocking out carping book reviews and turgid 'think-pieces' cobbled together from other people's thoughts for the *TLS* or Sunday review sections, and if there was time, just if, fitting in the odd graduate seminar or highly publicized lecture. What a world of difference there was between being a head of department like Thorncote and the butt of the department like himself.

'Get much work on the book done over the summer?' Tod asked.

The Book, Daniel thought. Sounded like The Bible. He'd been working on it for so long now, it was no longer necessary to specify *which* book. Not 'your monograph on Poe' or 'your study of Poe as Romantic Rationalist', but simply The Book. It was that final chapter that was causing all the problems, the one where everything was meant to come together and cohere into some kind of unified whole, illuminating all that had gone before. Without that it was no more than a collection of unconnected essays on well-trodden themes: Poe as inventor of the detective story, Poe as visionary poet, Poe as hack journalist, Poe as inspiration for the *Symbolistes*.

'Did a bit,' he said. It wasn't entirely a lie. Since the dreams had started, he'd been using the book to provide a sort of reference point, an anchor, a toe-hold on reality. He knew that if he could see the pages of his script before him, could read the words he'd written and recall having written them, having framed them in his mind, if he could hold all fifty thousand words in his hands, could scan them from start to finish, pausing to read at will, well, he could hardly be dreaming, could he?

So at least he'd thought until a couple of nights ago. Then he had a dream in which he was sitting at his desk at home, reading over his final chapter, Chapter VII. He was particularly pleased with what he'd achieved there, every word seemed just right, he felt he'd finally got to the root of Poe's troubled psyche. Among other things it contained the first full account of the circumstances surrounding Poe's mysterious disappearance and death, and an explanation of that curious repeated cry on his deathbed, which turned out to have been not 'Reynolds!' as previously thought, but '*rené!*' – reborn.

This was a major discovery. Not only did it link up with Poe's obsessive fascination with the idea of rebirth, reincarnation and life-in-death, explored in some of his most famous stories – 'The Colloquy of Monos and Una', for example, set in the afterlife, actually begins with the question ' "Born again?" ', to which comes the reply, 'Yes ... "born again". These were the words upon whose mystical meaning I had so long pondered ... until Death himself resolved for me the secret' (the phrase returns later in the story, this time in italics *and* quotes: 'That man, as a race, should not become extinct, I saw that he must be "*born again*" '). Not only that, but it also shed light on one of Poe's early pseudonyms, Henri Le Rennet, Henry the Reborn, a pseudonym being in a sense the mark of a new identity and Henry the name of Poe's poet *manqué* brother, under whose initials, W. H. P., Poe's early poem 'Dreams' appeared. It was as if Poe foresaw (in a dream?) his brother's untimely death some few years later and wished to express, through his assumption of Henry's name and initials, what he saw as the rebirth of the latter's poetic spirit in himself. It all hung together.

Waking in the morning, or believing himself to have woken – the best he could hope for these days – he was seized by a kind of desperate panic. He flew to his attic study, hoping against hope that somehow the chapter would be there, that perhaps he'd risen in the night and produced it in a sort of somnambulistic trance or spontaneous burst of automatic writing. But he knew what he'd find even before he opened the heavy grey box-file in which he kept all the drafts of his script. There was no Chapter V I I; it ended at Chapter V I. He tried for some time to reconstruct his memories of the dream, but to no avail, they evaporated as he wrote, grew wispy and transparent and fled with the dawn. It occurred to him that this was how Coleridge must have felt after being deprived of the memory of his dream of 'Kubla Khan' by the visit of that bastard from Porlock. It was all there, perfectly composed, just waiting to be transcribed, and now he'd blown it and it was gone forever. It was as if, he felt, Poe himself had entered his house, entered his dreams, and given him the material for his book, only he'd been too dense to realize it. He said nothing about any of this to Tod.

'Oh, before I forget, Tod, how are you fixed for Saturday? Can you still make it? Emmy got the tickets yesterday, so – '

'Sure, sure, no problem.'

On Saturday they were going to see a production of *Waiting for Godot* (Emmy had never seen it before) at the Gulbenkian, and Tod, as usual, had offered to baby-sit. He was a godsend as far as baby-sitting was concerned. Far from regarding it as a chore that one reluctantly performs for old friends, he seemed actually to enjoy it. Funny sort of bloke, Daniel thought. In all the years they'd worked together, he'd never once known him to have a woman. In fact, he didn't seem to have many friends of either sex apart from Emmy and himself, though there was nothing especially disagreeable about the guy. OK, he was no Greek god exactly, but he was slim, well groomed, intelligent, considerate. As Emmy often said, he'd make someone a good husband one day, a phrase Daniel couldn't help finding slightly insulting. Perhaps he was gay, but if so he kept it well hidden. Asexual, more like. Some people simply aren't interested in sex. At least, he never brought up the subject with Daniel, never responded to Daniel's playfully sexist remarks about the charms of some of his more appealing and well-endowed female students. Sex just didn't seem to be a part of his world. Daniel mentioned this to Emmy once. Perhaps he has his mind on higher things, she said. Is art more noble than sex? Daniel wondered sometimes.

There was a timid knock at the door.

'No rest for the wicked,' Tod said.

'Once more to the breach,' Daniel said.

'What've you got?'

'Final-year modernism option. Bloody Hemingway. Come in,' he called.

Tod got to his feet and stood back to allow the line of four scruffily dressed students, three female, one male, to enter. 'See you later,' he mouthed soundlessly and closed the door gently behind him.

'Well, how did you get on with *Islands in the Stream?*' Daniel asked, forcing himself to adopt what he hoped was a convincing pretence of interest, when the students had removed their coats and shuffled into their seats and arranged their books and bags and assorted study paraphernalia in an untidy circle around them. 'It's a bit long, I know, but you've had all summer to read it.'

A series of confused and alarmed glances passed rapidly between four sets of eyes.

'We thought you said *The Old Man and the Sea*,' the male student volunteered. 'Does it make any odds?'

5

Daniel hated doctors. He'd always hated doctors for as long as he could remember. Doctors and priests were the bane of his life. He sometimes wondered whether both weren't put into the world specifically to cause pain, physical distress in the one case (all that jabbing, prodding, probing with cold instruments of torture), spiritual anxiety in the other (ignore my words and you go to hell). Doctors were bloodsuckers, corrupters, castrators: why else should we speak of 'doctoring' reports or 'doctoring' cats? They got under your skin and bled you dry, that's why they used to be known as leeches. They made a living out of other people's suffering, rode on the backs of sickness and death.

Perched on the corner of this sticky vinyl bench in a dark and musty waiting-room, queueing for the Friday morning surgery – why did they call it that? They didn't perform surgery there, did they hope thereby to elevate themselves in the eyes of the public to the ranks of their more esteemed co-torturers? – Daniel was reminded of all the times he'd accompanied his mother to the doctor's as a child. Not on his own account, he'd always been fairly healthy as a boy, but on hers. She'd made a career out of illness, as she'd made a career out of religion; was that why priests and doctors were so closely associated in his mind? Her migraines, her depressions, her anxiety attacks, her agoraphobia, she seemed to have been ill from the moment he was born. (In fact, as he later learnt to his everlasting torment, his delivery had led to complications depriving her of the possibility of further children, so in achieving life he effectively murdered all future brothers and sisters.) Perhaps she needed those illnesses, perhaps they gave a meaning, a purpose, a justification to her life, stopped her from dwelling on the emotional and sexual sterility of her existence. It couldn't have been easy for her after Daniel's father died (a man who'd never had a day's sickness in his life, then suddenly dropped dead one morning at the wheel of his baker's van). It was only later, after Daniel left home to go to university, after he'd achieved a degree of physical and psychological distance from his mother, that he began to realize what a desperately lonely life she must have led. Doctors and priests were no substitute for the satisfactions of family life. The Family of God and the Family of Man were all very well, but they couldn't make up for a dead husband and a barren womb.

He leant forward to pull a magazine from the deck of uninspiring reading-matter spread across the low deal table in front of him, averting his face and holding his breath as he did so, trying not to make it too obvious to the other sick people lined up along the wall like victims of the Inquisition that he wished to avoid breathing in what he imagined as the bacteriological miasma hovering in the centre of the room. What a brilliant invention doctors' waiting-rooms were! This was meant to be a place where people came to be cured of their various ailments. I know, let's put them all in a room together so they can exchange bacillae before they go in. Brilliant! Ever hear of an unemployed doctor? Ever wonder why?

He perused the cover of the grubby, tattered magazine he'd picked at random from the table. *Woman's Realm.* Flicked idly through it. Problem pages, diet plans, horoscopes, recipes, fashion. Women really were an alien species, weren't they?

The snuffling, unshaven giant hunched on Daniel's right suddenly erupted in a convulsive volcanic sneeze, sending a shower of tiny mucus particles raining down on the magazine table. A bout of restrained coughing and general shifting of backsides ensued among the other members of the sick community. Daniel let his *Woman's Realm* slide unobtrusively to the floor, wiping his hands squeamishly on his trousers.

At that moment the surgery door opened and a hobbling, white-haired old man emerged clutching a prescription. He made his way in a painful, shuffling gait past the receptionist's glass-screened cubbyhole and round the corner out of sight. Daniel waited patiently to be called.

'Mr Fowler?' the receptionist announced in a bored nasal whine.

He stood up and strode purposefully towards the surgery door, where 'Dr Glazier' in uneven black plastic lettering spelt out the identity of its incumbent. He'd seen Glazier a number of times recently, mostly in connection with Liam, and had no great affection for the man. A dour-faced old Scot with weatherbeaten features that looked as if they'd been hewn out of Aberdeen granite, he seemed to operate according to the assumption that pain and sickness were part of humanity's common lot, the norm rather than the exception, and any alleviation that might be produced in them as a result of his own intervention a rare and fortunate accident. Daniel knocked and entered in a single movement.

Glazier was seated behind his desk, writing something on a card. Daniel sat down on the creaking high-backed chair opposite, waiting for him to finish.

'What seems to be the problem, Mr Fowler?' Glazier said without looking up.

Daniel bided his time; he wasn't going to have a conversation with a man only half of whose mind was engaged. 'When you're ready,' he said.

Glazier stopped writing, looked up, taken aback. Capped his pen, sat back in his chair. 'I'm all yours.'

'Thank you. Well the thing is, I've been sleeping very badly recently.' No, that wasn't it. 'Or not so much sleeping as dreaming. It's hard to explain but – ' How was he to put it, how make Glazier understand the severity of his problem, the disastrous effect it was having on his life? 'You see, I keep dreaming I've woken up and then it turns out I haven't, I'm still asleep, and then I wake up again, or at least I think I do but – '

'Yes,' Glazier interrupted. 'Are you under any special stress at the moment?'

'Well I'm quite busy at work, I suppose.'

'And what work do you do again? Schoolteacher, isn't it?'

'I teach at the university.'

'Ah yes, well that would be very stressful, wouldn't it?' Was he being sarcastic or what? 'You probably just need to relax a bit more. Have a hot bath and a cup of warm milk before you go to bed. If that doesn't work,' he reached for his prescription pad, 'take one of these each night before turning in. They're a mild sedative, they should ensure you get a good night's sleep. You'll probably find that when you're not under so much pressure the problem will disappear.'

'Actually, I really didn't want any sleeping pills. I took some once before, years ago, after my mother died, and they really knocked me sideways. As I said, the problem's not so much the sleeping, more the dreaming. I was hoping there might be something else you could do.'

'Such as what?'

Daniel stared back at him incredulously. 'Well I don't know. You're the doctor.'

'Exactly. And I'm giving you the benefit of my considerable experience.' For a moment their gazes locked, like two prize-fighters at the start of a match. Daniel broke the contact, glancing pusillanimously away, and the contest was decided.

'Give them a try,' Glazier said, generous now in victory, tearing off the top sheet from his pad and handing it to him with a practised flourish. 'If you find the problem persists, come back and see me in a couple of weeks and I'll see about referring you to a consultant. We'll keep that as a last option, though. OK?'

Daniel briefly debated with himself whether to press his case further or let it go at that. 'OK,' he said, 'I'll try

25

them. Thanks,' he added grudgingly.

'How's little Liam getting on by the way?' Glazier asked as Daniel got up to leave. 'Any improvement with the bed-wetting?'

'Well it goes in phases, you know. He's not too bad at the moment.'

'He'll grow out of it, you'll see. A bit highly-strung, that's all.'

Daniel drew up a quick mental list of all the technical terms Glazier had used during their appointment, a doctor's dictionary: grow out of it, highly-strung, stress, hot bath, warm milk. Ah, the miracles of modern medicine!

Leaving the surgery, holding his breath again as he ran the bacteriological gauntlet of the waiting-room, he already began berating himself for having let Glazier get off so lightly. Why hadn't he stood up for himself? Why had he allowed himself to be fobbed off with a bottle of pills, to be mollified by talk of Liam? Why did he always get this feeling, whenever he'd just seen a doctor, that he'd been conned?

6

Tod didn't want to go home, he never did. He liked it here at Dan and Emmy's, it was more of a home than his own place. The glowing gas fire bathing him in warmth – the nights were drawing in already, there was an autumn chill in the air – the Mozart string quartet on the stereo, the ambient disorder of daily life (scattered toys, unwashed dishes, a half-eaten apple on the table), the sense of those two slumbering angels dreaming childish dreams above his head. Everything here was somehow vital, weighted with life. Sometimes when he was alone here like this he'd just wander from room to room touching things, picking them up, putting them back, pretending they were his own, imagining how it would be to live in such a rich and full, such a companionable environment. He envied Daniel. How lucky he was to have a wife like Emmy, intelligent, attractive, generous, kind. And to have such smashing kids – especially Sean, the older one, he found Liam a little hard to communicate with, he was so shy, so timid, a bit like Tod himself in fact. To be surrounded by so much warmth, so much energy, so much palpable reality. What did Tod have to compare with that? He had his draughty, poorly furnished house that no one ever visited, his phone that never rang, his novel that no one knew he was writing and that he was sure he'd never finish, his cupboard of videos and magazines for weekend entertainment. Entertainment! Torture, more like. How empty, how sordid. How had his life come to be like this? He'd never planned it that way, he'd never wanted to end up like this, alone, unmarried, unloved. He wanted a wife, kids, family holidays by the sea with sandcastles and kites and thermos flasks of tea. He wanted to be a pater-familias. He wanted to be Daniel.

He turned back to the pile of closely written pages balanced precariously on his knee, full of insertions, deletions, reinstatements, re-deletions. It was hopeless, he wasn't a writer, he never would be, no matter how he tried to delude himself. His characters simply refused to come to life. They weren't even characters in the proper sense of the word, in the sense of flesh and blood creations with histories beyond the page. What they were were literary conceits, amalgams of adjectives attached to proper names. Every now and then they'd twitch into a semblance of real life, some fortuitous phrase or incident would inject them with spirit, galvanize them into action, so they staggered and stumbled around for a couple of pages like coin-fed automata till the money ran out, the spark was consumed, and they slumped back into their original inertia, all lolling heads and splayed limbs with the stuffing spilling out. It was all a sham, a mockery. It was a lot easier to criticize literature, he realized, than to write it.

Perhaps he lacked the necessary life experience to write about real people, people with marriages and divorces and kids, as he was attempting to do. Perhaps he'd do better to make his novel more autobiographical, to write about his own life, his relationship with his students, say, or with Dan and Emmy. But who would read that, who would be interested in that? What he ought to write was a racy historical romance with a barely disguised version of Emmy as its heroine. That was something he could pull off, that was something he could expand into. He could capture her forever with a few well-chosen phrases, make her live before the reader's eyes: the sway of her hips, the shimmer of her hair, the sparkle of her smile in moonlight, the way her eyes glittered with promises of secret pleasures as she swooned in her dark lover's manly embrace. But that was another book he knew he'd never write.

Sighing, he transferred the bundle of scribbled notes from his knee to the carpet and levered himself up from the sunken armchair, every joint in his body seeming to crack as he rose. Soon he'd be forty and his life hadn't started yet.

He slouched through to the kitchen to pour himself a glass of milk. As he crossed the hall he saw Sean descending the stairs in his pyjamas.

'Uncle Tod, Liam's crying. He woke me up. I think he's wet himself again.'

Tod had never been faced with this situation before. What were you supposed to do? Sponge down the mattress (hopefully there was a rubber sheet), find some clean pyjamas and bedlinen, wash little Liam's loins? Oh God.

'OK Sean, you go back to bed, I'll see to it.'

Just then a car pulled up in the street outside. Doors slamming, engine still running. Tod checked his watch: ten past eleven. With any luck it would be Dan and Emmy's taxi. He waited till he heard the key in the lock, then crossed swiftly to the lounge to return the pages of his novel to his briefcase, replacing them on the carpet with a wad of students' essays.

'Sean, what are you doing up?' he heard from the hall.

'Liam's wet himself apparently, Emmy. I was just about to go up, I – '

'It's all right, Tod, I'll see to it,' she said. 'Back to bed now, Seanny, there's a good boy. It's very late.' She disappeared up the stairs at a trot.

Daniel looked awful. He could barely keep his eyes open as he staggered into the lounge and slumped into the chair where Tod had been sitting. Was he drunk or what?

'How was the play?' Tod asked.

'Dunno,' Daniel mumbled, eyes closed. 'Fell asleep in the second act. Emmy wasn't very pleased. Apparently I was snoring.'

'So you never found out whether Godot turned up in the end?' he tried, but Daniel didn't laugh, didn't even reply.

'Well, I'll be shooting off then. You look done in.' He

gathered his papers and briefcase. 'Say goodbye to Emmy for me, won't you?' Daniel grunted, or perhaps it was a snore. He closed the door softly behind him as if he was leaving the house of the dead.

7

Sheer physical exhaustion of this magnitude, the shutting down of all the faculties of sense and speech, the vice-like tightness around the eyes, as if every muscle was stretched and taut and ready to snap, the continuous, intolerable thudding and thumping that made his head resemble a carpenter's workshop full of buzz-saws and power-drills and clanging hammers – or would have done, had he been capable of such an elaborate metaphor in his paralysed, enervated state – physical exhaustion of this order Daniel had never experienced before. He hadn't known what it meant to feel tired. He'd thought tiredness was what you felt when you nodded off in front of the TV. He hadn't realized it could take the form of a physical force pinning you to your seat, bearing down upon you with the weight of the universe, so that even the act of raising your arm to rub your bloodshot eyes demanded a colossal effort of will, a battle with gravity. He forced himself, impossibly, to attend to what was being said, to keep the faces before him from floating and blurring and dissolving in a featureless haze.

'Yes, er, yes, good point,' he said. 'How does, er, how else does Henny, Henny Jayes, how else does he, er, explore, er, themes of, of incense and cruption?'

An embarrassed silence filled the room before an anonymous voice, no doubt taking pity on him, broke it.

'Well, take *The Portrait of a Lady*, for example. I think there he – '

Yes, take it, Daniel thought, take it, please.

The dreams had stopped of course. But then everything

had stopped. Sleep had become a bottomless pit, a yawning vortex that sucked him in each night the moment he crawled into bed and spat him out with the alarm the following morning. Nothing filled that void, no images trespassed on that blank expanse of lost time, no dreams-within-dreams or dreams of waking or waking dreams, nothing. But oh, this tiredness, this appalling fatigue. How was it possible to sleep for eight or nine hours a night and yet feel as if you'd only slept for two? And which was worse, the sophisticated torments of his former state or the lifeless suspension of his present? Like a choice between purgatory and limbo.

A sudden terrible thought surfaced in his mind: what if all this is still part of that original dream, what if I haven't woken from it yet, what if I'm dreaming this too? It was too awful even to contemplate and he forced it hurriedly back underground.

'. . . concepts of the self,' the voice concluded. He knew it must have concluded because he was vaguely aware that for some moments now it had been silent in the room.

'Very true, very true,' he managed to say. He summoned up his last reserves of energy for a final attempt at articulate speech. 'Well, that about, er, wraps it up. You can, can leave a bit early today. Er, next week we'll, er' – what the hell were they doing next week? – 'we'll carry on where we left off,' he said limply.

They filed slowly out of the room, casting curious backward glances at him as he pretended to look through his notes. The door closed with a click. His head fell on to the desk, on to a paperback copy of *The Ambassadors*. He was distantly aware of a string of saliva stretching in a thin wet bridge between the corner of his mouth and the book, but was powerless to do anything about it.

8

The first time Philip made a pass at her, she affected a show of moral outrage. In fact, it wasn't so much a pass – what an old-fashioned word; did men still make passes these days? – more a direct assault from the rear. She'd been standing at the photocopier behind the stacks in the resources room, xeroxing some hand-outs for her students, when he came up behind her. She didn't hear him approach, but as she bent over to collect the pile of papers from the delivery tray, she felt a hand brush her thigh and flip up her loose cotton dress to reveal a flash of her pantie-clad bottom beneath. She whipped round, ready to bawl out whoever it was, to deliver a powerful dose of vitriolic, but when she saw him standing there, cutting such a ridiculous figure with his hands raised above his head in a gesture of surrender, that stupid boyish grin on his face, her anger softened and turned to something like forbearance. He probably tried it on with every woman he met; some men needed that constant confirmation of their sense of themselves as sexual operators, it was a weakness really. Still, she didn't intend to let him get off without at least a pretence of indignation. Defending her honour, as they used to call it.

'You've got a cheek,' she said.

'So have you. Love those cute cotton panties.'

'I could report you for sexual harassment.'

He smiled. 'You could, but you won't.'

'What makes you so sure?'

'You wouldn't stitch me up like that. Christ, there's little enough fun round here as it is. Just a bit of harmless horseplay, that's all. Anyway, you probably enjoyed it.'

She ignored this last slur. 'It may be horseplay to you. It happens to be my body.'

'And a very nice body it is too.'

'Listen, I'm not some cheap tart you're chatting up at a disco. You don't talk to me like that.'

Why am I reacting like this, she thought, getting so uppity and self-righteous? God knows, things like this happened to her seldom enough. Anyway, he was right: she had enjoyed it after a fashion, enjoyed his interest in her if not his coarse way of expressing it. Who was she trying to kid?

'OK, truce,' he said. 'No more liberty-taking, no more sexual harassment. But at least you can agree to have a drink with me sometime to show you've no hard feelings.'

Would there be any harm in having a drink together? Possibly. 'You realize I'm married, I suppose?'

'What difference does that make? I'm not asking you to get a divorce, just go for a drink with me.'

'Then you won't mind if my husband comes along too?'

He smiled again, that disarming saccharine smile he knew exactly when to take out and put on. 'Wouldn't be the same, would it?'

'I think you should look round for someone your own age,' she said. 'Someone who's available.'

'Everyone's available. At a price.'

'Is that so? Well, I won't ask what the price is. You think quite a lot of yourself, don't you?'

'If you don't, no one else will.'

There was a certain creepy quality about him, she had to admit, a sickly, self-satisfied smugness, a cocksureness. Yet for all that he was attractive. Perhaps it was simply that it was flattering to receive attention from a man so much younger than herself.

'Well, I've enjoyed our little chat,' she said. 'But if you'll excuse me, I have a class waiting. Don't you do any teaching round here? Or do you just hang around the photocopier all day like a grubby little schoolboy in the playground waiting for girls to bend over?'

'Ouch,' he said. 'I thought we'd called a truce. That was unfair. A severe blow to my vulnerable male ego.'

She shook her head. 'To think of everything the women's movement went through, to end up with someone like you. If you're an example of the New Man, give me the old one any time.'

He shrugged and turned to leave, no longer smiling. 'Suit yourself.'

Have I offended him? she thought. I didn't intend to, it was meant as a joke, surely he could see that. This is ridiculous. Why should I be the one to feel guilty? Isn't that typical?

9

Tod parked his Ford Fiesta in the empty space in front of the drive and checked in the rear-view mirror to make sure his tie was straight before going in. Perhaps he should have worn the simple, pale blue one after all. God, he hated these dos. Of course, it was nice of them to have invited him; Saturday was the worst night of the week to be stuck in alone when you knew everyone else was out having fun. It was just that he was so nervous when it came to meeting new people, especially when it was patently obvious that Dan and Emmy were trying to fix him up. Sally, Dan had said her name was when he asked whether Tod would be free (as if he had any doubts!). An old schoolfriend of Emmy's, recently divorced. Perhaps she'd be feeling demoralized, lacking confidence – women usually did after their husbands left them, he supposed – perhaps they thought he'd be able to inject some sparkle back into her life, give her back a sense of her own worth. Well, we'll see. He pulled out his bottle of Blue Nun in its crinkly mauve crêpe paper from under his seat – was that the right sort of wine to bring? He didn't know about these things – steeled himself for the coming encounter with his possible future wife by inflating his chest with a lungful of stale air, and opened the car door.

It was Emmy who greeted him. 'Oh hello Tod, you're nice and early.' Oh God, he'd got the time wrong, he'd come too early again. 'Sally isn't here yet. Daniel's just getting changed. I'll take that, shall I? Oh, Blue Nun. Lovely.'

She relieved him of his coat and led him into the lounge. 'Make yourself at home. Daniel will be down in a minute.

Now, what would you like to drink?'

'Oh well, anything, whatever you've got.'

'Well, say. Wine, beer, gin and tonic?'

'Oh, er, wine I think, if that's OK.'

What were they going to do about Tod? He was always so jumpy, so nervous, he never seemed able to relax. At least, that's how he was with her. Daniel said he was different when it was just the two of them together. And he had no dress sense at all, how was he ever going to find a woman, dressed like that? That navy blue blazer with that red striped tie, he looked like a football manager. Poor Tod!

Daniel appeared in the doorway, looking haggard and drawn.

'Hello Dan. How's things?'

'Not bad, not bad. Bit knackered but not bad.' He lowered himself into his favourite winged armchair, opening his top button and loosening his tie.

'Here you are, Tod,' Emmy said, returning with a precariously brimming glass of red wine. 'Is red OK? There's white if you'd rather.'

'No no, I prefer red.'

'Have you checked on the boys?' she said to Daniel in a confidential undertone. 'No point starting anything till they're asleep.'

'Both soundo,' Daniel said, yawning.

'Well, this is nice,' she said, seating herself next to Tod on the sofa and taking her own glass of wine from the side table. 'Cheers, Tod.'

'Oh, cheers. Not drinking, Dan?'

'No, I'm off it at the moment. Doctor's orders.' He didn't elaborate further and Tod thought it impolite to pry.

'Sally should be here soon,' Emmy said. 'You'll like Sally, Tod. She's very well read. And she's got a terrific sense of humour, hasn't she, Daniel?'

'What? Oh yeah, yeah.'

Why did they have to make a pitch for her like that? He'd decide himself whether he liked her or not. Anyway, maybe

37

she wouldn't like him. He'd hardly blame her if she didn't. What did he have to offer a woman, in real terms? Security, stability, fidelity, certainly, but what else? He was quite aware that most people regarded him as a rather stuffy, earnest, uptight (that was the modern word) sort of character. Was it his fault if he happened to be interested in serious subjects, things that mattered? And what were the chances of finding a woman who shared those interests? Emmy said Sally liked to read, but what did that mean? In his experience when women said they liked to read it meant the latest Jackie Collins or Sidney Sheldon. Airport novels. Emmy was the exception there. She enjoyed poetry, she liked drama, especially Shakespeare, she even knew something about the writers of the thirties and forties that were his own special interest. Pity she didn't have a sister.

The moment Sally arrived he knew it was a mistake, an awful, ghastly mistake. Not that she wasn't attractive. Quite the contrary. Many men, he supposed, would have found her sexy and desirable. But he wasn't many men. That sort of big, blonde, bountiful femininity had never appealed to him. Statuesque, that was the word to describe her, as if her body had been modelled in imitation of some overblown male ideal. But Tod preferred statuettes to statues. He liked women with slender, girlish, even boyish figures, women with small, delicate features, Pre-Raphaelite women, women who didn't parade their sexuality like a trophy. Apart from anything else she was too tall, he could never imagine himself with someone so tall. She was nearly as tall as he was.

For an embarrassing twenty minutes that seemed to stretch into hours they sat together in the lounge, Tod perched bird-like on the edge of the sofa with Emmy and Sally on either side of him, Daniel sprawled lumpishly in his armchair, exhausting their common fund of polite drawing-room conversation. The weather, some pop star's fund-raising efforts for the Ethiopian famine victims, that play on TV last night. 'Well, I don't know about anyone else,' Emmy announced finally, mercifully, 'but I'm getting a bit peckish. Shall we go through?'

Emmy had obviously gone to a lot of trouble in her preparations. The dining-table alone deserved an award for culinary design. Starched Irish linen tablecloth, raffia placemats, wicker bread trays, an array of gleaming cutlery, peaked napkins neatly furled in crystal glassware, candles, coasters, carafes. Such a home-maker and hostess she was. Why was Dan acting so damned surly? He didn't know when he was well off, that was his trouble.

'You sit there, Tod, next to Sally, and I'll sit here so I can get to the kitchen. Daniel, light the candles, would you, please?'

The dinner passed in something of a haze. Tod wasn't used to drinking and by the time they reached the main course he was already on his third glass of red wine (his bottle of Blue Nun, he noted, was never brought out). So light-headed did he feel, in fact, and so nervous, that he was scarcely even aware of what he was eating. Some kind of soup first, followed by a dish with – what were they? – aubergines in it. 'I hope you don't mind vegetarian food, Tod, only Sally's a vegan,' Emmy said. 'Really?' Tod said. 'That's, that's very interesting.'

Throughout the meal Emmy made patient and well-intentioned efforts to engage Tod and Sally in some form of meaningful dialogue together, but Tod diligently resisted her efforts, deflecting the conversation back each time on to Daniel or Emmy herself. 'Sally and I were at school together, you know, Tod,' she'd say. 'Sally was always the bright one.' 'Oh I find that hard to believe, Emmy,' he'd reply. 'I mean ... well, you know what I mean.' Or, 'Sally works up near where you live, Tod, in the day-care centre at Sturry.' 'Really,' he'd say, looking at Daniel. 'Apparently Harry Thorncote's thinking of moving to Sturry soon, did you hear?' Daniel, he noted, had begun to drink, despite his earlier disclaimer, but it appeared to be doing little to lighten his spirits. Eventually Emmy seemed to understand that her efforts were doomed and she fell silent. For the first time Tod felt able to relax.

'I'll make some coffee then, shall I?' she said when they'd eaten dessert, a fresh fruit cocktail that Tod wasn't able to finish. His head was beginning to swim. 'Daniel, help me clear some of these away, would you?'

Daniel raised himself unsteadily to his feet and began clattering the dessert dishes noisily together.

'I hear you've just got divorced,' Tod came out with when he and Sally were finally alone together and the silence was becoming unbearable. It was all he could think of to say.

'That's right.'

'I'm sorry to hear that,' he said.

'Don't be. Best thing I ever did. Good riddance to bad rubbish.' She drained her Perrier water. 'You've never married then?'

'Oh no,' he said, attempting a breezy nonchalance, 'foot-loose and fancy-free, that's me.'

'Quite,' Sally said.

In the kitchen Emmy was getting mad. 'Fat lot of bloody good you were. I'm exhausted.'

'You're exhausted,' Daniel said.

'Yes, I'm exhausted. You haven't got a monopoly on tiredness, you know. All that preparation, all that cooking. Might as well not have bothered. What is it about Tod, why is he such hard work?'

'He's just nervous around women, that's all. You never give him a chance to relax.'

'Oh, so it's my fault, is it? If I hadn't kept the conversation going it would have been like a wake out there. What must Sal think? I didn't hear you contributing much, you could have helped out.'

'I'm not in the mood for socializing, you knew that, I told you that. These bloody pills.'

'If they make you feel that bad, stop taking them.'

'What, and go back to the dreams, you mean?'

'For God's sake, Daniel, you're like a child sometimes. I

40

don't have a magic wand I can wave to make you feel better again. If you're that worried about the dreams, go back to Doctor Glazier and ask him to make you a referral. He said he'd do that, didn't he?'

'Yes, I guess so.'

'Anyway, I thought you weren't going to drink tonight. That hardly helps.'

'I had to have something, it was deadly out there.'

Emmy took a paper filter from the packet on the kitchen table and unfolded it into the coffee maker. 'Hope they don't stay too long. Can we get rid of them, d'you think?'

'God knows. Tod's not the sort of person who takes a hint.'

He came up behind her and folded his arms round her waist. 'How about if we tell them I'm not feeling well and I've gone to bed?'

'*We* tell them?'

'OK, you tell them. I'm sorry, love, I'm shattered, would you mind?'

She sighed. 'Go on. Go to bed. I'll tell them.'

He kissed her gratefully on the neck.

Tod and Sally were maintaining an oppressive silence when she returned to the dining-room with the coffee tray. She wondered if there'd been some kind of disagreement between them – that is, if Tod had got as far as actually opening his mouth in the first place.

'Daniel makes his apologies,' she said, 'but he's not feeling very well, so he's turned in.'

'Thought he was looking a bit peaky,' Tod said.

'I'd better be going as well actually,' Sally said. 'Didn't realize what the time was.'

'Really? Oh that's a shame. Well, if you're sure. What about you, Tod? Are you OK to drive?'

'Actually I'm not sure. Drunk a bit more than I normally do. Maybe it's best if I wait awhile till it wears off, drink some of your lovely coffee.' How pleasant it would be, he thought, to spend some time alone with Emmy, to have a quiet intimate chat, to talk about their lives, their hopes, their dreams, their regrets. He'd enjoy that.

A quick exchange of glances passed between the two women.

'I could give you a lift if you like. Sturry's more or less on my way.'

Bless you, Sal! 'Oh, that'd solve a lot of problems. Be silly to risk driving, Tod. You could pick the car up tomorrow.'

'Yes, perhaps you're right,' he said uncertainly.

'Well, I'm sorry Daniel was such a bore,' Emmy said, a perfunctory cup of coffee later, as she led them to the door. 'He's not himself at the moment. He's been having trouble sleeping and the doctor's put him on some kind of sedative. Personally I think the dosage is too high.'

'Your company more than compensated for Dan's lack of sociability,' Tod said pompously.

'Yes, well, goodnight then. Night, Sal. Night, Tod.' She offered her cheek to each of them in turn.

Tod breathed in her perfume, filling his lungs with her fragrance.

She locked the door behind them and leant back against it with a sigh, closing her eyes. A sinkful of dirty dishes awaited.

PART TWO

My Dreams became the Substances of my Life.

Coleridge, letter to Thomas Poole, 3 October 1803

10

'Tell me, when did all this start, Daniel?'

'Oh, about a month ago, I think, though it's hard to be exact. Time has become such a weird thing for me, Doctor. I keep thinking, you know, perhaps this is all part of the same dream and in a minute I'll wake up again, I mean really wake up. Or perhaps I won't wake up for another ten or twenty years and find I'm only one night older. A sort of Rip Van Winkle in reverse.'

'Yes.'

Dr Leonard Eidel nodded ruminatively. Despite the name, Eidel was anything but the Mittel-European *Herr Doktor* of lean features and gimlet eyes that too many old films had led Daniel to expect. In fact, shaking hands with him on first entering the consulting room, Daniel had had an incongruous vision of him as a butcher in a blood-stained apron. He had a butcher's hands, a butcher's grip (though the fawn suit and red tie he wore may also have contributed to the impression). There was something too fleshly about the man, about the ruddy cheeks and sagging dewlaps, the spreading paunch and hairy hands, something too carnal for him to be a healer of the spirit.

Daniel's attitude to psychiatrists was much the same as his attitude to doctors in general. If anything, he trusted the former even less than the latter. At least medical doctors dealt with things that could be seen and touched: skin, bone, blood, muscle, vital organs. Whereas the psychiatrist dealt in – what did he deal in? – complexes, personality disorders, states of mind. What a woolly and presumptuous profession it was: prescribing the patient not antibiotics or analgesics or analeptics, but words. Talking cures. Or in extreme cases violent bolts of electric shock administered direct to the brain. Perhaps psychiatry would one day achieve respectability as a science. For the moment, as far as Daniel could see, it was still stuck in the Dark Ages.

He forced himself to shelve his misgivings and attend to the word-medicine being dispensed him by the fat man behind the desk. Give the guy a chance, he told himself. Don't dismiss him out of hand. Hear what he has to say, then dismiss him.

'First of all, let me reassure you on two counts,' Eidel was saying. 'What you're experiencing now is not a dream, it's real, quite real. I am real, this desk is real, this hospital is real – all too real, I sometimes think – though from what you've said I can appreciate this might not convince you. Second, the phenomenon you describe is in fact not unknown. It's called "false awakening" and many people experience it to a mild degree. The difference in your case is that it appears to have become habitual.'

'Can you help me, Doctor?'

'That remains to be seen.' He got up from his chair and walked to the window, where he stood for some moments apparently gazing into the far distance before turning back and perching one buttock on the corner of his desk, a sequence of actions undertaken for no other reason Daniel could see than to give an impression of measured deliberation. 'I'd like, if you're willing, to see how you respond to hypnosis.'

'Hypnosis?'

'Yes, have you been hypnotized before?'

'No. No, I haven't.' Daniel averted his gaze to take in the row of framed diplomas lined up along the wall, the two brown leatherette sofas in the corner of the room, the low, chrome and glass coffee-table between them, the framed print of a fashionable Magritte – a house-front sunk in night-time shadows beneath an azure sky crossed by wispy white

46

clouds – on the wall above, the gun-metal filing cabinet, the bookcase, before returning in an arc to Eidel. The Magritte print set off a train of associations in his mind, leading him, via the cover of the old Jackson Browne album *Late for the Sky*, to his memories of a girl called Mara with whom he shared a damp basement-flat in Crouch End and an interest in French new-wave cinema (they saw *Last Year at Marienbad* six times) during his final undergraduate year in London. She took a job in Geneva after graduating and they never saw each other again. He wondered idly now what she was doing and whether the point of the Magritte print here, in Eidel's office, was to serve as some sort of symbolic representation of the human mind, with its airiness and light above, and huddled shadows below. Could he trust a man who thought in such simplistic terms, who saw symbols wherever he looked?

'Let me explain what I'd like to do. You remember how you told me that each time you wake up, or think you've woken up, you can look back on your dream and spot all its "flaws", as you call them, all the things you miss or overlook when you're actually in the dream, and how you then use this information to identify it *as* a dream? Well, what I'd like to do is to make you receptive to such cues while you're actually in the dream state. And this we can practise under hypnosis. Have you heard of the term "lucid dreaming"?'

'Lucid dreaming.' He found himself lapsing for some reason into a sort of echolalia.

'Doesn't matter. It's simply a dream in which the subject is aware he's dreaming and able to exert some measure of control over his own actions and reactions. Many people have dreams in which they wonder whether or not they're dreaming. The lucid dreamer no longer wonders, he is sure.'

This all sounded a bit too science fiction for Daniel's liking, the plot of another hammy horror film from the seventies starring Susan George and Oliver Reed. 'I don't know, I just want to get a good night's sleep, that's all.

Perhaps I should go back on those tablets I got from Doctor Glazier?'

'That's no solution, Daniel. Do you really want to go on taking sleeping pills for the rest of your life?'

Daniel was forced to admit that he did not. But as he went on to explain, he was also rather wary of further stirring up the can of worms his dreams had unwittingly opened. Who knew where it might lead? Both his mother and grandmother had suffered from mental illnesses of one kind or another. That way madness lies. He voiced his doubts to Eidel.

'According to the records I was sent by Doctor Glazier, Daniel, your mother suffered from agoraphobia. There is nothing in the annals of psychiatric medicine to suggest that agoraphobia is hereditary or connected in any way with your present sleep disorder. However, if that's how you feel, I suggest you ask Doctor Glazier to renew your prescription.' He began shuffling the papers on his desk.

Daniel thought of Emmy, of the boys, of his work, of the future that lay in store for them if his condition persisted. He owed it to them as much as to himself. 'OK, when do we start?' he made himself say, with an air of mock-dramatic resolve.

Eidel grunted softly, presumably as a token of satisfaction. 'How about now?' he said.

'Oh good, you're back, you can have a look at the washing machine, I can't get any hot water. How did it go? Liam, put that down, will you, and get on with your lunch.'

Daniel had rescheduled his classes for the day so as to leave the afternoon free. Returning now to the routine anarchy of the midday meal, he was tempted to invent an excuse to take him back to his office.

'OK, I suppose. He put me under hypnosis.'

'Oh, I've always wanted to be hypnotized, what was it like?'

'Mummy, what's hippozits?'

Sean, the elder of the two, laughed scornfully. 'Not hippozits, stupid. Mummy, he thought he said hippo-zits.'

'Quiet, both of you, Daniel's trying to speak.'

It was a cause of some private niggling regret to Daniel that Emmy's ex-husband Michael, who lived in Ireland and saw the boys only two or three times a year, should continue to be honoured with the title 'Daddy', while Daniel, who saw them every day, who fed them and clothed them, who . . . well, Daniel was just Daniel.

'Oh it was OK. He put me back into a dream I had last night and asked me to give a sort of running commentary on it so as – '

'Liam, *leave that alone!* How many more times do I have to tell you?'

' – so as to spot anything that might sort of prove it was a dream.'

'That sounds interesting. Did it work?'

49

'Mummy, I can't eat any more.'

'All right, you can get down. Go and put something on the video, you two. Give Daniel and me a bit of peace.'

'Yippee!'

'I want to choose.'

'No, me, me!' They raced each other out of the kitchen.

Emmy smiled. 'They've been a couple of buggers this morning. You know what it's like when they're not at school. Be pleased when half-term's over and I can get back to work. Anyway, you were saying.'

'Well, that's all really. I had to describe everything that happened till I noticed anything strange, then sort of focus in on that. Then we discussed it afterwards. Got another appointment for next week.'

'It's worth persevering with. Better than taking those pills.'

'I guess so. He also wants me to keep a record of my dreams. Told me to get up in the middle of the night if necessary and write everything down.'

'That sounds a good idea.'

'Yes, only – '

There was a sudden piercing scream from the lounge, followed by the sound of voices raised in dispute and a single set of rapidly approaching footsteps.

'Mummy, Liam wouldn't let me put on my tape of *The Incredible Hulk*. He wanted *Winnie-the-Pooh*.'

'You know he gets scared by that tape, Seanny. Try and show a little understanding, he's younger than you, remember.'

'He's just a stupid cry-baby. And now he's gone and broken the video.'

Daniel finished his sentence silently: only how will I know if I'm really writing down my dreams or just dreaming that I am?

'Well, I'd better go,' he said.

'I thought you were taking the afternoon off.'

'Yeah but I remembered, there's a departmental seminar

50

this afternoon. Some visiting professor from Harvard or somewhere. Better not miss it, it's on Poe. Probably have to go for dinner afterwards as well. Bloody nuisance actually.'

From *The Case of Gabriel Flowers*

A slight, soft-spoken man in his early thirties, Gabriel was referred to me by his GP following a period of acute sleep disorder, which a course of amylobarbitone had done little to relieve. It transpired that he was suffering from a particularly severe and ongoing form of 'false awakening': that is to say, he would regularly experience dreams in which he apparently awoke and got up to go about his daily affairs, only to find himself at some point again waking up, aware that his present anxieties, otherwise displayed few obvious neur-otic symptoms. I had heard some time previously of Dr Isabel more false awakenings before the final, authentic one took place. Not surprisingly, as a result of these experiences, Gabriel had been left in a highly distraught state of mind.

My initial impression of Gabriel was of a rather reserved and independent-minded man who, making allowances for his present anxieties, otherwise displayed few obvious neur-otic symptoms. I had heard some time previously of Dr Isabel Calder's work with lucid dreamers, and it struck me that one way of tackling his problem might be to explore techniques of lucid-dream awareness so as to enable him to distinguish between his false awakenings and the genuine ones. I knew that in some cases this could be achieved through hypnosis – the so-called 'hypnotic cueing' technique in which the patient re-experiences his dreams under hypnosis, being cued to attend to any unnatural features they may possess, such as, for example, lack of colour vision or obvious logical inconsistencies – and I decided I would propose this to him as a possible *modus operandi*.

Before doing so, however, I wished to learn a little more about him – more, that is, than was contained in the brief medical profile I had received from his G P. I asked him about his early childhood, which he assured me had been very happy and untraumatic. He had experienced, he said, only two major periods of disturbance in his life, and both came later. One of these was social and sexual in nature and was brought about by his leaving the sleepy (I noted the word) Shropshire village where he had spent his first eighteen years to begin life as an undergraduate amid the more permissive and promiscuous atmosphere of the University of London. It came as a shock to him, he said, to discover that women were no less interested in sex than men were, and apparently derived equal pleasure from the act. The sexual favours he had enjoyed up till then, as he put it, had been precisely that, favours extracted from an unwilling accomplice through superior force of will, through bribery, blackmail or sheer wheedling persistence. 'I had a dispensing-machine attitude towards sex: put in enough money – a ticket to the pictures, a choc-ice, a hot-dog – and the thing ought to deliver.'

The other principal source of conflict in his life had been religion. Gabriel explained that he had been brought up in a strict Catholic home and accepted the devotional duties imposed upon him by his mother (his father died when Gabriel was aged six) until well into his teens. During a turbulent six-month period in 1967, however, which he seemed to associate with his having just read James Joyce's *A Portrait of the Artist as a Young Man*, he lost his faith. This placed considerable strain on his relationship with his mother and caused her a great deal of distress, from which she had apparently still not recovered at the time of her death in 1982. It was only much later that I realized the crucial importance of this religious 'apostasy' of Gabriel's ('apostasy' was the word he himself used) to his present problems. Indeed, in many ways it provided the key to the entire case.

53

I also tried to elicit from him whether he was under any special stress at home or at work. He replied that his job was no more stressful than most others and his marriage no less successful. Something in the tone and phrasing of this statement, however, suggested to me that he was not being entirely honest, a suggestion borne out by the fiercely defensive attitude he struck when I inquired about his sexual relations with his wife. So defensive did he become, in fact, that I realized there would be little point in pursuing such a direct line of questioning. Instead I shifted to his relations with his stepchildren (two boys, aged seven and eight), whereupon he returned to the more relaxed manner he had shown before. He did confess, however, that it was a cause of some regret to him that he would probably never have children of his own owing to his wife's unwillingness to extend their family. Once again, it was only later that I understood the extent to which his relations with his wife and his feelings of thwarted paternity lay at the very root of his neurosis.

As a way in to my first hypnotherapy session with Gabriel, I asked him how much he could recall of his dreams of the previous night. This turned out to be very little – all he could recollect was something about missing a train – but it was a start and I decided to make it the text for the remainder of the session. He proved at first to be a somewhat refractory hypnotic subject, though with practice his receptivity improved. My post-session notes have enabled me to construct the following abridged and approximate record of our dialogue:

> LE: I want to put you back into the dream about the train that you had last night. You are very relaxed. You can hear everything I say, but you are also in the dream about the train. Tell me what you see. What do you see?
>
> GF: Smoke.
>
> LE: And where is the smoke coming from? Follow it to its

source and tell me where it's coming from.

GF: Funnel.

LE: What sort of funnel is it? Is it a ship's funnel?

GF: No. Train.

LE: What sort of train is it then?

GF: Steam. Steam train.

LE: A steam train. Does this strike you as strange? [No answer.] Doesn't this strike you as strange?

GF: Steam train.

LE: Yes, it's a steam train. But there aren't any steam trains these days, are there? They're all electric, except in museums or on private railways. Is it a private railway?

GF: Don't know.

LE: Or perhaps it's from a long time ago. How are the people about you dressed? Are there any people about you?

GF: Old. Old clothes. Top hats and tails. Frilly dresses. Crowds.

LE: There are crowds of people, are there?

GF: Crowds.

LE: And where are you? Are you in the crowd or are you on the train?

GF: In crowd.

LE: And what are you wearing? Are you dressed in old clothes too?

GF: Walking stick.

LE: A walking stick. Why do you have a walking stick?

GF: Limp. Hurt knee. Ow!

LE: Your knee hurts, does it? And that's why you have the walking stick, to help you walk? Do you remember hurting your knee?

GF: Got to see someone. See someone. Train.

LE: Who do you have to see on the train?

GF: See someone. Train. Leaving.

LE: Yes, but who do you have to see?

GF: Girl. On train.

LE: There's a girl on the train you have to see, is there? Can you make it to the train in time?

GF: Trying. People. Crowds.

LE: Are you trying to push your way through the crowds?

GF: Falling. Trying. Falling.

LE: Why do you keep falling?

GF: Stick. Rubbery. Soft. Falling. Train leaving. Got to, got to – leaving, girl's leaving. [Begins sobbing.]

LE: It's all right, Gabriel, there's no need to cry, you're here with me, it's all right. You're having a dream, that's all, it's only a dream. And the dream's beginning to fade now, it's getting dimmer and dimmer, and you're falling into a deep, deep sleep. A nice, warm, comfortable, refreshing sleep. In a moment I'm going to wake you up and when I do you'll remember everything you've seen in the dream and everything you've told me. You're beginning to wake up now. Very gently, very gently. I'm going to count to three and when I get to three you'll wake up and remember everything that's happened. One – you're waking up now. Two – almost awake. Three – open your eyes.

It should hardly be necessary to point out that the symbolic content of the dream confirmed my suspicions that Gabriel was experiencing sexual problems in his relations with his wife, the limp and the soft stick suggesting impotence. The common dream motif of the missed train, with the girl he tried but failed to meet, also hinted at a regret over lost erotic opportunities with other women, perhaps because of the constraints on sexual freedom imposed by his marriage and the conventions of respectable society (the crowd in evening dress barring his route to the train). I tried to elicit from Gabriel the associations that he himself placed on these symbols, but our discussion made little headway as he immediately objected to my use of the word 'symbol', maintaining – if I remember his argument correctly – that the search for symbols in literature or dreams was a futile and self-defeating procedure, aimed at generating fixed meanings when the whole power of images lay in their ambiguity. When I casually inquired whether he did not consider that the limp and the stick that kept going soft in his dream might have associations of a phallic nature, he again adopted that defensive attitude I had noted before, laughing and asking me in turn whether the tailcoats in the dream were not also phallic and whether a shooting stick would not have made a better phallic symbol than a walking stick. 'And what about Freud's cigars?' he added with a flourish, as if that settled the matter. I could see that his rudimentary understanding of psychoanalytic theory and practice, doubtless gleaned from one of those popular introductions to Freud that have been the curse of psychoanalysis over the years, might prove a considerable barrier to his further treatment and cure.

At the end of the session I suggested to Gabriel that he keep a journal in which to record his dreams each night or morning after they occurred. I impressed upon him that it was essential he wrote down the dreams the moment he awoke, at whatever hour of the night or day it might be, and that the journal was to be for his benefit not mine (though he was free to show it to me if he so wished). The journal would provide him, I said, with a convenient means of measuring his development, in terms of lucid-dream awareness, in the weeks and months that lay ahead. This suggestion, at least, he seemed to welcome as sensible and worthwhile.

13

'Good holiday? Refreshed and relaxed and ready to do battle again?' Philip inquired as they took their places at the front of the coach while their noisy, high-spirited charges squabbled and jockeyed for seats behind them. What was it about coach outings that turned even the most exemplary group of students inside the classroom into a band of mindless hooligans as soon as they left it?

'Some holiday. If you had kids you'd know. They have holidays, you just exchange one sort of work for another.'

'Ah, the trials of motherhood,' he said and patted her lightly on her trousered knee. 'Where would we be without our mothers, eh?'

She removed his hand and crossed her legs. 'Don't patronize me,' she said. 'I hate the way you do that.'

He turned and faced the window. 'If you weren't so hostile towards me the whole time, maybe I wouldn't feel the need to. I don't get you, I really don't. Are you like this with everyone or is it just me?'

Well, she thought, which was it? Is this the sort of person I've become? Do I come across as some kind of mean-spirited grouch, always putting a dampener on things? Is this how I appear to others? Or is it just him, rubbing me up the wrong way, bringing out the worst in me?

The drive to Broadstairs took a little over half an hour. They were going to visit Bleak House before it closed to the public for the winter. Emmy had been on the excursion several times before, but had no hesitation in signing up for it again. It made a pleasant change from the usual round of classroom activities, the grammar exercises, the role-plays, the tense drills, the endless games of Hangman and Twenty Questions. Besides, whatever the problems of organization and control that were involved, it was fun to see the students in a more relaxed, less formal setting.

One of them, a tall Swedish youth with a fuzzy blonde moustache, now approached along the aisle and stood with a hand on each seatback as he addressed himself to Emmy.

'We're having a discussion,' he said, with only the slightest trace of an accent. 'What does the expression "what the dickens" mean? Lasse says it comes from "what the dickheads".' A flickering smile played at the corner of his lips as Emmy tried to restrain her amusement and Philip gave vent to his in a loud, chuckling snort. It was a question she'd never been forced to consider before and she was pleased when Philip fielded it for her.

'That's quite a thought. Actually I believe it's a corruption of "what the devilkin", an old form of "what the devil". In Swedish you'd translate it as *vad fan* or *vad helvete*.'

'*Vad fan! Vad helvete!*' the youth shouted down the aisle to hoots of laughter from the back of the coach.

'Well well, who's a clever boy then?' Emmy said when he'd gone. She was genuinely impressed.

Philip patted her knee and smiled. 'Don't patronize me, please.'

As the coach pulled up by the gardens above Viking Bay, Emmy got to her feet and attempted to quell the babble of voices filling the air around her.

'Before we get off,' she called out, then repeated a few decibels higher, 'before we get off, there's a couple of things I want to say. First of all, we're *all* going to visit Bleak House. I don't want to see anyone trying to slip off to amusement arcades or the beach. You can go there afterwards if you like, but not before. We'll meet back here' – she looked at her watch – 'at a quarter to five. Is that clear? A quarter to five.' Few of the students seemed to be paying any attention, but she ploughed on doggedly. 'Secondly, Bleak House is a private museum; the owners still live there. They therefore expect visitors to treat the place with respect. So: no running, no shouting, and no touching any of the exhibits. Is that understood?' God, she sounded like a proper martinet. 'Now, leave the coach in an orderly fashion – orderly! – and keep to the pavements, the roads round here are very narrow.'

Philip led the dawdling party of youngsters along the prom and up the winding path to the clifftop, while Emmy brought up the rear. Perched high above the harbour with its castellations surmounted by a Union Jack on a white flagpole – why the national flag? Weren't writers meant to belong to everyone? – Bleak House had the look of a small coastal fort rather than a literary monument. Come to think of it, hadn't it been built on the site of an old fort? She recalled reading or hearing that somewhere – perhaps that explained the castellations and the flag? A squat, brown brick building with a bowed front, it appeared to be thrusting out its chest as if bracing itself against the chill North Sea winds. It was certainly well named. Buffeted by the elements in winter, it was hard to imagine a more exposed setting for a house, even if today, with its windows winking in the low, late autumn sunlight, it presented a more benign aspect. Like most people, she thought, it had two faces, one light, one dark, which it showed to the world in rotation and rarely if ever combined.

Keeping company with two Greek girls at the back of the group, she stopped with them from time to time to admire the various scallops, conches and other shells set in the stone of the high garden wall bordering the house. One particularly large and impressive shell, nacreous and inward-curling, resembled a human ear. She pointed this out to the girls and made a joke about walls having ears, but the witticism was lost on them. At the head of the group, confident and brash, Philip's voice was blown back to her in snatches by the wind. Why *am* I so hostile towards him? she thought. Of course, he's a chauvinist and thinks far too much of himself, but that isn't it, surely? Perhaps it's because I'm afraid of letting him think I'm attracted to him. Am I attracted to him? Am I afraid of letting him think so? Ten years ago I'd probably have fallen madly in love with someone like him, with his independence, his self-assurance, his social ease. Am I getting old? Have I lost the ability to respond as a woman, instead of as a wife and mother? Is this what marriage and kids and divorce and remarriage do to you? Have I become my own mother?

Philip wrote out a cheque for the admission charges and led the party through the turnstile into the neatly laid out garden with its inappropriate cannon, then through a porch into the main entrance hall, where they were met by the bright, breezy figure of the woman from the turnstile. Was she the owner of the house? Emmy had never worked out her exact role. The speech she gave always had a proprietorial ring to it, at any rate, and was always more or less the same. How many of you have heard of Charles Dickens? Can you tell me the titles of any of his books? Do look at the furniture as you go round the house and note, particularly, the collection of stuffed animals – the Victorians were very fond of stuffing animals (Philip glanced across at Emmy, suppressing a smile).

When she'd gone, Emmy and Philip led their group into the ground-floor room rather grandly billed as the 'Maritime Museum'. Like the 'Smugglers' Cellars' beneath the house, with its ghastly papier-mâché mannequins, it had nothing whatsoever to do with Dickens. It was as if the owners of the house considered the literary connection insufficiently interesting in itself and hoped to attract more visitors by broadening the house's appeal. Emmy tried as she always did to interest the students in the various encrusted artefacts unimaginatively displayed under glass cases, though she herself found them as dry and dusty as she did all museum pieces. The students, too, appeared unimpressed, and by the time she came to mount the wide staircase leading to the old part of the house where Dickens's bedroom and study were situated, she found herself virtually alone. Most of them, she suspected, had bypassed the upstairs rooms completely – who

61

could blame them? What were they to Dickens or Dickens to them that they should visit his house? – and gone direct to the Smugglers' Cellars.

She passed along the dim corridor, its gloom barely relieved by the ornate lamps that burned all day, even in summer, and paused outside the tiny study with its view out over the North Sea like a blank page waiting to be filled. Philip stood with his back to her, gazing out of the window, apparently lost in contemplation of the scene. She continued on into the bedroom, her favourite room, from where a commanding view of the beach, now deserted except for a couple walking a dog, and the broad sweeping prospect of Viking Bay was to be had. The two Greek girls she'd been speaking to before turned as she entered and hurried off, whispering, along the corridor, leaving her alone.

She stood for a while behind the low-slung rope cordon, surveying the interior of the small, densely-furnished room. Surely it hadn't been as cluttered as this in Dickens's day? Some of the furnishings, it was clear, had been brought in from outside to give the place an air of authenticity – the great brass bed, for example, which a sign informed her came from the Bull Hotel at Rochester and in which Queen Victoria had also slept (though not, Emmy assumed, at the same time). But what of the other items: the telescope on its tripod pointing out to sea, the various mirrors (was Dickens so vain as to need three mirrors?) that, so another sign usefully pointed out, 'many times reflected the face of Charles Dickens', the shoes and boots on the floor, the foot-warmers, the chamber-pot under the bed? Did they really belong here or was it all a sham, a stage set manufactured for the twentieth-century visitor who wants only an illusion of historical accuracy, who is content with lies so long as they mimic the truth? How difficult it is to see behind appearances, how hard to penetrate surfaces. Even with someone we see every day, how can we be sure whether the face we see is real or only a mock-up meant to deceive, a disguise so perfect it's indistinguishable from the real thing? All we ever really have to go on are artefacts – even words, even gestures are artefacts. No one can ever know another person's feelings, all we can know is the expression of those feelings, and expressions can always be faked. Is my life any more authentic than this room? Is the life I lead with Daniel? Are we living in our own Bleak House, a museum passing itself off as a family home?

'Don't know why we bother, I really don't.' She turned to find Philip, hands in pockets, close behind her. 'They're not interested in Dickens, couldn't give a toss. Most of them don't even know who he was. I found one of them sitting on the bed when I came up here, trying on a pair of Dickens's shoes. Suppose one of us had better go down to the bloody Smugglers' Cellars before they wreck the place.'

'Yes, I'll go.' She made to leave but he reached out an arm to detain her.

'Why are you so unhappy, Emmy? You're not fooling anyone, you know, you're an open book.'

'Ha ha,' she said, 'very apt,' thinking of the first editions of Dickens's works open in display cases around the house.

'I wasn't trying to be funny.'

'What makes you so interested anyway? There's lots of unhappiness around, what's so special about mine?'

'I like you,' he said simply, 'that's what. And I'd like to know you better. Come out for a drink with me. Please.'

She hesitated, looking away at the large wall mirror framing a reflection of the bed, herself and Philip captured in a frozen tableau like a painting by Vermeer. 'Give me your phone number.'

He took a pen and shiny black diary from his inside jacket pocket, tore out a page from the back, began scribbling. How many names and phone numbers had that little black book held in its time? What had become of them all?

'When will you phone me?'

'I don't know,' she said. 'I don't know if I will yet.' Soon, she thought. Maybe.

The two Greek girls reappeared suddenly in the doorway, as if from nowhere, smiling, saying nothing.

14

Daniel's first lucid dream worthy of the name occurred, aptly enough, on Bonfire Night, the night of light. In the dream he was lecturing to a class of students on, more aptly still, the role of dreams in literature. We can imagine how the lecture might have gone.

'Writers love dreams. Open virtually any novel and somewhere in it you will find an account of one of its characters' dreams. Open a title catalogue in any public library and look at all the books containing the word 'dream' in their titles. From Shakespeare to Joyce, from *A Midsummer Night's Dream* to *Finnegans Wake*, dreams and dream narratives have endlessly inspired the literary imagination. Why should this be so?'

He paused and looked up from the sheaf of handwritten notes clutched like paper armour at his chest to let his gaze wander in leisurely survey over the rows of bowed heads and bored faces confronting him across the room. What did they care for his dreary pontifications, these lolling youths with their ink-stained hands and pasty complexions and faraway, lustreless eyes? They had their own dreams. Which were? Sex, probably. Sex and money: what else? Rock video dreams, all spangled surfaces and ping-pong hollow inside.

'One obvious reason is that dreams are ready-made narratives. However obscure or bizarre or perverse their content may be, dreams tell stories. They provide the writer with material and the writer is always hungry for material.' Brief flurry of pens on paper in the studious, myopic front row: 'Dreams in literature – Function: 1) Provide material.'

'But what sort of material do they provide? Certainly, no one ever wrote a detective novel or spy story in their dreams. Dreams, notoriously, flout all the conventions of traditional, "realistic" fiction, with its heavy reliance on causal sequence and linear plot structure, its striving for rounded characterization and reality effects, its denouements and epilogues. This is not the stuff dreams are made on. Dreams are ambiguous, fragmentary, problematic, open-ended, opaque. They omit connections, they juxtapose seemingly unrelated images, they shuffle space and scramble time. Unlike novels, dreams do not need to persuade us of their "reality". Every writer's ideal reader, the dreamer's disbelief is always already suspended.'

First signs of impatience among the audience. Fidgeting, yawning, talking at the back, wrists openly or furtively consulted. Daniel noted with a slight unease but without surprise that the two students chiefly responsible for the interruption were Joyce and Shakespeare, the twinkling, weasel-eyed Irishman beating his ashplant rhythmically on the floor as he apparently explained the laws of prosodics to the serene, unmistakable Bard chewing the end of his quill beside him. Typical, he thought, that they should turn up for the very lecture in which he gave their work a mention.

'It is this tolerance of unreality, of absurdity, that makes the dream peculiarly suited to the needs of the modern world. Modern life, in other words, has become so fractured and fragmented that the dream has come to seem, paradoxically, a realistic mode of expression. Hence the especial popularity of dream narratives, dream sequences, dream effects, in contemporary literature and film. Hence expressionism, surrealism, absurdism, dada. Hence the fashionable devices of alienation and defamiliarization – the *topos* of modern fiction is the *topos* of dreams. Reality has become so dream-like that there is no longer a clear distinction between the two. Distinctions belong to the daylight world, not the night-time realm of shadows. The dream is the twentieth-century fiction *in epitome*.'

He paced slowly across to the far side of the stage, as if physical motion alone could enliven this dry peroration. Checking his watch, still twenty minutes to go. Fuck it, skip to the last page, wrap it up. This is beyond all but the best of them anyway.

'Dreams, then, are a special kind of narrative. Like poems and novels, they consist of a surface "plot" both masking and revealing hidden meanings. Like works of fiction, they can be "interpreted" and their "symbolic structure" or "underlying themes" exposed. One should bear in mind also that the psychological condition of the dreamer has much in common with the accounts given by writers of their state of mind while composing. As the dreamer has no control over the nature of the material represented in his dreams, so the writer typically portrays himself as a passive instrument, a medium, a vessel, a channel, through which unconscious content may be given artistic form. The state of inspiration, writers tell us, is akin to a sort of waking dream.

'What I am suggesting is that the act of dreaming represents an ideal analogue of the process of artistic creation, just as the dream work and literary work are themselves analogous. Dreams are visual poems, as poems are paper dreams. What attracts the writer to dreams is the nightly confirmation he finds in them of the infinite fertility, the endless fecundity, of the human mind, and of his own mind in particular. In dreams we tell ourselves stories, compulsively, garrulously, like a drunk at a bar; each person is his own dream factory. No matter that these stories are confused and lack endings, for so are the stories of the drunk, so are the stories of life. So too, sometimes, it must be said, are lectures.' Shuffle notes, return pen to top pocket, look up forbiddingly. 'Any questions?'

'That's a load of pigsballocks, man, and you know it.' It was Joyce again, standing now, ashplant raised like a cudgel before him, spectacles glinting in the late afternoon sun streaming low through the slats of the window blinds. 'Sure enough, literature's a dream, a collective dream spun by the

66

human race. Not an original thought, but OK. But your modern fiction's no ordinary dream, it's a nightmare. There's a world of difference betwen Bill's dream play, say, and my nightmare novel. We see the world in different terms, we have a different view of history. What's that quote of mine you fellows always trot out on these occasions? "History's a shite affair from which I'm dying to escape." It's like those books your man Kafka over there writes. The *Metamorphosis* is no dream, it's a fucking nightmare. What d'you say, Frank?'

The cadaverous-looking man in the corner coughed into his fist and nodded seriously. 'I have to say, I – '

'Or Edgar Poe. Is Eddie here? Tell him, Ed.'

For the first time Daniel noticed that his entire audience seemed to be composed of celebrated dead authors, like a gallery of dust-cover portraits suddenly come to life. There was foppish Proust, there old man Tolstoy, there a gaggle of Romantic poets passing round the laudanum and laughing. A slight, dapper man in a black frock-coat with a broad brow and thin moustache rose unsteadily from his aisle seat and looked uncertainly about him. So this was the divine Edgar.

'Well I don't rightly know, y'all,' he began in an absurd southern drawl.

'Bejaysus and begorrah!' Accents were deteriorating rapidly now. 'The point's patently bloody obvious, man. Dreams don't tell stories, they don't "narrate" as you say. Dreams play games, they play tricks, they're what a cretinous critic like you would probably call "ludic", they're – '

'What's that?' Daniel was surprised to hear himself speaking again.

'Ludic, man, ludic.'

There was something familiar but not quite right about the word, something he was supposed to remember, something –

As if a point had suddenly been switched in his brain, Daniel achieved lucidity. Another voice, another self, another identity within him took over, not his dreaming self.

67

It said: Be calm, Don't panic, This is a dream. These dead authors you see around you, from different centuries and different countries, They aren't real, They're part of the dream, That's why they're here, all together in a room, speaking English. Don't panic, You can control this, Remember what you've learnt, You're in charge, It's a dream, You —

There was a knock at the door. The Liberal Studies secretary, whose name he couldn't recall just now, entered the room and walked briskly up to the stage where Daniel stood with both hands gripping the lectern. She whispered in his ear.

'I've just had a call from the hospital. Your wife's gone into labour. They think you should be there.'

The next thing he knew he was sprinting down the aisle past a blur of faces towards the swing-doors in the centre of the auditorium. He flung them open and emerged in a brightly lit hospital corridor. White walls, nurses, patients in wheelchairs. Running, breathless. 'My wife. Maternity ward. Can you tell me.' Headlong into another dream, as real and opaque as any other.

15

Eidel seemed to like that dream. At least, he listened with unusual attentiveness to the brief and muddled account Daniel gave of it at their meeting the following Friday, then nodded and murmured and scribbled something on the notepad he kept before him on the desk. This, by Eidel's standards, constituted a major display of interest. Daniel supposed it must be hard being a psychiatrist, forced to listen to other people's problems all day. It must be hard not to become bored by the sheer ubiquity, the uniformity, the banality of human suffering.

'Am I allowed to ask what you've written?' he asked from his chair across the desk.

'You're allowed to ask anything, but I'm not obliged to answer. These are *aides-mémoire*, Daniel, that's all. Lines of inquiry that may need to be followed up, leads that may turn out to be false. There's no reason why you should bother yourself about things that may have no actual bearing on your case.'

'You make it sound like a job for the CID. Actually I can see what it says anyway. What's a "posterity dream"?'

'Paternity dream, Daniel, it says paternity dream. Does that strike you as an unreasonable rubric for what you've just told me?'

'No, I suppose not. Except that it does seem to miss out all the earlier, lucid part of the dream.'

'You think that's the most important part?'

'Well, I don't know. It was certainly the most lucid. And

that's the point of all this, isn't it? Becoming lucid in my dreams, I mean?'

'The point, Daniel, is to find out what's at the root of your problems and what can be done to overcome them.'

'Well, yes, of course, I just meant, well, you know.' Eidel sometimes had this effect on him, of reducing him to stammering inarticulacy.

Daniel liked to think of himself as essentially of a generous nature, and his attitude to his therapist at this early stage of their relationship was one of guarded trust, cautious confidence. I place myself in your hands, he wished to say. I will do anything and everything you require of me in the service of my treatment unless you give me reason to do otherwise. I will suspend, I will place in brackets, my natural resistance to the sort of psychoanalytic symbol-mongering I suspect you like to go in for. I will answer honestly and frankly and to the best of my ability any questions you consider it necessary to ask me. The rest is up to you.

'I think it's time we took a closer look at this dream of yours.' Eidel gestured with an outstretched arm to the two small leatherette sofas and coffee-table where he conducted his hypnotherapy. 'Ready?'

'As ever.'

Daniel found the hypnosis taxing at first. It was like trying to be in two places at once. On the one hand he was expected to remain in communication with Eidel, to listen to his instructions and respond to his questions ('Isn't it strange that he should be writing with a quill?' 'Do Irish people really speak like that?'). On the other hand he was also expected to enter back into the dream, to re-enact it, give himself up to it. He was left with a curious sense of being both in the dream and outside it at the same time; as if he contained two selves, one waking, one sleeping, two sentries who never met but passed each night and morning when they relieved one another from duty. And now, suddenly, they were expected to stop, chat, share a cigarette, exchange photos of their wives and children.

When the hypnosis was over they would sometimes do some free association work using elements from the dream. This was the only part of the therapy Daniel actively enjoyed. He couldn't help thinking of it as a sort of mental chess in which the object was to outwit, to outmanœuvre the other player by coming up with an association at once instantaneous and plausible yet unforeseen. It was like plot construction in fiction. The best plot was that which constantly surprised the reader yet seemed at the end the natural, indeed the inevitable, product of its premises. So Eidel would say 'secretary' and Daniel would say 'bird'. Eidel would say 'liberal' and Daniel would say 'party'. Eidel would say 'labour' and Daniel would say 'love'. Eidel would say 'love' and Daniel would say 'lost'.

Whatever time remained at the end of the consultation would be given over to the discussion of more general and, as it seemed to Daniel, often highly tangential issues such as his relationship with Emmy or his mother or his early experience of sex. He had to admit, he found it hard to see the relevance of such matters to his present sleep problems, and sometimes parried Eidel's questions by raising these reservations with him. But for the most part he indulged the doctor's overly familiar methods as one would the bad table-manners of a good friend.

'Do you masturbate, Daniel?'

'Sometimes.'

'Do you prefer masturbating to making love with your wife?'

'Occasionally.'

'Do you feel any guilt on that account?'

'Now and then.'

'Do you find it hard to talk about these things?'

'No.'

One thing that did impress him about Eidel was the uncanny ability the man apparently possessed of knowing exactly – and without once, it seemed, consulting a watch – when their fifty-minute hour was up. Clocks were banned during consultations: he wanted Daniel, he said, to feel 'unconstricted by time' ('Shouldn't that be "unconstrained"? Or "unrestricted"?' Daniel asked pedantically), and made him leave his watch with the receptionist at the beginning of each session. Yet every time Daniel strapped his watch back on his wrist at the end of the appointment, it always said nine or ten minutes to the hour. He began to suspect Eidel of having concealed a timepiece somewhere about the room or his person, of playing a cheap trick. Only weeks later did it occur to him that from the window of his third-floor office Eidel must have been able to see one of the faces of the hospital clocktower, rising like a hackneyed symbol of something above the other buildings of the complex. But so much had happened in Daniel's life by then that it scarcely seemed of interest.

16

From *The Case of Gabriel Flowers*

Lucid dreaming, it should be understood, is not an all-or-nothing affair. There are an infinite number of stages, of gradations, between the usual sort of unselfconscious dream we are all familiar with and the pure clear self-awareness of the expert lucid dreamer. Dreams can be more or less lucid.

A good example of this is provided by the following part-lucid dream of Gabriel's, which he reported early on in his treatment and which first alerted me to certain salient features of his case. In the dream he was lecturing to a class of students, among whom he noted the figures of James Joyce and William Shakespeare. Joyce was making a nuisance of himself by ignoring Gabriel and talking with Shakespeare, beating his walking stick up and down on the floor as he spoke. Then he stood up and became abusive, challenging Gabriel's authority to teach and brandishing his cane in the air. At this point Gabriel seems to have shown the benefit of some of the techniques we had been practising under hypnosis by taking his first tentative steps into the lucid state. He explained it, typically, in literary terms, as another 'voice' arising within him and wresting control of the dream narrative from his dreaming self. The anxiety generated by such states can be intense, however, and it is unusual for lucidity to last more than a few moments in its early, developing phase. In the present case it appears to have been interrupted by the entry on to the dream stage of a

73

new character, the departmental secretary, who informs Gabriel that his wife is at the hospital and has entered labour. He rushes from the auditorium and emerges, breathless and excited, in a hospital corridor. Here the dream ends.

It struck me as significant that the dream should break off at this particular and critical juncture (that it was the dream itself rather than Gabriel's waking memory of it that was incomplete was sufficiently established by repeating the dream under hypnosis). It was as if his conscious (lucid) mind was not prepared to allow the dream to develop for fear of the anxiety it might generate by exploring themes of birth and fatherhood. I remember making a note to this effect on my jotter when Gabriel recounted the dream to me. I also remember he was curious as to what I had written and tried to make out what the note said, but misread 'paternity dream' as 'posterity dream'. The slip, as so often, is a revealing one, for in a manner of speaking Gabriel was correct. Indeed, one could almost say that what the dream amounted to was a demonstration of the equivalence for his unconscious mind of posterity and paternity. I suggested, accordingly, that it might be useful to see the dream as representing two possible forms of posterity, of vicarious survival into the future: on the one hand, literary 'immortality' through the survival of an author's books (thus the dead writers brought back to life in the classroom), and, on the other hand, continuation of the blood-line through paternal issue (his wife's impending delivery). The answer to the question posed by the dream – how can my place in posterity best be ensured? – is supplied by his action at the end of the dream: by abandoning the classroom for the hospital, he is effectively choosing life over art.

The dream in fact exhibits a highly symmetrical structure, with the pairing of Shakespeare and Joyce representing a further father–son relationship paralleling that of Gabriel and his child *in utero*. This may seem less fanciful when one recalls that Shakespeare occupies a privileged position in

Joyce's work (as Gabriel would have been well aware), and that one of Joyce's central themes, so I believe, is said to be the 'search for a father'. It is entirely natural that the dreams of a literary specialist like Gabriel should utilize literary material to dramatize personal conflicts.

What particularly interested me about the dream, in the light of the above, was the importance Gabriel seemed to attach to Joyce's cane, especially bearing in mind the role played by a walking stick in his earlier missed-train dream. The beating of the cane up and down on the floor suggested masturbation and, thinking I might be able to lead the discussion into areas so far unexplored, I suggested that perhaps what was being indicated was another familiar aspect of father–son relations, namely the son's assertion through symbolic masturbation of his superior potency to the father. I remember Gabriel laughed at this and said something I didn't understand about Bloom and the influence of anxiety, presumably another reference to Joyce. I asked him how he himself would read the dream and he replied, ingeniously if evasively, I thought, that if a 'reading' of the dream was necessary it would make more sense to see the point of all the stick tapping and waving, for example, simply as a gratuitous visual pun on the name 'Shakespeare'. Similarly, the passage from lecture theatre to hospital at the end of the dream might be explained by means of the suppressed link 'operating theatre'. 'Maybe dreams aren't fables with a meaning,' I remember he said. 'Maybe they're jokes with a point, and the reason they're often obscure is that we don't always get them.'

I was not convinced by Gabriel's argument, nor do I believe, at heart, was he. Something told me that his resistance to accepting a symbolic interpretation of his dreams was actually a defence against the *import* of that symbolism. Fables have morals that must be understood, jokes can be laughed off.

17

Tod couldn't make up his mind whether to have peas or beans with his fish. He stood at the canned vegetables section of Sainsbury's, hovering, debating, picking up first one then the other. He had a repertoire of about five or six dishes – fish and chips, cheese omelette, beefburgers, cornish pastie, sausage and mash, and if he was feeling specially adventurous, pizza – that he repeated each week in more or less strict rotation. Tonight it was fish again.

'I'd stick with the peas if I were you.'

He recognized the voice at once and swung towards it with a smile already enlivening his features.

'Hello, Emmy, didn't know you shopped here. Hello there, Sean.'

'Hello, Uncle Tod.'

Emmy stood with her hands on the bar of a shopping cart piled high with what looked, to Tod, like a month's groceries.

'How are you getting that little lot home?'

'Oh I'll take a cab, it's not far.'

'I'll drive you if you like.'

'It's OK, Tod, thanks anyway. I've still got some things to buy. Besides, it'll take an age getting this lot through the check-out.'

'Well, if you're sure.'

'Yes. Thanks.'

'I'd have thought Dan could have given you a hand with the shopping.'

'Oh, he's at home with Liam. Liam's got another cold and the winter hasn't even started yet.'

'Poor little blighter. Seems to catch anything that's going round, doesn't he?'

Sean had wandered off along the aisle to where the cakes and biscuits were stacked. They stood for a while without speaking, unsure whether or not the conversation had ended.

'Mummy, can I have these?' Sean shouted, holding aloft a packet of marshmallows.

'No, put them back, we've got plenty of cakes already. Actually,' she said, lowering her voice, 'I'm a bit worried about Daniel. Does he seem to have been acting strange to you recently?'

'What, the tiredness, you mean?'

'No, that's better now. He's stopped taking the pills.'

'Oh, what then?'

'Oh I don't know, he's been having this sort of recurring dream. He's started seeing a psychiatrist, didn't he tell you?'

'No, no he didn't.' Well, that was a turn-up for the book.

'It's probably nothing. It's just that he doesn't seem to want to talk about it, he keeps so much to himself these days. I just wondered if he'd said anything to you about it.'

'No, but then I haven't seen much of him lately. Been so bloody busy at work, 'scuse my French.'

What a queer fish he was, Emmy thought. Did he really feel he had to apologize for saying the word 'bloody'?

'Well, I'll let you get on with your shopping, Tod. Sean, come here darling.' Sean came running back with two packets of marshmallows in his hands.

'Oh Mummy, please!'

'No, I said. Now put them back.'

Tod thought of offering to buy them for him as a present, but then thought better of it. Mothers could be awfully touchy where their children's diets were concerned.

'Well, bye then, Tod. You must come over for dinner again some time.'

'Yes, thanks, I'd like that,' he said. 'Bye, Sean.'

'Bye, Uncle Tod.'

She left him as she'd found him, standing there hovering,

moving his weight from foot to foot, a can of beans in one hand, a can of peas in the other.

PART THREE

All days are nights to see till I see thee,
And nights bright days when dreams do show thee me.

Shakespeare, Sonnet 43

18

On Wednesday 21 November 1984, at Leonard Eidel's
suggestion, Daniel went along to the studio flat of another
psychiatrist, a Dr Isabel Calder, in North London, where a
group of lucid dreamers met once a week to discuss their
experiences while Dr Calder taped the proceedings and took
notes for a book she was writing. Daniel was sceptical about
attending at first, having a deep-seated mistrust of all forms
of 'personal growth workshop' or 'fringe therapy' ever since
a traumatic experience at an encounter group during his
undergraduate days when he was subjected to a painful and
unjust inquisition by the other members of the group for
refusing to 'let go', as they rather quaintly termed it (actually
his behaviour was the result of plain bashfulness: he had
joined the group because a girl he was infatuated with also
attended, but finding himself expected to interact with her
in all sorts of embarrassing ways, he froze). Unable to defend
himself against the massed emotional artillery assailing him
from all sides, he crumpled first into silence and then copious
tears, and vowed thereafter never again to lay himself open
to such a humiliating and pointless pillorying. However,
Eidel assured him that Dr Calder's meetings bore not the
slightest resemblance to encounter groups, so he agreed.

The meeting was scheduled to begin at seven-thirty, but
Daniel missed his train and arrived almost an hour late. He
was greeted at the door by an effusive and genial-looking
woman hardly older than himself (for some reason he had
expected a rather crabby spinster), who briefly introduced
herself – 'Call me Isabel' – and directed him to a vacant

beanbag in the main living space before retiring to a desk in a corner and inviting the group to continue.

'You were talking about scene-shifting, Colin.'

'Yeah well, I was saying, I don't know about anyone else but I find that if I sort of cover my face with my hands in the dream like this' – and he provided an unnecessary illustration of the technique – 'well, nine times out of ten I can change the scene. I mean I can't tell what the next scene will be or anything, but I can make the old one, you know, go away.'

He searched the faces of those around him for support until a teenage girl badly scarred with acne nodded and said quietly, yes, she could do that too.

'Comes in handy sometimes,' Colin continued, relaxing now, enjoying the sense of confirmation. 'The other night I dreamt I was falling off this sort of mountain ledge. I remembered about the hands business just in time.'

'That raises an interesting point,' Isabel Calder interjected. 'It's something we haven't talked about much before. Perhaps I could ask how each of you deals with situations of danger and distress in your dreams?'

'Ignore them, that's the best way,' a paisley-shirted youth drenched in hair gel volunteered after a short silence. 'I remember I once dreamt I was in a Western shoot-out, in a wagon-train surrounded by Indians. I got an arrow in the bum. I told myself it was a dream and pulled it out.'

'Cupid and his bow perhaps,' a fierce-looking woman in thick-framed spectacles commented without any trace of irony.

'Life as a pain in the arse more like,' someone else said.

'Another time,' the youth continued without responding to either remark, 'I dreamt I was walking across a desert and this tiger leapt out at me, blocking my way. I told it it was just a dream tiger and if it didn't move I'd have to shoot it. When I looked down I noticed I had a rifle in my hands and when I looked up again the tiger was gone.'

'Very violent dreams you have, Timmy,' the fierce-looking woman said. 'Are they always as violent as that?'

'These are the mild ones,' he said, sniggering and looking about him. 'You should hear some of the others. I remember once ...'

The conversation continued in this desultory and anecdotal fashion for some time, while Daniel contented himself with adopting the role, or at least the pose, of non-participant observer, much as he supposed Isabel Calder thought she herself was doing. In fact, he had little choice. Daniel's own lucid dreaming was still at such a primitive stage – momentary flashes of self-awareness, brief intervals of clarity no sooner achieved than lost – that he felt unqualified to contribute to the discussion. He was here as an anthropologist, he told himself, an ethnologist, a witness of the customs and ritual practices of some newly discovered tribe. In this capacity he wondered what common factor, if any, accounted for the peculiar ability apparently shared by all those in the room. Of the eight or nine people present, men and women were fairly evenly balanced. The participants seemed to represent a broad cross-section of social types, though it struck him that none looked older than forty. He tried fitting occupations to each of them – the secretary, the teacher, the shop assistant, the bank clerk, the student – on the basis of their clothes, posture and accent, aware that the parlour-game in which he was indulging was about on a par with the level of the discussion going on around him. But then something strange happened: it was as if his thoughts had been read and echoed.

'Don't you think it's all a bit amateurish, though, what we're doing here?'

It was the first time the girl had spoken. She was half-obscured from Daniel by the angled shadow of an open door, and he had barely registered her presence. She sat forward in her chair to speak, and Daniel too leant forward to see and hear her better. Quite attractive, he thought, in a rather severe, austere sort of way, but not really his type (what was his type? Was Emmy his type?). As he did with all women except the excessively ancient or infirm, he drew up a quick mental audit of her credits and debits: pretty face if a bit thin, under-nourished, almost sculpted; smoky, smouldering eyes, though a touch too much mascara for his liking; long, straight, black hair, almost Oriental, as if ironed; lovely skin, just that one mole on the neck; short dress, long shapely legs tucked beneath her; clothes simple and stylish but perhaps too self-consciously chosen to show off her figure, which they did, he was forced to admit, to agreeable effect. Maybe it was the prude in him, a trace of his strict Catholic upbringing, but he always felt somewhat threatened by women who wore skimpy jumpers and no bra. The word 'trollop' articulated itself in his mind, spoken in his mother's voice. He realized with a start that he'd been staring at the girl and that she was now returning his gaze as she spoke.

'I mean all of us here have a certain talent, a skill, a gift, call it what you like. We can all exert a certain control over our dreams. Some of us can perform unusual mental or athletic feats, some can sustain injuries without feeling pain, some can even act out their fantasies, whatever they may be.' There was a wheezy chuckle from the youth with the hair gel. 'But all we're doing is playing. It's just playing. We've no idea how this thing really works, of its possibilities, its uses, how it can be applied to our daily lives. I know that's part of the reason for these meetings and Isabel's research and so on, but I can't help wondering if we're going about it the right way, if this is the best way to explore and develop this thing. I'm sorry, I realize I must sound very critical, but I just wanted to make my feelings known.'

The other members of the group took up the criticism, agreeing, disagreeing, half-agreeing, and for the first time Daniel felt his own interest personally engaged.

'What did you mean when you spoke about applying lucid dreaming to our daily life?' he asked at the first convenient lull in the debate.

'I don't know, you tell me, I'm just throwing out ideas. But if lucid dreaming isn't to become just some sort of curious psychological backwater, then it must have some application to our everyday, non-dreaming lives. I mean it's all very well to be able to fly and visit exotic places and, I don't know, make love to Madonna – '

'Prince, actually,' the gelatinous youth corrected her, to a mixture of embarrassed titters and groans.

'See what I mean? If that's the limit of our aspirations we might as well all go home.'

Sensing evidently that tempers were beginning to fray and personal hostilities threatening to lower the tone of the discussion, Isabel Calder proposed they adjourn to the pub before last orders, a suggestion that was greeted with general and enthusiastic assent. Daniel explained, however, that he had a train, actually two trains, to catch, that he'd found the evening most illuminating and thought-provoking, and that he'd do his best to attend subsequent meetings, when he hoped he'd be able to contribute more to the discussion. End of speech. Bye, everyone.

As he walked to the door he threw a sidelong glance at the liquorice-haired girl shrugging herself into a functional but inelegant duffel coat in the hall. Their eyes touched, wavered, held each other for a second, before he pulled away. Something seemed to pass between them, he couldn't say what. Some sense of recognition perhaps. No, not recognition, more a kind of precognition, a vaguely unnerving sense that this person would assume a critical role in his life, that in some as yet undefined way her destiny would become entangled with his own. Was this mere fancy on his part, one more trick of the imagination? What faith could he place in his perceptions now when he knew how unreliable they could be? Well, time would tell. The next time he saw her – assuming he did see her again – he'd know better, perhaps it was just the mood of the moment, sometimes everything you did seemed weighted with significance.

On the train going home, though, he began to have second thoughts about continuing with the workshops. He had a busy time coming up over the winter: on top of his teaching there was the MLA conference paper he'd agreed to write on 'Melville and the Problematics of Naming' (a title he'd thought up at short notice and now regretted as he wasn't sure what it meant), as well as his book on Poe to finish. Yes, that MLA conference. Why had he applied to attend? He didn't want to go to Washington, even though his expenses would be covered by a travel grant from the department and even though, from a career point of view, it would probably be a good move, his first international conference, the chance of interesting an American university press in his book on Poe. But it would mean flying out on Boxing Day and then back on the 30th, ruining both Christmas and New Year. What he wanted was a rest, feet up in front of the telly, a complete break from work, not to sit on some tedious panel discussion along with half a dozen other pompous academics all pretending – or perhaps they really believed it? – that the meaning to our lives was to be found in some handful of Great Books, to be endlessly pored over, analysed, explained, annotated, assigned a canonical Truth.

No, he was too busy for all this workshop nonsense. Besides, had he really learnt anything from the evening, anything he hadn't known before? Did he really want to get involved with these people? Was there anything to suggest that such informal group discussions would benefit him in the long run? No, on all three counts. Dreams, after all, are a private affair, perhaps the most private affair of all. What was it Conrad said? 'We dream as we live – alone.' Or was it the other way round? Whatever. Hard enough to share one's thoughts and feelings; what hope of sharing one's dreams?

19

From *The Case of Gabriel Flowers*

It was around this time that I first became aware of the central role played by religious symbolism in Gabriel's dreams. A minor example, excerpted from a much longer entry for 17 November in his dream journal, may help to make this clear:

Walking in a churchyard, looking at the names and dates on the headstones. One in particular attracts my attention. I stop and read it: Virginia Mather 1829(?)–1982. Her longevity strikes me as remarkable but I do not question it further. I walk on and notice something clinging to a tree in the distance – a squirrel is it? – moving, wriggling. I approach closer and see that it is in fact a cat, a tiny tortoiseshell kitten, attached to the trunk by four rusty nails, one through each paw, covered with blood but not quite dead. It is mewing softly, as if imploring me to put it out of its misery. I look around for some implement or tool with which to perform the task and notice another rusty nail on the grass at the base of the tree, presumably dropped by the kitten's torturers. I pick it up and gently insert it into the beast's blood-stained belly, on its left side where it can less easily see what I'm doing, its head being twisted the other way. I turn the nail in the wound in order to penetrate further and a jet of clotted gore spurts from the hole, splashing across my hand. I hold the nail in place till the kitten stops mewing and drops its head. I turn and run back the way I have come, resting finally on a headstone to catch my breath and wipe away my tears with my bloody hands. It is the same stone I stopped at before, but this time when I read the inscription the absurdity of its dates strikes me more clearly. I look around and realize I am lucid ...

Gabriel presented this dream to me, verbally, at our next meeting some days later (23 November, according to my records), asking me with a rather unconvincing jocularity whether I thought the rusty nail was a phallic symbol and whether he perhaps had latent tendencies towards bestiality. We spoke about the dream at length and in the course of my questions I elicited from him the information that he himself had owned a tortoiseshell kitten in his early teens. When I inquired what became of the kitten he suddenly grew very nervous and hesitant, revealing finally that it had been run over by a car in a street near his home. Probing further, I learnt that a couple of days after the kitten went missing he prayed to the Virgin Mary for its safe return. It was on the day following this prayer that the kitten's mangled body was discovered in the gutter by a neighbour's child and returned to Gabriel in a shoe-box for burial. This event, he told me, marked the beginning of his rejection of his mother's faith.

I now had everything I needed to piece the dream together. Its most significant elements appeared to be the crucified cat, the nail with which Gabriel finished it off, and the strange inscription on the headstone. When one understood that the crucified cat was an obvious Christ symbol,* and

* Cf. T. S. Eliot's phrase 'Christ the tiger' in his poem 'Gerontion'. Cf. also the following passage from a little-known tale of Edgar Allan Poe's, 'A Dream', recounting a dream of the Crucifixion: 'It seemed that I was some Pharisee, returning from the scene of death. I had assisted in driving the sharpest nails through the palms of Him who hung on the cross ... I could hear the groan that ran through his soul, as the rough iron grated on the bones when I drove it through.' Gabriel's dreams, as has been noted before, often seem to employ a

88

that the nail corresponded to the spear which the Roman soldier at the foot of the cross plunged into Christ's left side, then the meaning of the inscription on the headstone itself became plain, being a condensation referring both to the Virgin Mary or Holy Mother (Virginia Mather) and to Gabriel's own mater/mother, the death-date on the stone, 1982, being the year of Gabriel's mother's death, and the birth-date a numerical anagram of this. Thus, the death of Gabriel's childhood pet and the failure of his prayer to the Virgin Mary became associated in his mind not only with his symbolic death to Catholicism as a source of truth and comfort (the buried Madonna and Gabriel's own role as Christ-murderer), but also with the death of his own mother (since his turning from the Church effectively 'killed' his relationship with her). For the first time in my treatment of Gabriel I felt I was beginning to approach the true source of his problems.

I also felt it was time that Gabriel meet some other lucid dreamers with whom he could share his experiences and from whom he might learn to develop his own abilities further. It is true that he was still at a comparatively primitive stage of lucid-dream awareness, but it was for precisely this reason that I believed he might benefit from contact with other lucid dreamers more experienced than himself, such as those attending Isabel Calder's London workshops. When I presented this idea to him, he seemed initially quite enthusiastic, and I had high hopes that the endeavour might prove a successful one, both in terms of providing Gabriel with a source of emotional support and reducing his feelings of isolation (which I could sense he was already beginning to develop, despite my assurances that lucid dreaming was in

subtext of extravagant literary allusion, with Poe (on whom he was writing a book at the time) and Eliot as favourite sources. I am indebted for the above material and for much of the other literary information contained in these notes to a close friend and colleague of Gabriel's, who wishes to remain anonymous.

no way freakish or unnatural), as well as by way of supplying Dr Calder with another valuable subject for her research project, whose small sample-size was proving something of an obstacle to its progress. However, when I spoke to Gabriel after he had attended his first meeting, I could sense at once that he had not found the experience an especially rewarding one. He himself denied this, in fact, insisting on the contrary that it was simply a matter of the time-commitment involved, and the constraints of his present work-load, that would make it impracticable for him to attend future meetings. Nonetheless, subsequent conversations I had with Dr Calder confirmed my first impressions: she reported that Gabriel had appeared bored by the whole enterprise, arriving late, leaving early and contributing little to the discussion.

20

2.35 a.m. Period of confused non-lucid dreaming. Reading a book on logic where I find the following syllogism: All men are mortal. No man is an island. Therefore water is precious. Puzzle to work this out but fail.

5.20 a.m. Extraordinary dream, most lucid so far. Almost total recall.

In my office marking essays on Shakespeare. 'Everybody agrees, with the possible exception of Joyce, that Shakespeare is the greatest writer who never [*sic*] lived.' Knock at the door.

– Come in.

I turn and before I can say anything – Oh it's you, she says, what a coincidence.

– Well hello, what are you doing here?

Surprised, but only mildly so, to find the raven-haired girl from Is. Calder's standing before me. Tweed jacket, white T-shirt, tight-fitting blue jeans, tote-bag. Take all this in while asking her:

– Are you a student here?

– No, but I'm thinking of applying for next year. It's a few years since I sat my A-levels but I think my grades should be good enough. The secretary said you could give me some information about the course. What a coincidence, she repeats.

– Yes well, come in, come in. Sorry, I don't know your name.

– It's Ellie. Well, Mary-Ellen actually, but I prefer Ellie. People always bring up that old song otherwise. You know, 'I'm shy, Mary-Ellen, I'm shy'. Silly really.

She laughs, a nervous, fluttering giggle.

– It's a lovely name. Sit down, sit down.

Getting up from my chair, closing the door behind her.

– D'you mind if I smoke?

– No, go ahead, I'll get you an ashtray.

I spot one, full of crushed butts, on top of a book on my desk. *Foul Johns*, by 'The French Loo-Attendant's Woman'. Must have been left by one of my students. I empty the ashtray and pass it to her with a smile.

– Thanks. D'you have a light? Seem to have run out of matches.

Patting my pockets mechanically – Sorry, no I don't.

From one of my jacket pockets a rolled-up newspaper sprouts like a stick of celery. Remove it and place it on the desk, intending to read or eat it later. She returns the cigarette to its packet and the packet to her jacket pocket (lot of jackets, packets and pockets here – any sig.?).

– I'll just take this off. It's so hot today, isn't it?

– Shouldn't complain, I suppose, I say platitudinously because my mind is elsewhere. Notice her T-shirt is one of those very thin, almost transparent cotton ones, nipples standing out erect and well-defined like rosebuds wrapped in gauze. She notices my noticing and follows my gaze to her chest, thrusting it out the better to examine herself. Runs her hand lightly over one breast.

– Is it a bit too thin, d'you think? Wasn't sure whether to wear it or not, but it's so hot. Can you see right through it?

Flustered, waving my hands. – No, I mean yes, I mean it's very becoming.

Laughing again, fingers still at her breast. – Not embarrassed, surely? You don't strike me as the easily shockable type.

– Oh I am, very easily, very shockable. Catholic

upbringing and all that. You never really shake off your upbringing, do you? At least I haven't. I mean – tempted to make a joke about being shy, Mary-Ellen, shy, but resist.

– I thought all professors were supposed to be sex maniacs. Sublimating their libidos in libraries. Seething cauldrons of writhing lust bubbling behind the scholastic exterior. (Words to that effect anyway – this dialogue very approx.)

– I'm not a professor actually. Not even a doctor.

– Doctors are worse. Always getting struck off!

Something about the improbable turn the conversation has taken jolts me into the lucid state. Like a veil lifted, a lens rubbed dry. Ah yes, of course, pity, explains everything. Realize it no longer frightens me, as it did at first, to take that plunge into the unknown, that acknowledgement of one's own unreality, that's required of the lucid dreamer.

She appears to notice the change in my expression. – Is something the matter?

– Not really. Knew it was too good to be true. Had me going there for a bit.

– What do you mean?

– This, I say, pointing vaguely about me. You.

– Me?

– Come on, drop the pretence. Turn into a bicycle or something. We both know this is a dream.

– I see. She hesitates, looks away, then back at me. – But you can see me, can't you? Hear me? Feel me? Takes my hand and places it against the underside of her breast, soft, warm, pulpy, heart tap-tapping convincingly beneath. Leans towards me, hair grazing my face. – You can smell me, can't you? Parts her lips. – Taste me? *Mills & Boon* in Dreamland.

I pull away. – This is ridiculous. Notice the newspaper still on the desktop where I left it. What was it Eidel was always telling me? If you see anything in writing, read what it says. Pick it up, scour the front page.

– Here, I'll prove it. The *Guardian*, right? Now look at the date: Sunday, 4 July. But the *Guardian* isn't published on a Sunday.

– Could be a misprint. The *Guardian*'s full of them, everyone knows that.

– OK, what about the headlines? 'M-Way Pile-Up: 6 Missing.' Is that a misprint too?

– Perhaps it was foggy and they wandered off and got lost. It's easily done.

– Oh you're impossible!

Another change of tack. – OK, suppose I am impossible, suppose I'm not real, whatever that means. Does it matter? Doesn't it feel real? I'm still here, aren't I? Alone, with you, now? And I know you want me, I'm not blind. As I want you. I wanted you the moment I saw you last night, as soon as I saw you were different from all the others. That's why I'm here. Remember what I said about exploring and developing this talent we have? Help me develop it, Daniel, help me explore it.

– Oh this is crazy. In the first place you don't exist. In the second, well, I'm married.

– Happily?

– Happily enough.

– What does that mean? Don't you want more than just enough? Don't you want it all?

– Look, Ellie, whatever your name is, whatever, whoever you are, I'll make it clear. I'm not the sort of man who has affairs, I'm just not like that, I'm a one-woman man, dumb as that sounds. I would never do anything to risk hurting my wife, to risk losing her. She's loyal, honest, generous, kind, qualities I admire. These things count for a lot.

– But that's the whole point, you wouldn't need to risk hurting her or losing her. Other men have to sneak off, make excuses, tell lies, lead double lives. All you have to do is close your eyes and dream. Don't you see, it's perfect?

94

All I saw was trouble. – Please go now, I have a class in five minutes. We're doing Eliot's *Cocktail Party*, I add irrelevantly. (I admit this is odd, I seem to have momentarily lapsed into believing in the dream again, but such lapses seem not uncommon.)

– There's just time then, she says and begins unbuttoning her jeans.

I watch, helpless, aroused despite myself, as she kicks off her shoes, steps out of her jeans and lifts her T-shirt over her head, suddenly naked except for her thin cotton panties, as wispy and insubstantial as tissue paper. In fact, I see now they are tissue paper.

– Do I please you?

Hooking her thumbs in the sides of her briefs, slowly working them down, her gaze never leaving my face, watching for my reaction.

I think: This is the first time I've seen another woman unclothed since I met Emmy. How beautiful she is, how –

Pull her towards me, recklessly, impatiently, claw off her panties, pantingly, wrestle her on to the desk, books and papers tumbling to the floor. Unzip myself, spread her thighs with my knees, jab myself inside her. Close my eyes as I enter, but she resists. Moaning, struggling – 'No! Stop it! Don't!' – battering her fists against my shoulders. 'Get off me! Off!' Open my eyes and find myself on top of Emmy, pinning her to the bed.

– God, Daniel, you could have woken me first! You could at least have woken me!

What is happening to me?

Two songs kept circulating in his brain the following day at work, like a loop of tape endlessly repeating itself. The first was 'Dream Lover', he couldn't remember who by. Nor could he recall most of the words, only the refrain: 'Because I want – a girl – to call – my own – I want a – dream lover – so I don't have to – dream alone.' The second was the old Everly Brothers hit, 'All I have to do is Dream', which Ellie had virtually quoted to him, perhaps unconsciously (but whose unconscious? Hers or his?), the night before. The words to this had lodged more firmly in his brain:

> When I feel blue – in the night
> And I need you – to hold me tight
> Whenever I want you
> All I have to do
> Is dream
>
> I can make you mine
> Taste your lips of wine
> Any time – night or day
> The only trouble is – Gee whiz!
> I'm dreaming my life away

He recalled at least three Roy Orbison songs on similar themes. It seemed that just about every pop star of the late fifties and early sixties was carrying on imaginary love affairs in his dreams. He wondered how many times in his life he'd heard all those dream songs without ever really listening to the words. Could it be that the Everly Brothers and others had stumbled years ago on to the same phenomenon he was experiencing now? In which case, did the line about 'dreaming my life away' contain a prophecy of his own fate?

No, it was absurd. His whole life was absurd, a drama played out in the absurd theatre of his mind. What was happening to him? Did he honestly believe this girl was anything more than some beautiful–grotesque phantom of his own unconscious? Did he even believe that his dream of the previous night had in actuality the sort of narrative coherence he'd attributed to it when reconstructing it for his journal? Looking back on it now, it was impossible to say. The dream itself had all but vanished from his memory, leaving only his recollection of the written record he'd made. In another's place would he have attached any credence at all to the idea that some remarkable cross-over between dreams and reality had occurred? Wouldn't he have put it down simply to an over-active imagination? But still the doubts remained.

Along with the doubts went an obscure lightness, a sense of buoyancy, of anticipation, of unpredictable events about to unfold, something he hadn't felt in years. Whatever was happening to him – and something clearly was – he felt sure it wouldn't leave him unaltered. Perhaps this was how the caterpillar felt when it began spinning its waxy cocoon, how the spider felt when it span its first web, unaware of why they were acting as they were, conscious only of a vague inner imperative compelling them to do so. And what sort of tangled web will I myself weave, Daniel wondered, what improbable form will my metamorphosis take? Butterfly or dung beetle? Either way it would mean a new start. Even if last night's dream proved in the end as chimerical as any other, it had value as an omen, an augury, a sign that developments were afoot. His life was about to enter a period of profound and lasting change, of that he was certain. As if, curiously, the last five years with Emmy were now proving to be the bright hallucination and his new inner life the dense, palpable reality.

97

He decided to say nothing about these feelings at his regular Friday-morning consultation with Eidel. In fact, he chose not to mention his previous night's dream at all, at least not for the time being; there was no knowing what elaborate fiction about his unconscious wishes the ingenious doctor would wring from it. Instead he offered him a selection of other dreams and dramas, all more or less innocuous, from earlier in the week. These included a strange semi-lucid dream about a graveyard and a cat nailed to a tree, which Eidel questioned him on in detail. He seemed to think it was connected in some way to Daniel's feelings about his mother and his attitude to the Catholic Church. Let him spin his fancy yarns, Daniel told himself, let him get his kicks where he can. We all need our fantasies.

During the afternoon Tod wandered into his office to return a book. 'Bumped into Emmy the other day,' he said, apropos of nothing. 'In Sainsbury's.'

'Oh yeah?' Daniel said, sensing this must be a prelude to something. 'How is she?'

Tod laughed. 'As a matter of fact she seemed a bit worried about you. I was wondering – I don't mean to pry or anything, you know that, Dan – but, well, if you ever want to talk about anything, well, you know where I am, don't you?'

Daniel thanked him for his concern – it was really rather touching, like a starving pauper fussing over a well-nourished friend's lack of appetite – and assured him that, should he need to confide in someone, Tod would be the first person he'd turn to. 'Maybe it's the old mid-life crisis getting to me,' he concluded vaguely. 'Anyway, it's all under control,' he added, 'I've become an honorary American, I've taken an analyst!' And nothing more was said.

Riding the crowded bus home from town after work, Daniel felt sixteen again, wondering if his date would show.

22

From *The Case of Gabriel Flowers*

The longest and most striking dream recorded in Gabriel's journal, and one that is in many ways a classic of its kind, is dated 22 November. Gabriel said nothing to me of this dream at the time. In fact, only at our final meeting did he confess to any of the erotic dreams discussed below, and even then he refused to elaborate on them in any detail. Had I had access to his dream journal during the period of his treatment, I might have been able to help him more than I did.

There is, however, a problem with this journal, which accounts for the limited use I shall make of it in the form of direct quotation. As mentioned previously, Gabriel was a specialist in American literature, and his training in narrative methods seems to have carried over into the style he adopted when making a written record of his dreams. Never have I witnessed such obvious and imaginative secondary revision of manifest dream content. This is particularly evident with regard to the large chunks of dialogue appearing in the journal entries. It is true that many of the dreams concerned were lucid, a fact which might account in part for their structural coherence and apparent completeness of recall. Nonetheless, it is highly unusual even for lucid dreams to exhibit the kind of systematic organization and strict intelligibility they are given in Gabriel's reconstructions. Consequently, at the risk of being accused of some sort of 'tertiary revision' of my own, I have chosen to extract and paraphrase what I take to be the essence of the more interesting of these dreams (following Stekel's 'simplification' procedure), before offering a tentative, but I believe plausible and accurate, interpretation of their latent content based on my understanding of the broader clinical issues involved.

(*There follows an abridged version of the dream recorded at 5.20 a.m. on 22 November 1984; see Chapter 20.*)

Even the most committed anti-Freudian could hardly fail to recognize the abundance of overt sexual symbolism in the above dream: the phallic symbols of the cigarette and rolled-up newspaper, for example, or the vaginal symbols of the cigarette packet and pockets (indeed, Gabriel himself comments on these elements at one point in a kind of authorial aside, suggesting that at an unconscious level he was aware of their import, despite the superficially mocking tone he adopted when discussing dream symbolism in general). Nor, again, can one miss the impotency-motif implied by Gabriel's failure to satisfy the girl's request for a light for her cigarette. There is, however, a great deal more to the dream than this rather pedestrian account of sexual symbolism might suggest, and much of this deeper significance is contained, I believe, in the dream's verbal rather than concrete symbolism. If we are to arrive at a proper understanding of the dream, in other words, we should consider how its latent content is encoded at a verbal or linguistic level.

There are three main sources of verbal symbolism in the dream, leaving aside the more obvious sexual symbolism of the *Cocktail Party* reference: the name of the girl, the headlines on the newspaper, and the title and author of the book on which the ashtray rests. I propose to examine each of these in turn.

The girl introduces herself as Mary-Ellen or Ellie, names that would appear to condense a double or perhaps triple meaning. The first reference is of course to the Virgin Mary again, here represented under her darker, sexual aspect, combining elements of both Heaven (Ellen) and Hell (Ellie). The second reference is to Gabriel's wife, Emmy, there being as it were only one short alphabetic step between this name and Ellie (an association reinforced by the fact that the initials of Mary-Ellen spell M-E or Em-my). Finally, it may not be too far-fetched to see in the name Ellie an additional, highly economic reference to my own name, via a play on the initials L. E. That is to say, the names chosen by Gabriel's dream-seductress point to her symbolic role as a representative of his ideal mate: a combination of his wife, the Virgin Mary (a displacement of his mother), and his therapist/nurse.

Let us now turn to the newspaper headline, 'M-Way Pile-Up: 6 Missing.' Here I would again point to two possible significations, both of which may be present simultaneously. The first and perhaps dominant symbolic sense of the rubric, I would propose, centres on Gabriel's relations with his wife, here represented by the monniker 'M' or 'Em'. Added to this is the obvious number-symbolism of '6', suggesting 'sex'. A loose translation of the headline, therefore, might read as follows: 'Emmy's way (i.e. life with Emmy) leads to an emotional pile-up in which sex is missing.' Once again it is Gabriel's potency problems that appear to lie at the root of his anxieties, problems here based on the emotional or sexual demands made of him by his wife.

For the secondary associations of the headline it is necessary to recall that Gabriel's father died when the boy was aged six; moreover, although Gabriel himself claimed that his alienation from his mother dated from his teens and was prompted by religious conflicts, it seems reasonable to suppose, in view of the early death of his father, that the real cause of this alienation was Gabriel's guilt about the Oedipal desires he experienced towards his mother. It seems likely, therefore, that the true beginning of his problems with his mother dated from the time of his father's death. Consequently, the 'M' in the headline may be understood as standing for 'Mother' as much as for 'Emmy', and the following secondary translation proposed: 'Mother's way (i.e. life with Mother) led to an emotional pile-up in later years, all stemming from when I was aged six and my father went "missing".' The headline operates as a kind of symbolic shorthand, condensing references to both marital and parental conflicts.

Finally there is the question of the ashtray and book. The ashtray is of course a clear vaginal symbol, being a hollow round receptacle for collecting the ejected matter (semen) of a cigarette (penis). Furthermore, not only is the ashtray itself a 'dirty' object – significantly in the dream it is 'full of crushed butts' – but it is placed on top of a book whose author and title, inverting those of a popular novel dealing with repressed sexuality, associate it both through the *Foul Johns* and the 'Loo-Attendant' with excrementa. As if this were not enough, the title of the book also plays on Gabriel's own surname (which is actually even closer to the word 'foul' than the pseudonym, Flowers, I have adopted here). Clearly, the effect of Gabriel's strict religious upbringing and his unresolved Oedipal feelings towards his mother – unresolved because of his absent father – was to associate sex for him, particularly his own sexuality, with dirt and filth, resulting in his present potency problems. This is why he must empty the ashtray before offering it to his (Virgin) Mary, as if attempting to cleanse or purify their relationship of all sexual and cloacal – or genital (cigarettes) and anal (butts) – content.

It is now possible to spell out the broader implications of the dream based on what we have understood of its latent symbolic structure. We know that Gabriel is experiencing severe sexual problems in his marriage, perhaps because of some unconscious identification between his wife and mother. As a result his blocked libidinal impulses are redirected to other women outside the marriage, represented in the dream by the figure of the ideal mate, a composite of his wife/mother, a darkly sexual Virgin Mary (also containing elements of his mother), and his analyst or nurse. This liberated and rechannelled sexual energy is the contribution of his id. However, against the libidinous id stands the strict censuring judge of the superego with its accusing finger of guilt. Gabriel's guilt is a complex web of factors, woven of a number of strands: the unescaped legacy of his Catholic upbringing, according to which marital infidelity is a sin, his equation of sex and dirt, and the presence in his dream-mate of a triumvirate of taboo sexual objects, namely his mother, the Virgin Mary, and his (male) nurse. Consequently, when sex is proposed to him by the girl in the dream, its initial effect is to reactivate his feelings of impotency (the failure to light the cigarette) and lead him to decline the offer of intimacy because of a fear of castration by the *vagina dentata* (the cigarette is returned to its packet and the packet to a pocket, symbolizing the closing of the *labia minora* and *majora* around the castrated cigarette/penis). However, the id is not so easily denied and reasserts itself through a renewed sexual advance. This time Gabriel is more responsive, even going so far as to take the initiative (the exhibition to the girl of the phallic newspaper). Significantly for an Americanist like Gabriel, the paper is dated 4 July, or Independence Day, though the promise of incipient sexual emancipation this seems to hold out is threatened by moral and religious constraints (the paper is a 'Sunday' edition of the *Guardian*). But the id is strong and the guardian weak and Gabriel succumbs, surrendering to an explicit erotic climax. It is worth adding that the attempted rape of his wife, whether fantasized or real, with which the dream ends suggests an unconscious acknowledgement on Gabriel's part of the critical role played by his wife/mother in the formation of his sexual neuroses, so that the rape functions in effect as an act of punition or retribution whereby he is able to reassert his regained potency and attack the source of its repression. The forces of the id at this stage are clearly in the ascendant; but the resourcefulness of the superego is not to be underestimated, it will in due course strike back.

23

She could have spoken to him at work, but she waited till she was back home, till Daniel was ensconced in his study upstairs and the boys watching children's TV in the lounge, then phoned him from the extension in the kitchen. It was too risky at work, anyone might have overheard. The phone bleated plaintively, monotonously, three or four times. He probably wasn't home yet.

'Hello?'

'Philip, this is Emmy.'

A slight pause. 'Well, this is a pleasant surprise.'

'Look, do you still want to go out for that drink?'

'Sure. When?'

'How about tonight?'

'Tonight?'

'I usually go to my health club on a Friday. It's easy for me to get away.'

'Well, I don't know, I was sort of busy tonight.'

'Forget it,' she said. 'It doesn't matter.'

'No, no, don't ring off, please. OK,' he said, 'how about if I meet you, say, in the Olive Branch, by the cathedral? Say, eight o'clock?'

'No, it's too central, I might see someone I know. There's a pub called the Wife of Bath just past Westgate Tower. Do you know it?'

'I'll find it.'

'I'll see you there around eightish. I have to be back by eleven though, you understand that?'

'That gives us three hours,' he said. 'That's OK. See you at eight then.'

'Bye,' she said.

She was trembling all over like a guilty schoolgirl. It had never struck her before just how easy it was to be unfaithful. But that was jumping ahead. She hadn't been unfaithful yet. Not yet.

24

Friday night was Emmy's night out. A game of squash and a sauna followed by non-alcoholic drinks at her health club was her preferred form of recreation, to Daniel's secret admiration and envy. Daniel's Friday-night routine was always the same. Having suppered and showered and bedded the boys, he'd make himself some sandwiches and stretch out on the settee with a few beers to watch TV. Not as invigorating as a visit to a health club perhaps, but in its way just as restoring; he needed this time on his own, this time when he could be himself totally, without regard for anyone else's wishes, could watch what he wanted on TV, could pick his nose and belch and fart without fear of reproof, could revel in pure slobbery.

Tonight there was a programme he particularly wanted to see, a film about George Orwell's life on the remote Scottish island of Jura, a period of Orwell's life that had always fascinated him. He despatched the boys to bed early, using a system of monetary reward he'd devised some years previously and was frankly rather proud of. The system worked like this. At the start of the evening two piles of 10p pieces, ten in each, would be placed on the boys' bedside tables. If they weren't in bed by eight o'clock half the pile would be removed. Thereafter, each time they got up or called out or made a disturbance, a further 10p would be deducted. Whatever money remained in the morning was theirs. For under two pounds one could purchase perfect freedom.

By 8.15 he had everything ready. Four bottles of chilled imported lager lined up at the foot of the settee. Fire up high, lights down low. Two chicken-liver pâté sandwiches on a plate on his chest. Stretch out. Relax. Enjoy.

The Orwell documentary didn't start for another forty-five minutes and he spent some time idly switching channels with the remote control before settling on an old re-run of 'Porridge'. He'd seen the episode before but laughed again. Then a game show came on and he lost interest. He rested back on the cushions. He felt so tired, so tired. If he could only close his eyes for a few minutes, just to refresh himself.

He awoke some time later with a confused awareness of loud, too jolly music playing somewhere in the room, accompanied by elaborate sound effects. Hammering, screeching, explosions. He came to with a start, then fell back on the sofa, cursing. He'd evidently slept right through the documentary because a cartoon, unusual for so late in the evening, now filled the screen. The modern morality fable of a Tom and Jerry cartoon. Dramatizing the eternal conflict between – what? – good and evil, brains and brawn, mice-men and fat cats, indomitable Spirit and malign Nature? Unrealistically, the rodent always got the better of things. What was that if not a wish-fulfilment dream? In fact, take away their stock plots, Daniel thought, and cartoons were very like dreams, governed by the same sort of logic, a logic of phenomena, a phenomenologic. Thus Tom will be flattened by a steamroller in one scene only to reappear in the next miraculously restored, his injuries healed or forgotten. Thus Jerry will step off a precipice and on to thick air, suspended by the force of his own ignorance; only when he looks down and, with a gulp, remembers gravity, will nature take its course. So it is in dreams. There is no reality in dreams beyond the reality we ourselves construct, phenomena are granted or denied existence by our own awareness or non-awareness of them. Dreams are a solipsist's dream, or night-mare, Berkeley's *esse est percipi* framed in terms we can all understand. He was about to follow up the implications of this interesting line of thought – if we can banish unwelcome elements from our dreams by succeeding in failing to become aware of them ... – when his meditation was interrupted by a raucous buzz at the front door.

Still half-asleep, he went to answer it, assuming Emmy must have forgotten her key and regretting the poor use he'd made of his precious evening alone. But it was Ellie, not Emmy, who stood before him on the porch, bathed in a nimbus of moonlight.

'What are you doing here?'

'That's a nice welcome, I must say. I thought you'd be pleased to see me. We never got a chance to say goodbye properly yesterday.'

'Well I am pleased, yes, of course. But not here. Emmy's due back any minute. How did you know where I lived anyway?'

She smiled. 'See how convincing I am!'

This threw him for a moment. 'Convincing?'

'Daniel, I promise I'll never interfere in your real life. Listen: every time you see me you can be sure it's a dream. This is enough for me. I have a life beyond my dreams too, a life that's – well, a life like any other, I suppose. I don't want to complicate things.'

'As if they aren't complicated already, you mean?'

'Look, let's go for a walk. There's a park over the road, isn't there?'

'Yes, but I can't just leave the boys, I – '

'Daniel! You're as fast asleep as they are. You won't be leaving them.'

He pondered this for a moment. 'I suppose so. I'll get my coat.'

She laughed, and when he returned he understood why. It was a gloriously sunny day with only a few puff-pastry clouds drifting lazily across a porcelain-blue sky. He draped his coat on a gatepost.

'How did you do that, with the weather?'

'You'd be surprised some of the things I can do. I'll teach you if you'll let me.'

They crossed the road and entered the deserted park

through its double wrought-iron gates, hand in hand as if out for a Sunday stroll. Past the daffodil beds, past the duck-pond and the bandstand, up the hill to where the towers of the cathedral could be seen rising distantly through the shimmering haze. As they walked she spoke to him of the pleasures of dream-life.

'This is all so new to me,' Daniel said. 'I don't understand any of it. How can it feel so real? How can we be sharing a single dream?'

She nodded sympathetically as if she herself had once been beset by similar doubts. 'Let me put it like this. At the dream-level we're all connected, OK? All dreams run from the same power-source, all dreams are shared dreams. Of course, we aren't normally aware of this because the same dream will still look different from two points of view and because we usually have no control over who we share our dreams with, we dream at random. How many times have you said to yourself, Why did I have that dream last night, of that old friend of mine I haven't seen in years? Your friend probably wondered the same thing too. Only if we're conscious, if we're self-conscious, if we're lucid, can we choose our dream partners, can we target our energies to a particular person. I see it as a kind of auric projection: our psychic energy travels out from us in waves or pulses, it meets other energies of a similar wavelength, and sometimes chance pools of it collect. These pools we call dreams. Lucidity simply reduces the element of chance, gives us control over that power of projection.'

Daniel was silent for a moment. 'I still don't see it. What about dreams of the dead?'

'What about them?'

'Well, doesn't that imply – ?'

'Yes, Daniel, it does imply. Did you think dreams were a prerogative of the living? Why shouldn't the dead dream too? There's bugger all else for them to do.'

'I don't know, that takes some swallowing. I'm not sure I fancy the idea of spending an eternity in dreams.'

'Why not, for God's sake? It's a lot more fun than lying rotting in the ground, isn't it? Honestly, Daniel, I don't think you realize how lucky we are. Compare it with the real world, what you call the real world. Think how it always frustrates your plans. Things happen when you don't want them to, and don't happen when you do want them to. Life's the bad dream, not this. Look around you. Isn't it wonderful? Here we can do what we like, we decide, we choose. Here we're masters of our own destiny, here anything's possible.'

'Anything?'

'Well, almost anything. Tell me,' she said, standing close against him and draping her arms round his neck, 'what would you like to do today?'

'I don't know, I thought we could just walk and talk, you know.'

'Oh Danny, you're hopeless!' The diminutive surprised and pleased him: only his mother and one or two schoolfriends had ever called him Danny. 'Don't you want to make love?'

'Well yes, of course, but I wasn't sure – '

She kissed him wetly and noisily, playfully, on the lips. 'What's your wildest sexual fantasy?' she said.

He reddened. 'Well, they're all pretty wild.'

'How wild? Come on, shock me.'

'Well, one thing I've always wanted to do is ... God, I feel awful even saying it ... it's ... well, I'd like to sort of make love on the altar of a church.'

She looked disappointed. 'Is that all? Oh well, maybe you'll become more adventurous later. Mighty oaks and all that.' And he noticed that there was indeed a towering oak near where they stood. 'Close your eyes.'

'What?'

'Close your eyes.'

He closed them.

'Now open them again.'

He did so and found they were standing in the nave of an enormous vaulted cathedral. Canterbury Cathedral?

Possibly. A cathedral, anyway. Stained-glass windows of intricate design shed a prismatic glow over the rows of empty pews. Candle-light illuminated the niches high in the wall where a line of carved figures gazed down, a silent audience of stone. The smell of incense hung heavy in the air. Ellie was dressed in a white muslin frock, a virgin all ready for sacrifice. Together they mounted the altar.

'Would you like to do it during a service? We could have a mass going on if you want. Evensong? Matins?'

'God no, please, this is fine.' He stood for a moment admiring her. 'Oh Ellie, you look so beautiful. I'd forgotten how it felt to really want someone.'

'Undress me then,' she said and raised her arms over her head for him to lift off her dress. Beneath it she was naked. Delicate, fragrant and golden in the filtering light. He fell to his knees and covered her with kisses, breathing in her perfume, unable to get enough of her, assuaging the thirst of a lifetime. Probing her with his tongue, blind and reptilian, gnawing, feasting on her flesh, while she gently caressed his head, pressing him deeper inside her. He grappled her to the floor, growing harder and hotter by the moment. Unbuckling his belt, he was about to pin her beneath him when she appealed to him to slow down, take it easy, relax, make it last.

'Yes, you're right.' From a font that appeared to have suddenly materialized nearby he scooped a handful of holy water and doused it over the bulbous end of his purple-throbbing penis, a battered thumb that had to be plunged in cold water to kill the pain. And she was his oasis, oh his adorable oasis! He scooped another handful of spring-cool water and sprinkled it between her thighs. She gasped with a shock of delight and raised herself on all fours, face pressed flat to the smooth stone flags, gazing back at him with the imploring eyes of a child about to be beaten, who welcomes the punishment as atonement for her sins.

'Now?' he managed to murmur.

'Not yet.'

He eased her buttocks gently apart, exposing the scarlet buttonhole of her anus. He wanted to taste it and did so, running rings round the tender red rim, encircling it, anointing it, with the point of his tongue. Her cries escaped like sudden prayers, echoing in the lofty vaults above them.

'Worship me,' she demanded. 'Worship me.'

He returned his attentions to the seat of her passion, now swollen and dewy with desire, fitting the contours of her lips to his own, lapping and flicking at her clitoris till it too was red and inflamed. He ran his hands over the downy, soft thighs, into the damp delta between her legs, on to the sleek, dangling breasts, rich and full as wineskins, with their rosily erupting nipples. She reached through her legs and took hold of him, impatient now for the moment of possession.

'Jesus,' he breathed as he slid inside her.

A tortured cry broke from her lungs, mounting higher as he ran her through. A rhythm achieved, a benediction bestowed. A passion tide. He looked down at her face, the curled lip of ecstasy imparting a savage quality to her features. Bunching the fingers of one hand, he crammed them inside her mouth, wishing he could fill all her orifices at once, could impale her from every angle with swords of flesh like one of those illusionists with a woman in a crate. Yes, he was worshipping her with his body, as she was worshipping him, folded together in the embrace of some sacramental rite, kneeling before her holy vessel as she knelt before the sceptre of his godmanhood, exploring and exploding deep inside her, transmitting his seed to the bottom of her womb, ripping through her immaculate flesh like a barbed and venomous spear.

25

From *The Case of Gabriel Flowers*

The following night, according to his journal, Gabriel again had a lucid dream involving the girl calling herself Mary-Ellen or Ellie, and the contest being played out in the theatre, or battleground, of his mind between guilt and desire, super-ego and id, took another decisive step forward. The dream is the most overtly sexual of any of those recorded in the journal. Indeed, so erotic is it that at times it reads less like a dream report and more like a conscious exercise in pornography, a masturbatory fantasy. The account is distinguished by an almost total lack of narrative action and a corresponding fascination with the detailed description of sexual organs and acts. The four-page entry can be reduced to the following simplification:

> In Canterbury Cathedral with Ellie, who is dressed in white like a sacrificial virgin. A statue of the Madonna gazes down at us, hand raised as if bestowing a benediction. We mount the altar and undress, then engage in energetic foreplay. I sprinkle holy water from a font over both our sexual organs. We have intercourse.

What is interesting about the dream, however, is not so much its manifest content (or lack of it) as the language in which it is recorded. The sexual activity occurring in the dream is presented in powerfully religious terms. Thus words like 'anoint', 'sacramental', 'passion', and 'worship' are repeated with a regularity bordering on the obsessional. In part, of course, this is the conventional language of pornography and therefore almost to be expected in the context of an erotic fantasy, dreamt or otherwise; besides which it is clearly the result of secondary revision on Gabriel's part. Nonetheless, it serves to underline the fact that the dream derives much of its effect from its subversion of traditional religious values. The demons of the id have been let loose with a vengeance, and react against the forces of guilt that have kept them repressed (Gabriel's Catholic upbringing) by deliberately flouting the most sacred of religious taboos. Thus the girl loses her components of mother, wife and nurse, and is transformed into nothing more or less than the Dark Virgin, madonna and whore combined (represented by the white dress and the statue of the Holy Mother blessing the lovers' sexual activity). What appears to be happening here is that, by consummating his relationship with the girl in the immaterial setting of a dream and the sanctified environment of a church, Gabriel is casting himself in the role of Holy Spirit and the girl in the role of Virgin. The dream becomes in effect a symbolic re-enactment of the Immaculate Conception.

Nor is that all. The other main source of verbal imagery in the dream report derives from the languages of sadism and bestiality: thus we find a high incidence of words like 'gnawed', 'devoured', 'tortured', 'animal', 'savage', etc. Furthermore, the vaginal penetration is presented as taking place from the rear and the penis itself transformed into a metaphorical 'spear'. Once again one must bear in mind that this is the conventional *topos* of pornography. However, in view of Gabriel's earlier dream of the crucified cat, in which his apostasy from Catholicism and alienation from his mother were both expressed in terms of his torture and murder of the cat/Christ figure, one cannot help feeling that – as he himself may have unconsciously recognized – a symbolic identification has taken place between the nail/spear of the earlier dream (the 'tool' as he called it there) and the penis/spear of the later one. So complete is the id's reaction against the moral and religious constraints that have held it in check that Gabriel becomes, in effect, both progenitor and murderer of Christ simultaneously.*

<hr />

*The setting and content of the dream also hint at two possible subtextual allusions: to T. S. Eliot's play *Murder in the Cathedral*, about the assassination of Thomas à Becket in Canterbury Cathedral, and to a famous scene in Matthew Lewis's 1796 novel *The Monk*, where the hero dreams of his beloved, dressed in white, being 'tortured' upon the altar of a cathedral by the 'odious caresses' of a lascivious 'Monster'. I am reliably informed that Gabriel was familiar with both works.

26

She made sure she didn't get to the Wife of Bath until ten past eight to allow him plenty of time to arrive before her. She hated going into pubs alone. It was different for men. A man could go into a pub by himself and no one would turn a hair; he was there for the beer, or to meet his pals, or escape from the kids. When a woman did the same it was automatically assumed she was there to be picked up or, worse, was actually on the game. On the game! What a phrase, a man's phrase. It wasn't a game for the women who did it, it was work, serious dirty work.

She paused outside a darkened shop window across the street to examine herself in the reflection from a street lamp before going in. She liked the way she looked tonight. High heels suited her, made her legs seem longer, gave her that extra couple of inches and enhanced the curve of her breasts and behind, or would have done without her coat on. Had it been risking it to wear her best silk blouse and her good black skirt with the slit up front and back? She was supposed to be going to her health club after all. But Daniel didn't say anything, he was too preoccupied with himself these days, barely seemed to notice when she left. She leant closer to the window for a final check on her make-up, but it was hard to make out anything more than a general blurred impression of glossed lips and darkened eyes. Well, her hair looked OK anyway. When she was a child, people had always said her hair was her best feature, which struck her now as something of a double-edged compliment. Still, it had meant she'd always looked after it, trimmed her split ends, kept it long and well conditioned. She ran her fingers through it now to give it that slightly mussed, negligent look that she felt showed it off to its best effect, then turned to cross the street.

There were two bars in the Wife of Bath, why hadn't she thought of that? Public and saloon. But surely he wouldn't go to the public bar, you didn't meet a date in a public bar, he must know better than that. (A date? Was that what tonight was? She hadn't been on a date in years.) She pushed open the saloon door, preparing her smile.

A group of three youngish men at the bar turned their heads in unison towards her as she entered, appraising her with a leisurely up-and-down of their eyes. She cast about over the deserted tables and chairs. Shit, he wasn't here! For a moment she hesitated in the doorway, unsure what to do. Perhaps she ought to go away and come back in another ten minutes. But then she might miss him. God, I have every bit as much right to be here as they do, she thought, returning the three men's single gaze, why am I so nervous all of a sudden? She threw back her head and strode purposefully towards the bar. 'Vodka and tonic please, with ice.' The three men grew silent beside her.

Maybe it was a mistake to have arranged to meet here. They should have met somewhere more crowded, somewhere with people, music, noise. How were you supposed to conduct an affair in this cathedral-like silence.

She took her clinking drink to a table in a far corner away from the bar, feeling the three men's gaze on her back as she walked. Removed her coat, draped it across the worn velveteen stool by her side. Delved into her bulging shoulder bag containing her towel and gym wear and the flat shoes she'd changed out of (what a charade this was!), searching for the cigarettes and matches she'd bought on her journey across town. She oughtn't to smoke, she knew, it was bad for her asthma, but at times like this it was indispensable.

Cigarette in one hand, drink in the other, she began to relax. She'd said 'eightish' after all, not 'eight' – or did he say that? Well, it was still barely ten past. She sat back in her chair and gazed around her at the framed prints of characters from the *Canterbury Tales* adorning the gaudily papered walls, making a pretence of interest. The three men at the bar resumed their huddled conversation.

By twenty past eight he still hadn't arrived and she'd almost finished her drink. The bastard, he wasn't going to show up, he'd done it deliberately because of the way she'd snubbed him before. She thought of all the effort she'd put into her preparations, all the agonizing over what to wear, of how nervous she'd been ever since the phone call. Of the hour in the bathroom with her waxing stick and tweezers. Of how she'd smuggled her stockings and suspenders out of the house in her shoulder bag so she could change from her tights in the cramped, smelly cubicle of the ladies' toilets at Westgate Gardens. Getting made up in the mirror over the rusty sink, drawing curious looks from the other women who came in (please don't let me see anyone I know!). And all for what? To be leered at and whispered about behind their hands by those three oafs at the bar whose pregnant wives were probably at home cooking supper for their loutish kids. She'd give him another ten minutes, then she was leaving.

Five minutes later he arrived. He smiled briefly, wanly, across at her, raised a hand in greeting, and went straight to the bar to order a pint.

'Sorry I'm late,' he said matter-of-factly, pulling up a stool across the table. 'Bloody car wouldn't start. Been here long?'

He might have come up with a better excuse than that! Probably trying to get rid of some other young floozie – some *other* young floozie? What am I saying? – making an excuse about his sick mother. Sick mother, that was closer to the truth. If Sean and Liam could see their sick mother now.

'You look sensational,' he said. She softened at this, despite herself. When was the last time anyone had told her she looked sensational?

She saw his hand disappear beneath the table and felt it alight on her knee, slide smoothly under her skirt and ascend the inside of her thigh. 'Ooh, stockings!' he said. 'Good girl!'

She pushed him away, crossed her knees, looked over at the bar, at the backs of the three supping men. 'Control yourself, for God's sake.'

They sat for a moment in frosty silence. Briefly she was tempted to get up and walk out, go home, before it was too late, leaving him to lament his loss. But she'd come this far, the hard part was over. If she left now, she'd never know what she was missing. Besides, it wasn't necessary that she like him as a person; it was a meeting of bodies she wanted, not a meeting of minds. 'You know I have to be back by eleven? I told you that.'

'Better not waste any more time then, had we? Come on, drink up.'

She drained what little melted ice remained in her glass; he hadn't even bought her a drink. 'Where are we going?' she said, her mind throwing up gruesome visions of sweaty gruntings and fumblings in the back seat of a car in some darkened, prophylactic-strewn lane.

'My place. OK?' He took three long gulps in quick succession from his pint and replaced it empty and froth-lined on the table. 'Aaah.'

In the car park she stood by the side of his maroon Ford Fiesta, waiting for him to open the passenger door. He lifted the locking pin. 'It's unlocked.' She waited. He shook his head, smiling, then leant across again to pull the handle. 'Your car awaits, Madame.'

As she backed in through the open door, keeping her knees together and swivelling round on the seat, he calmly rested his hand on her breast and gave it a gentle squeeze.

'Hands off! If you want anything to happen tonight, I suggest you keep your grubby little paws to yourself till we're indoors. I have a reputation to protect.'

He shrugged, 'Just trying to be friendly,' and started the engine.

Leaving the car park, it struck her that she had no idea where he lived.

'Not far,' he said. 'Herne Bay.'

Herne Bay! That was miles away. She calculated rapidly. It was twenty to nine now. They'd have to leave by ten thirty if she was to be back by eleven. That would give them approximately an hour and a quarter. It wasn't long.

They drove for a while in silence. 'You know, I don't know anything about you. I'm not even sure why I phoned you.'

'I am.'

'Oh really. Enlighten me, please.'

'You want an affair,' he said. 'No strings. Nothing that would threaten your marriage, you've invested too much in it for that. Just a bit of good old-fashioned rutting.'

'Please!' she said. The trouble was he was right; that was precisely what she wanted. 'You could try and make it a bit more personal. I don't even know who you are.'

'What's to know?'

'Oh, just trivial things. Like where you come from, what you're doing here, what you want out of life.'

'A good time, I suppose, doesn't everyone? Look, since you're interested: I went to university down here at the end of the seventies, spent a couple of years teaching in Sweden, couple in Japan, and now I'm back here. End of story. Satisfied?'

If he went to university here at the end of the seventies, he might have been one of Daniel's students, they might know each other. God!

They drove along Herne Bay sea-front, eerily quiet as it always seemed at this time of the year, even on a Friday night, then turned into a side street off the prom and pulled up outside an old Victorian three-storeyed terrace.

'Big place,' she said. 'D'you live here alone?'

'Not all mine, unfortunately. Just the first-floor flat.'

She followed him through the gate and along the path, read the name in black type under the middle of the three lighted doorbells. P. Rice. How apt! What price would she have to pay for this, what payment would be exacted from her for what she was about to do?

The front door opened into a small vestibule with the

downstairs tenant's door leading off to the left. She followed him up the narrow, poorly lit staircase, both walls bare of decoration. At the top of the stairs he unlocked his door and stood back to usher her in ahead of him. '*Entrez*,' he said.

She emerged in a long, carpeted hallway with rooms leading off from the right and a large sitting-room with cane furniture visible through the open door at the end. Against the hall wall was a narrow high table with a number of unopened letters resting on top and a long, gilt-framed mirror above.

He took her coat and hung it on a hook on the back of the door together with his own, then turned back to her and began unbuttoning her white silk blouse.

'Don't waste much time, do you?' she said, letting him do it, thinking, This is what you came here for, isn't it? This is what you wanted.

'This is just an aperitif,' he said. 'Something to sharpen the taste buds. The main course will follow presently.'

He removed her blouse and let it fall to the floor. 'Cute little bra, but it'll have to come off, I'm afraid.' He unhooked it, dropped it on top of her blouse, began fondling her pouting breasts, kissing them, nipping them, wetting her nipples with his tongue, drawing them out with teeth and lips. This is like a movie, she thought, like a dream, stroking his hair, running her fingers through his tight brown curls. He sank to his knees and unzipped her skirt at the side, working it down over her hips, lifting each ankle in turn for her to step out of it. Hold your stomach in, she thought, hold it in. 'Wow, now that's what I call sexy!' Eyes fixed on her thin, lacy suspender belt and matching lace briefs with tie-sides and red embroidered rose on the front (a present from Daniel – 'A red, red rose for my red, red rose' – oh God!). 'Seems almost a shame to have to take them off.' He pulled one bow with finger and thumb, watching as the front flapped and fell open. Pulled the other, let them slide unaided to the floor. Leant towards her and covered her pubis with a long, slow lick of his tongue. Drew back for a more measured view, moaned softly, then returned again to nuzzle and lick, nibble and kiss. She felt herself growing quickly, embarrassingly wet – God, wet wasn't the word, she must be drenching him! He raised himself to his feet, moved her towards the hall table, swept the unopened letters carelessly on to the floor. Then, still in her stockings, suspenders and stilettos, she found herself lifted high into the air and deposited on the polished mahogany table-top, smooth and deliciously cold beneath her, the glass of the mirror chill against her shoulder-blades, fire and ice. He ran his hands up the insides of her thighs, spreading them wide, opening her up for inspection. Stood back and began unbuttoning his shirt, eyes travelling the length of her body, radiating out in leisurely sweeps before returning each time to her yawning, glistening centre.

'Puss puss puss,' he said.

27

'Ellie, Emmy, Emmellie,' he'd been chanting, intoning, reciting, when she woke him up the following night.

'I think you should move into the study, Daniel. I think that's best, don't you? That's the third night in a row.'

'I know, I guess so, I'm sorry. What can I say? I wish I could explain it but I can't.'

'Don't try. I don't know what you want from me, and I don't think you do either. You don't seem to want to make love any more. Instead there's these – these rapes.'

'Hardly rapes.'

'Well what would you call them? I'm asleep and then I wake up and find you on top of me.'

'I'm asleep too. Don't forget that.'

'So you say.'

'You don't believe me?'

'I don't know, I don't know what to believe. I don't seem able to reach you any more. If you're asleep, what's happening? I mean are you dreaming or what?'

'Yes, I told you.'

'What are you dreaming of, then?'

'Well, you, of course. Who else?'

'Don't say, "Who else?" like that. How should I know what you're dreaming of? It could be anything, anyone.'

'But it's not, is it? It's you, I've told you.' He got out of bed and opened the wardrobe door, piling sheets and blankets on to his arms. 'I'll make up the bed in the study then.'

'Not tonight. You don't need to do it tonight.'

'It's best.'

Emmy began sobbing quietly. Nothing could make him feel so desolate as the sound of her tears. It awoke all the paternal, protective instincts in him. She became his little girl who needed cradling against all the horror of the world, all the horror that was him.

'Don't cry, Emmy, please.'

'I'm sorry, I can't help it. First those dreams when you didn't know if you were asleep or awake, now this. Daniel, what's happening to you, what's happening to us?'

'I don't know.'

'Why don't you phone Doctor Eidel and see if you can bring your next appointment forward? Perhaps he can help. You have to do something, we can't go on like this.'

'I know, I will, I'll phone him on Monday, I promise,' he lied. He turned to face her. 'Can I have a pillow?'

'Of course, take both of them.'

'No, one's enough.' He tucked it under his arm and moved towards the door. 'Well, goodnight then.'

'Goodnight, Daniel. Daniel,' she called as he closed the door behind him, 'I love you.'

He heard her muffled sobs mount as he walked away.

PART FOUR

The glory dropped from their youth and love,
And both perceived they had dreamed a
dream.

> Browning, *The Statue and the Bust*

28

So this was what it had come to: abandoning the bed of his wife to be with the girl of his dreams. So much for not having to lead a double life! Could his life be any more double, any more duplicitous, than at present? During the day he went about his business as a respected member of the community: a married man with two children, a teacher, a man of learning. While at night, in some dreadful metamorphosis of the spirit, he became this other, this phantom, this bodiless daemon performing impossible sexual acrobatics in a world where the laws of the physical universe seemed no longer to matter or apply. Wasn't he as much of a cheat and two-timer as the most faithless adulterer? For God's sake, he'd even taken to wearing a condom in bed – affixed with a rubber band to prevent its slipping off during the early, unaroused stages of sleep, an expedient which only served to heighten his excitement when tumescence, as it always did, struck. This so as to avoid having to face Emmy at the end of the week with a sheet stained with the sordid evidence of his betrayals. What a wretch he'd become!

Yet he couldn't tear himself loose. On the contrary, each night he felt himself sinking deeper, succumbing more and more to the persuasive appeal of his dreams. At Ellie's suggestion their lovemaking grew more adventurous: she taught him how to do it underwater without the aid of breathing apparatus in some blue lagoon of the mind, and airborne without parachutes, floating like feathers on a cushion of air, Mother Earth grainy and mottled beneath them. It struck him that there must be some limit to the frequency and variety of their couplings, some limit to his own powers of recovery if not to Ellie's ingenuity. One night they made love six times, each time on a different continent (not surprisingly, the last of these, on a windswept Antarctic ice-sheet, proved finally impossible).

His work began to suffer too. How was he supposed to make sense of *Tales of Mystery and Imagination* or *The Turn of the Screw* when the screws were turning on his own life, when his own imagination was a mystery? His job started to seem an annoying excrescence on his life, a niggling irrelevance to the real drama of his days. He found himself falling prey to absurd feelings of paranoia. So it sometimes seemed that everyone in the university was aware of the intimate details of his inner life and was determined he should know it. One morning, for example, he was seated with Tod in the Senior Common Room, discussing a certain troublesome student, while opposite them a pair of drudges from Economics were puzzling over the *Times* crossword. 'How d'you spell "elemental"?' one of them asked. 'Is it ell-ay or ell-ee?' 'Ell-ee,' the other replied with an ambiguous grin, 'ell-ee-mental.' Daniel put down his cup, stood up and left without a word.

There was no one he could talk to about what he was going through. He couldn't talk to Emmy, for obvious reasons, and Tod was someone he'd never really felt able to confide in, despite the latter's recent, clumsy attempt at intimacy; their relationship simply wasn't like that. They could discuss at inordinate length the emotional complexities of a novel by James or Fitzgerald, but when it came to their own lives – well, that was another matter.

That left Eidel, but the little faith Daniel had once had in psychiatry and psychiatrists was rapidly beginning to be eroded. Psychiatry, psychotherapy, psycho-rape. Eidel seemed determined to reduce everything to Daniel's relationship with his mother and to relate this, in turn, to the sexual problems he imagined Daniel was experiencing in his marriage. He'd gone to Eidel with what he was assured was a relatively routine, more or less mechanical, disorder, but instead found himself being quizzed about remote events in his early childhood, matters that seemed of no conceivable relevance at all. In fact, he'd have been tempted to abandon the therapy altogether had he not been sure that Emmy would merely interpret this as further evidence of his cravenness, his inability to face up to his problems. It was one of the phrases she used, 'facing up to your problems', like 'coming to terms with yourself' and 'liking yourself' and 'getting in touch with your emotions', to cover up for her complete lack of understanding of what he was feeling.

The upshot of all this, as far as Daniel's relationship with Eidel was concerned, was that he began to censor what he told him, began, frankly, to lie, to invent. He didn't do this indiscriminately. For example, he was quite open about the fact that he no longer shared a bed with Emmy (though he kept quiet about the alleged 'rapes' that were responsible for this). Where he allowed himself licence was in the account of his dreams. There was something so rare, so pure, so, well, *personal* about his dreams of Ellie (with Ellie? from Ellie? even his prepositions were becoming problematic), that he was unwilling to contaminate them by sharing them with Eidel. Besides, did he honestly imagine that the learned doctor – a trained scientist, or pseudo-scientist, after all – would take seriously his claim to be partaking of a common dream-life with a woman he barely knew? He wasn't talking about simple telepathic dreams here – whose existence, apparently, even Freud had been prepared to concede (Daniel became an avid reader of books on dreams) – he was talking about a spectacular, unprecedented kind of joint astral projection. You had to admit, it took some swallowing.

So he said nothing about his night-life with Ellie. Instead he palmed Eidel off with other, more suitable dreams, real or imagined, hatched on the spot or cobbled together from the prop-shop of memory. There was a strange sort of fascination to be had from seeing how easily Eidel's attention could be collared and held in tow by introducing the most banal of symbols (a ruined column, a felled tree, a rusty nail) into his dream reports. There was something faintly prurient and offensive about the man's constant eagerness to talk dirty symbols.

Another of Daniel's stratagems was to question Eidel's questions, to defuse them before they could detonate, to make them the ground of a much broader inquiry into the nature of methods and meaning, psychiatry and semantics, verifiability, veridicality. It was an elaborate cat-and-mouse game they played between them, another Tom and Jerry cartoon.

'Why do you persist in hiding behind words?' Eidel asked him on one occasion.

'I beg your pardon?'

'Why do you hide behind words? Whenever you find yourself confronted with a difficult emotional situation, with a feeling you can't deal with or don't wish to recognize, you immediately domesticate it, you denature it, you disguise it with words. Words give you power over it, or an illusion of power. Like those pets people dress up in human clothes. But emotions don't wear clothes, Daniel, emotions are naked.'

'Oh that's very good, can I use that some time? By the way, let's get this straight, are you suggesting we conduct this conversation non-verbally? I mean, I can draw you a picture of how I'm feeling if you like, or do a mime. You know, "Give Us a Clue" or "Don't Say a Word" or whatever it's called. Two syllables. First syllable – '

'There you go again,' said Eidel.

'What?'

'Hiding behind whimsy.'

'I'm talking,' Daniel said. 'Talking. Isn't that what we're supposed to be here for?'

29

Sex, sex, sex, she loved it, couldn't get enough. She hadn't felt this good in years. The moment she stepped outside the house on the two, or with luck three, evenings a week that she managed to see Philip, she felt as if a cloud was being lifted from above her, as if a swift summer breeze was chasing away the brooding thunderhead crouched doom-laden over her head, bringing with it a stretch of clear, blue, open sky. If Daniel was going to lead his own secret life buried away up there in his study, doing whatever he did, then she would lead hers too.

They did it on the floor in the hall, in the kitchen bent over the table, on chairs and cushions, in the bath all covered in suds, all the places, all the ways, she'd never done it before with Daniel or Michael or any one of her meagre tally of previous lovers (what had she been missing out on all her life? Why had no one ever told her it could be like this?). He was insatiable, and so was she. As soon as they entered the door of his flat they'd be at each other's throats, tearing at each other's clothes – literally tearing, on two occasions he ripped the zips on her dress and she had to return with them pinned together, praying she'd have time to change before seeing Daniel.

She wondered how long it could go on like this. Nothing lasted forever, she was old enough to have learnt that. It was a fling, that was what they called it. Apt in a way, thinking of how she'd fling her arms round his neck, her legs round his waist, throwing herself at him. No, of course it wouldn't last. But right now it didn't matter, she didn't care. It was happening now, and now, for the moment, was all there was.

She adored pleasing him. Dressing in the sort of underwear she knew excited him, making up her face in the bathroom at his flat with scarlet lipstick and thick mascara when he wanted her to act the whore, putting lipstick on her nipples too when he wanted it (only she must never, ever forget to take it off before going home). Once he asked if he could shave her and for a moment she was tempted. Why not? She and Daniel weren't sleeping together, he'd never know, it would grow back. But that was stupid, there was no point taking unnecessary risks, keep a grip on yourself.

It wasn't easy. Sometimes she had to remind herself that she was a woman approaching forty, with two young children, a job, a home, responsibilities. What was extraordinary was that she felt younger, less responsible, less wifely – yes, that was it, less wifely – than she had at any time since her teens.

And what about her and Daniel? Would that continue, would that remain, would they still be together when this was all over? God knows, he wasn't the easiest of men to live with even at the best of times, and recently he'd become impossible. Morose, sullen, unreachable almost. Yet for all that, she felt a deep and genuine affection for him. Where did affection end and love begin? Or was there any difference, was love perhaps just affection plus sex? She certainly wasn't in love with Philip – lust, yes, but not love. And hadn't she told Daniel she loved him the other night? Or was that just guilt? Oh, who could say? There'd be plenty of time to mull that one over when the time came. For the moment you're feeling good, she told herself, don't spoil it, don't complicate things. Time enough for soul-searching when the storm clouds gather again, when the clear blue deepens to an unbroken tempest-grey.

30

Daytime existence for Daniel had degenerated into a series of shabby, unfurnished waiting-rooms. A gentleman-in-waiting, that's what he was. Waiting to sleep, waiting to dream. It was at night that he came truly alive, the days were mere gaps in time, dark hollows crossed by vague, evanescent shadows. Life had become a shadow-play.

He tried half-heartedly to plug these barren interstices between his periods of authentic living by returning to his book on Poe, but found himself unable to concentrate, distracted by the details of Poe's biography and what he saw as their uncanny correspondence with events in his own life. He'd never before realized, for example, how the names of virtually all the significant women in Poe's life seemed to consist of variations on the name 'Ellie' or 'Ellen'. To confirm this, he drew up a list of Poe's Women: Elmira Shelton, Mrs Ellet, Estelle (Stella) Lewis, Helen Whitman. His mother, too, was an Elizabeth, and his cousin-wife a Virginia Eliza (probably the most important woman of all in his life, his aunt and mother-in-law Mrs Clemm, was a Maria). Likewise in his stories and poems there were the Eulalies and Eleonoras, the Helens and Lenores, the Morellas and Annabel Lees. Then there were Poe's dream-poems – 'A Dream', 'Dreams', 'A Dream Within a Dream', 'Dream-Land' – and the prefatory note to what he regarded as his *magnum opus*, the mystical prose poem *Eureka*, addressed, he said, 'to the dreamers and those who put faith in dreams as in the only realities'. Even the fact that Poe died in the year 1849, a simple transposition of 1984, seemed to Daniel vaguely ominous and full of dark meaning.

Poe's relationship with Helen Whitman especially intrigued and disturbed him, reverberating as it did with so many strange half-echoes of his own relationship with Ellie. Mrs Whitman was apparently a rather unworldly character, deeply immersed in the spiritualistic current of her time. Soon after he first saw her, and before he'd even spoken to her, Poe sent her, anonymously, a copy of his famous love-lyric, 'To Helen', torn from a book of his poems. A month later he sent her a new poem, also entitled 'To Helen', which he claimed 'contained all the events of a *dream* which occurred to me soon after I knew you'. Their first meeting seems to have produced a remarkable effect on Poe, reinforcing his identification of her with the subject of the original, youthful 'To Helen'. 'I felt, for the first time in my life, and tremblingly acknowledged,' he says, in a letter in which a number of words have unaccountably been excised with a knife, 'the existence of spiritual influences altogether out of the reach of the reason. I saw that you were *Helen – my* Helen – the Helen of a thousand dreams – she whose visionary lips had so often lingered upon my own in the divine trance of passion – she whom the great Giver of all Good had preördained to be mine – mine only – if not now, alas! then at least hereafter and *forever*, in the Heavens.' He goes on: 'It is my diviner nature – my spiritual being – that burns and pants to com-mingle with your own.' And concludes, remarkably: 'My soul, this night, shall come to you in dreams and speak to you ...' As the affair progresses and Poe's proposals of mar-riage are rejected, his letters grow increasingly disturbed and gnomic. He assures her that he did not love his wife Virginia but married for the sake of her happiness, not his own. He speaks of unnamed 'fears' and a 'terrible agony ... known only to my God and to myself.' He takes a dose of laudanum in an unsuccessful attempt at suicide and tells her she is the only one who can save him from a fearful doom. An engagement is briefly agreed upon before Mrs Whitman breaks it off and ends the affair for good. Within the year Poe is dead. A decade later, in her book *Edgar Poe and his Critics*, Mrs Whitman pays homage, apparently without irony, to Poe's enormous imaginative power 'that made his dreams realities, and his life a dream'.

The tragedy of Poe's end filled Daniel with strange forebodings and increased the sense of isolation he felt in the face of his own bizarre dream-life. At home he became a ghostly presence, spending long hours closeted alone in his study inventing lectures to write and essays to mark, surfacing only at mealtimes and for the occasional half-hour of TV. There seemed to be a sort of tacit understanding between Emmy and himself that until the present crisis was over they would talk only of trivial, practical matters, live only on the surface as it were, avoiding deeper and more perilous waters. So at mealtimes, for the sake of the boys, they would adopt an exaggerated lightness of tone, what Daniel came punningly to nickname to himself their anti-gravity device. Subjects of conversation might include the competition on the back of the cornflakes packet or the number of shopping days left till Christmas, but not the reasons for Daniel's increasingly haggard appearance and elsewhere eyes, or the reasons he and Mummy no longer shared a bed. They kept up the pretence even when alone. Watching a film together, Emmy would point out the flaws in the plot and Daniel would nod and agree, or politely demur, and all the time both of them would be thinking, Why are we acting like this? Why aren't we talking about things that matter, about our inability to talk about things that matter?

Touching was another taboo. Moving about the same room together, they would manœuvre around one another in an elaborate dance, ducking and weaving and feinting like polarized magnets to avoid the embarrassment of accidental contact. Daniel wasn't sure who introduced these new rules, who established these limits on communication. Was it him? He certainly didn't recall making any conscious decision to that effect. It just seemed to happen that way.

One practical result of this new domestic regime was that Emmy took to going out on her own more often. She already had her Friday nights at the health club, now she took up yoga and weekend visits to the cinema with a friend called Dawn. Daniel was not a naturally suspicious man and Emmy had never given him cause to doubt her, so he saw no reason to believe she was being anything less than honest about the nature of her activities. In fact, so stooped was Daniel beneath the burden of what he regarded as his own act of betrayal, he would scarcely have recognized another's if held up and waved before him.

Only on one occasion did it occur to him, and then only fleetingly, that Emmy might have secrets of her own. It was a Saturday night and she'd gone into town to see a film with Dawn. Around eleven o'clock, having drunk the house dry of booze, Daniel decided to make a quick visit to his local, The End of the Road, to buy a few more bottles of beer before closing time. In the event he was too late, the mats were over the pumps, the truculent landlord already wiping the tables and abusing his tardier customers. Daniel turned back disappointedly into the frosty night air, cursing his luck and the stupidity of English licensing laws. As he did so he saw a car pull up at the lights across the street and an attractive well-dressed woman emerge, laughing, from inside. She bent down to say something to the driver through the open door before slamming it shut and watching as he drew away. Still smiling, she hopped on to the kerb and stepped-and-ran a few paces, awkward in her high heels, as the car turned and sped into the distance. Daniel wondered who could be driving. It had been too far away to make out the face behind the wheel, and to a dedicated non-motorist like himself all cars looked more or less alike. He noticed only that it was dark in colour, red or perhaps black, and what people called a hatchback.

'Walk you home, Miss?' he called as she passed the alley-way where he stood waiting in the shadows.

Her hand sought out her chest in an instinctive gesture of

defence, a look of sudden panic crossing her features.

'God, you frightened me. What are you doing here?'

'Getting some beer. Too late though, bloody landlord wouldn't serve me. Good film?'

'Oh, we didn't go actually. No, it was sold out so we went for a drink instead, then back to Dawn's. Richard offered to drive me home. That's Dawn's husband. Save on cab fare. Good of him really.'

'In a rush was he?'

That look of confusion again. 'No. Why?'

'Well, he could have driven you to the door. 'Stead of letting you walk the last hundred yards in the dark.'

'Oh that was my idea. There's usually a police car by the pub this time of night on a Saturday. Richard had been drinking a bit as well. Seemed silly to risk it.'

'Very thoughtful of you,' he said.

It occurred to him that if he seriously doubted Emmy's story he could check at the cinema to see if the film really did sell out. Or he could check to see if Dawn's husband Richard owned a hatchback, or even existed. He did neither. He had other things on his mind.

31

From *The Case of Gabriel Flowers*

Towards the end of November I began to notice a change in Gabriel's behaviour. The change was gradual at first, only becoming fully apparent at our final meeting some weeks later. It expressed itself in an increasing remoteness and reticence on his part, a sort of willed detachment, as if he were no longer interested in what our meetings might achieve, as if he had erected an invisible barrier between himself and the world, and between himself and me in particular, as if he had in some sense cast himself adrift. Sink or swim, his attitude seemed to say, I will do it on my own. The more intimate and confidential I encouraged him to become, the further he would withdraw behind his finely spun web of whimsy and conceit; the harder I tried to pin him down, the more stubbornly he struggled to escape.

This led to certain obvious problems, not the least of which was the problem of distinguishing exactly how much of what he was telling me was true and how much invention. For example, he admitted after some equivocation that he was no longer sharing a bed with his wife, but gave as the reason for this the fact that his rising in the night to write in his journal disturbed her sleep. I asked him why he could not keep a torch beside the bed – a torch, pen and pad were all that were required, I said – to which he replied that his wife was an extremely light sleeper and would probably wake anyway.

I decided to deliver an ultimatum of sorts. I explained

that I thought we had made considerable progress in the treatment of his problems – his lucid-dream powers were developing quite nicely now and the false awakening almost a thing of the past – but that I still believed there was work to be done. This work required different methods, I told him, with the emphasis no longer on hypnosis or dream analysis or free association but on good old-fashioned straight talking. What it required was honesty, I said, and unless I could be sure he was fulfilling his part of the bargain by being open and sincere with me I saw little point in continuing. Gabriel replied, typically, with a question. 'What is honesty?' he said. 'Define it for me. And tell me how a man can be expected to tell the truth when he doesn't know whether his whole life is a lie.'

The style of Gabriel's journal shows a corresponding change during this period. Where previously the entries gave the impression of having been composed as discrete narrative units, with a generous component of secondary revision, now they begin to look more like brief, coded messages, communiqués from the battlefront, scribbled under stress and in haste. Common words and names are abbreviated (notably the name E., with its ambiguous and multiple reference), punctuation almost non-existent. Some entries break off in mid-sentence, others consist of an illegible scrawl followed by a train of exclamation marks. Where they can be deciphered, the dreams show evidence of being over-whelmingly sexual in content, a chaotic Kama Sutra of the dream state.

It is clear to me now, looking back, that Gabriel's illness had by this time entered an obsessional phase. The obsession centred on his fantasies of sexual gratification with his dream-creation Ellie/Mary-Ellen/E., and like all obsessions was self-fuelling and self-fulfilling. That is to say, the more his waking thoughts dwelt on the erotic dreams he was having, the more likely he would be to have further erotic dreams, and therefore the more preoccupied with these dreams would he become. The circle is vicious and self-consuming. Denied normal expression, Gabriel's libidinal impulses effectively colonized his dreams.

As for the dreams he brought to his meetings with me, I had no way of knowing whether these were authentic or whether they had been concocted for my benefit in order to mask the true nature of his anxieties. I suspected the latter, an opinion which has since been largely borne out through a reading of his journal: little correspondence exists between the material he produced for me at this time and the dreams he recorded privately. In a sense this hardly matters. Lies are no less a fantasy production than dreams, and even the most consciously elaborated fiction will be bound to carry a residue, a seepage, of unconscious content (something of which Gabriel, as a professional reader of novels, should have been well aware). All the same, it raised difficult questions of interpretation and meant that much of the information on which I was basing my judgements was at the very least problematic. I began to feel less like a doctor treating a patient and more like a detective interviewing a suspect, trying to sift fact from fiction, false alibis from true. Perhaps after all this is what a psychiatrist most closely resembles: a psychic sleuth, a mind cop. Gabriel would doubtless have agreed. One of his more amusing puns was his dubbing of my profession the 'Freud Squad'.

32

She lay naked and half-asleep on top of the bed, still glowing, when lightning flashed behind her eyes. Opening them, blinking, shading them with her hand against the sudden light, she looked up to find Philip crouched at the foot of the bed, a Polaroid camera raised before him, its bleached tongue hanging loose as if drooling over what it had seen.

'What's the – what are you doing?'

Oh God, he's going to blackmail me, she thought, he's going to tell Daniel.

'A souvenir,' he said.

'What?'

'A memento. Something to remember you by.'

'You must be joking. If you think you're having a photo of me looking like this,' she gazed down at her body, splayed and open before him, 'what, to show your mates, I suppose, to flash around the pub?' She made a dive for the camera.

'Lay off, it's no big deal,' he said, holding it out of reach above his head. 'I'm not going to show it to anyone, don't be such a prude.'

A prude! she thought. Me! After all the things I've done with him.

'I'm warning you, Philip, if you don't give me that photo this instant, I'm leaving.'

He stood there silently grinning, camera still held aloft.

'Right.' She grabbed her clothes off the floor, where they lay as they'd fallen, in a heap, and began dressing. Or would have done, had she been able to find her panties.

'Lost something?' he said, that sickly smirk still pasted on his face.

'Look, I don't find this very funny. In fact I find it very childish. What have you done with them?'

'Done with what?' All smiles and innocence.

'You know what. My knickers. Another memento, I suppose.'

'Tell you what,' he said. 'I'll do a deal with you. You can have one of them back – the panties or the photo. Which would you prefer?'

This is ridiculous, I can't go home without any knickers on, she thought. (Is he still going to drive me home?) On the other hand, they're less incriminating than the photo. She gritted her teeth. 'Give me the photo.'

'Certainly.' He tore it from the camera, peeled off its protective fascia, and gazed at it for a few seconds before handing it to her. 'Shame. You've come out very well. It catches the essential you.'

'Bastard,' she said, ripping it in two, then two again, and stuffing it in her handbag (don't forget to throw it away – no, burn it!). She slipped on her suspender belt – the suspenders she wore for him! – and began pulling on her stockings, leaning forward on the edge of the bed. 'You know, I'd have given you a pair of my panties if you'd asked. You only had to ask.'

'Wouldn't be the same. I want to think of you going home to your darling hubby with no knickers on.'

'You're sick.'

'Want a lift home?' he said. 'Or would you prefer to ring for a cab?'

'Fuck you, I'll ring for a cab,' she said, sweeping out of the bedroom towards the phone in the hall.

'Doubt if you'll get one this time of night,' he called out behind her. 'Could always walk, I suppose – only take about three hours. Bit of an invitation to any potential rapists, though. Attractive woman walking home alone late at night.

With no knickers on. They'd probably say you were asking for it.'

She paused by the phone. You wait, she thought, you just wait. For what? What could she possibly threaten him with, other than to deprive him of her body, and that would probably be no great loss, he probably had several other women on the go. Men were such bastards. How did they get away with it, why did we let them get away with it?

She slouched back into the bedroom doorway. 'Please drive me home,' she said.

33

With no one else to confide in, Daniel found himself, absurdly, confiding in Ellie. 'What I want to know is,' he asked her in one of the brief interludes between their exertions, 'are you real or have I invented you?'

'Doesn't compute, sorry.'

'Come on, quit fooling about, this is important to me. Look, I'll spell it out for you. What I mean is, are you asleep somewhere now, like me? I know you don't want to tell me where, though I don't understand why – I suppose you have your reasons. But are you having this same dream? Are you, the sleeping you, hearing these words I'm speaking now?'

'D'you want a straight answer?'

'Of course.'

'Yes, I am.'

For a moment Daniel was satisfied with this response. But not for long.

'The thing is, how do I know I haven't simply dreamt you said that? Put the words in your mouth myself? I suppose what I'm really saying is, how can I ever be sure anything you say is true when the only time I see you is in my dreams? I mean, if I were to meet you – the real you, the other you, the you that's asleep now – if I were to meet you outside the dream and *then* you gave me the same answer or told me what you'd been dreaming about, well, that'd be different. I'd be able to check it against my own dreams, I'd know if it was true.'

'Would you?'

'Yes, of course I would.'

'How could you be sure you weren't dreaming that too?'

She brushed the coating of fine white sand from the backs of her legs and trotted down the gently sloping beach to the glistening, unnaturally blue water below where they lay.

'Why must you always be so intellectual about everything, so cerebral? Why can't you let yourself enjoy things as they are, without questioning them to death? Why don't you come in for a swim?'

On another occasion, when they were discussing how best to spend their dream, he said, 'I sometimes think it might be nice to do something normal for a change.'

'Normal?'

'Yes, you know, normal. We're always thinking up more and more, well, crazy things to do. I sometimes think it might be nice to stay in and watch TV together. Or go shopping, throw a dinner party, visit friends. Share our happiness with other people. All that.'

'We could do that, we could see other people. Did you mean famous people or people you know?'

'You don't understand, do you, you just don't understand. I don't mean imaginary people, I mean real people.'

'That again.'

'Yes, that again. It's important. Look, there's something else I can't figure out. If we're free to fill our dreams with anyone we like, can make them do anything we like, then why don't you simply invent me, or me you? Why do I actually need to be here? Why can't you just imagine me? What's the difference?'

Her eyes took on that pained, doleful, doe-like expression he'd already come to recognize as a sign of bruised vanity, or a posturing of such bruising. 'That's typical of you, that is. If there *were* no real difference, you wouldn't need to ask.'

He never entirely succeeded in working that one out.

'What would happen,' he asked her on yet another occasion, 'if I decided I didn't want to see you again?'

'Are you thinking of doing that?'

'No, but I'd just like to know, what would happen? I

mean, could I do that? If what you say is true, well, couldn't you turn up in my dreams anyway, regardless?'

'Like a bad penny, you mean? Yes, I suppose I could, if I wanted to. But I'd respect your decision. Look, Daniel, it's no different from any other relationship in what you call the real world. If you decided you didn't want to see your wife any more, or if I decided – well, she could still come and see you, I suppose, yes. But you could refuse to answer the door.'

'It's not the same.'

'Very well, it's not the same. I sometimes think the best thing would be simply to agree with everything you say, but I don't suppose that would satisfy you either. It seems to me I can't win.'

'It seems to me you won a long time ago.'

34

He decided finally, reluctantly, with misgiving, to unburden himself to Eidel, though some moral scruple in him, some wish to protect the guilty, prevented him from revealing Ellie's true identity. She remained for the purposes of the psychiatric session a dream-phantom with a name and face but no model in the real world; all resemblance to persons living or dead was purely coincidental.

'I can't seem to get her out of my head, it's crazy. I think about her all day and dream about her all night.'

'Does she threaten you in any way?'

'No, she excites me but – well, what does it all mean? I'm a happily married man.'

'You are?'

'OK, was, was. Was a happily married man, till these dreams started. I wondered whether she represents the sort of feminine part of my psyche, my anima, you know, and the sex symbolizes an attempt at a sort of reintegration of self. I mean the initials of Mary-Ellen spell M-E, don't they, ME?'

'Sounds to me as if you've been reading too much Jung, Daniel. I prefer not to think in such terms, I find it just muddies the issue. I think it far more likely that these erotic dreams are a symptom of some more general inadequacy in your marriage. I take it you haven't resumed sexual relations with your wife?'

Daniel laughed. 'How dull you make sex sound, Doctor Eidel. No, I haven't "resumed sexual relations" with her. I'm suffering from Lawrence's Syndrome, you know.'

'Lawrence's – ?'

'Sex in the head, Doctor Eidel. Sex in the head.'

Eidel shifted uncomfortably in his chair. 'Tell me, are you always lucid when this girl appears in your dreams?'

'Usually, yes. It's seeing her that sort of jerks me into the lucid state.'

'Then there's no problem, surely. You are master of your dream while you're lucid. If you don't want to see her again, tell her so or walk away. If you do want to, go ahead.'

'It's just that I feel so bloody guilty. I can't help feeling I'm betraying Emmy.'

'And that disturbs you?'

'Of course it disturbs me. We've been married nearly five years now and I've never once – I mean I've thought about it, naturally, but – '

'And that's all you're doing now, Daniel, thinking about it. You're not being unfaithful, it's a dream.'

'But it doesn't feel like a dream, it feels like – ' He decided to come clean; what was there to lose? One way or another this business had to be resolved. 'Look, there's something else I should tell you, Doctor Eidel. The thing is, this girl isn't someone I've just dreamt up, she's – well, I know her.'

'I see. Do you know her well?'

'No, I only met her once. She was one of the people at that meeting of Isabel Calder's I went to in London.'

'Well, there's nothing remarkable in that. You meet a girl, you find her attractive, and later you dream about her. In fact it makes more sense than your original account. Why didn't you tell me this before?'

'No, but there's more to it than that. You see, at that meeting she spoke about the possibility of applying lucid dreaming to her everyday life.'

'Yes?'

'Well don't you see? I think she's doing it deliberately. I think she has some sort of, oh I don't know, some sort of psychic power I suppose, and – '

'Oh come, Daniel. Are you telling me you're not respon-

148

sible for your dreams, that this girl is somehow projecting or insinuating herself into your dreams while you sleep at night?'

'Yes, exactly.'

'To what purpose? To corrupt you, to lure you from your wife, to try out her evil powers? Come, Daniel, you're an intelligent man – '

'Look, I can see you don't believe me but there's no need to be fucking patronizing. You think I'm crazy, don't you? Well it seems to me a perfectly reasonable explanation.'

'It seems to me, Daniel, a perfectly unreasonable explanation. It also seems to me a very convenient way of denying responsibility for your own sexuality and the evident problems you're experiencing in your marriage. You used the phrase "fucking patronizing" a moment ago. An interesting juxtaposition of terms. We've spoken before about how you regret not having children of your own, how sex is closely associated with *paternity* in your mind. And how your wife's unwillingness to bear you children has led to an unconscious resentment of her on your part. These erotic dreams are as much a symptom of this resentment as your impotency problems with your wife.'

'Impotency – ?'

'You don't seriously expect me to believe there's some supernatural agency at work here, do you, that this girl has the power to infiltrate your dreams, that you're the victim of an elaborate plot to control your mind? If we're going to work together and sort this problem out, Daniel, you really must trust in my judgement on this matter. I can appreciate it must be difficult for you to see things clearly at the moment – '

'I can see quite lucidly, thank you. I can see I'm wasting my time here for a start.'

'Is that what you think you're doing, wasting your time?'

'Yes I do.' He stood up, arms rigid, knuckles boring into the table. 'I'm sorry but I really don't think we have anything more to say to each other. Good-day, Doctor Eidel. I'll see myself out.' He'd always wanted to make a speech like that.

'Daniel, wait a minute.'

He slammed the door behind him, slammed another door shut in his life.

35

From *The Case of Gabriel Flowers*

My final meeting with Gabriel occurred on 14 December. I was immediately struck by the change that had taken place in his appearance since the last time I had seen him. He looked tired and drawn, he was scruffily dressed and unshaven, and he had what I can only describe, at the risk of sounding like a third-rate novelist, as a steely glint in his eye. He began by telling me in a highly agitated manner how he had recently been having a series of powerfully erotic dreams involving an unknown girl (only later in the session did he admit that he was slightly acquainted with the girl). When I tried to relate these dreams to the tensions he was experiencing in his marriage, and to reassure him that such unconscious fantasies were nothing to be ashamed or afraid of, he reverted to that confrontational attitude familiar to me from our previous encounters. However, whereas in the past there had always been something teasing, almost playful, about this reaction of his, I could see that this time he was in deadly earnest. He exhibited all the classic symptoms of acute paranoia, claiming that the girl was deliberately trying to infiltrate his dreams, that she was the agent of some supernatural power battling for control of his mind (in a sense, of course, he was correct, in so far as the girl embodied the menacing energies of his id, though there was nothing supernatural about this). The more I tried to calm him, the more defensive and hostile he became, apparently determined to regard me as part of the same sinister conspiracy bent on overthrowing his mind. It is plain to me now that what he was experiencing was the result of his guilt at the dream-feelings recorded in his journal, a guilt projected outwards on to some external and therefore, paradoxically, less threatening force. At the time, however, without the benefit of any detailed knowledge of those dreams, I was at a loss as to how best to proceed. I realized that, as with all paranoiacs, to deny my complicity in the conspiracy would merely serve to confirm him in his delusions, and I therefore chose to remain largely silent and listen. Unfortunately, this strategy proved hardly more successful and Gabriel stormed out of our meeting in a violent fit of rage. I never saw him again.

Naturally, I tried to contact him, but his work number always seemed to be engaged, and when I phoned him at home the following week he was out. Wishing to alert but not unduly alarm his wife, I supplied her with an edited version of recent events and urged her to ask Gabriel to call me at the earliest available opportunity. He failed to do so.

36

She went back, of course she went back, she couldn't keep away. After all, it wasn't such a terrible thing that he should want an article of her clothing, something to remember her by, like the lock of hair she gave her first boyfriend, Gerald, at school (he presented her in return with a tobacco tin containing a collection of yellowing toenail clippings, which she consigned to the dustbin the moment she got home). It was almost endearing in a way. Anyway, some people got a kick from things like that. Fetishists they were called. Well, there are worse crimes.

She caught a cab in town and went straight up to his flat as arranged, where they made love quickly and mechanically on his double bed.

Afterwards he was silent. 'Think I'll go buy some wine,' he said.

'OK, I'll take a shower.'

It was the first time she'd been alone in the flat. She wandered naked from room to room, opening cupboards, pulling drawers. It wasn't snooping exactly, she just wanted to learn a bit more about him. If he wasn't going to tell her, she'd have to find out for herself.

In the locker of his bedside cabinet she came upon a wad of airmail letters, tied with string, from Japan. Love letters, no doubt. She'd have liked to read them but there wasn't time. At the bottom of the wardrobe, under a pile of spare bedding, she unearthed a bundle of hard-core Swedish porn magazines. Some of the things they were doing there didn't bear thinking about. Animals and all. God, those Swedes!

She padded along the hall to the spare bedroom, where she recalled seeing an antique woodworm-peppered bureau. She had no idea what she expected to find. Nothing probably; it was like a game of treasure-hunt in which you weren't sure whether the person who set the clues had remembered to plant the treasure. She opened the bureau and rummaged about inside. Bills, receipts, typewritten letters, a bunch of keys, nothing of any interest. Tried the drawers. More papers, teaching materials, files. The bottom drawer was locked.

She took the bunch of keys from the pigeon-hole in the top of the bureau and tried each one in turn, but none of them fitted. Puzzled and intrigued, she hunted through the rest of the room – lifting ornaments, upturning vases, feeling blindly along ledges – careful to replace everything exactly as she'd found it. At last, in a wooden cigar-box on the top shelf of a bookcase, she located a solitary, slightly rusty, antique-looking key. She tried it in the drawer. It clicked open.

Nothing had prepared her for what her eyes encountered. The drawer was full of women's underwear: panties, thongs and G-strings mostly, some crotchless, but also suspender belts, garters, stockings, bottomless tights, peek-a-boo bras with openings for the nipples, a congeries of lingerie, sub-pornographic products of the male sexual imagination, each with its donor's name – Yuki, Katta, Denise – inscribed in precise lettering on a small white tag attached with string. She was reminded of the exhibits in a court case: Exhibit A, m'lud, the victim's panties. Near the top of the pile was her own pair of rose-embroidered briefs, tagged like all the rest, which he'd stolen from her. She lifted them up and held them to her cheek, drying the moistness brimming in the corners of her eyes. How could he! Another thought, more worrying, also occurred to her. All these contacts, all these partners – what had she been risking? Of course, after that first time she'd insisted he wear a condom, much to his displeasure. But it only took one exposure, they said. And then there had been the other things, the oral sex, the sperm he sometimes asked her to swallow. Even now that sperm might be at work inside her, attacking her immune system or whatever it was. Oh God!

She didn't want to see any more, didn't want to know any more, didn't want to think any more, but some impulse of self-torture made her continue to run her fingers through the jumble of delicate silks, nylon and lace heaped before her, all this finery, all this beauty, in the service of such ugliness. Her fingers touched on something sharp-edged and glossy.

Nervously, squeamishly, afraid of what she was about to find, she parted the lingerie and found it. A cache of dozens, maybe hundreds, of polaroid snapshots of naked girls and women, some apparently taken unobserved, others modelled in a variety of coy or obscene poses. On the back of each picture was a name – he couldn't even remember their names! – and a date, presumably the date when it was taken. Sometimes a descriptive epithet had been added for good measure: Anal Annie 8/6/83, Droopy Lena 17/10/81. She felt herself growing nauseous but was unable to turn away. How could he! she kept repeating to herself, how could he! Of course, she'd known all along he was an inveterate woman-izer, but she'd never imagined anything like this. This one – Tight Tina 27/7/84 – couldn't have been more than thirteen or fourteen. This one, she seemed to recall, had been a student at the school. This one . . . she didn't recognize herself at first, it looked so unlike how she imagined herself to be. Head to one side on the pillow, one leg drawn up, crooked at the knee, lens aimed mercilessly between her thighs. The bastard! He must have taken two photos of her that night; that was why he let her tear up the other one. She turned it over, numb with shock and rage, to confirm the date. She read: Wet Emmy 8/12/84.

She slammed the drawer shut, fighting back her tears – the bastard! the bastard! – seized with a violent fit of trembling. Stormed down the hallway and into the bedroom, stuffed the compromising photo into her handbag, trying to control her breathing as she dressed. She could feel an asthma attack coming on and rifled through her bag for her inhaler but couldn't find it, she must have left it at home. What have I done that he should treat me like this? What have I done? She thought of leaving him a note, something clever and withering – but no, he didn't deserve it! Besides, she was too angry. The bastard! Buttoning her blouse and grabbing her bag, she swung into the hall and towards the door. As she passed the hall mirror she stopped. On an impulse she took her lipstick from her bag and scrawled on the glass in sprawling red letters, 'Fuck yourself – Wet Emmy 14/12/84.' Replaced her lipstick, took out a tissue to dry her eyes and blow her nose (I must look a real mess, I can't go home looking like this!). Lifted her coat from the hook and slung it over her shoulders. Reached for the door handle.

As she touched it, it opened. He looked at her uncomprehendingly, placed his plastic Oddbins bag on the carpet by his feet, closed the door behind him.

'What is it? What's happened?'

She tried to push past him but he took hold of her arms, pinning them to her side.

'Let me go!'

'Not till you tell me what's happened.'

He was staring into her eyes. Then she saw his gaze shift, move past her, over her shoulder. There was a brief pause when nothing happened and then he hit her, slapped her full across the cheek.

'You bitch, fucking cheap little slut, snooping round my fucking things.' Hitting her, shaking her, slapping her up against the wall. She closed her eyes, trying to distance herself, telling herself, This isn't happening, I'm not here, It'll be over soon, I'll wake up, Stay Calm, Don't panic, Hold on. Suddenly he had hold of both her wrists, locking them together in a tight, painful grip, while his other hand was diving under her skirt and tearing at her panties. Oh God, no, please, no. She commanded herself to go limp. Don't fight him, it'll hurt less, Let him do it, Get it over with, Keep your eyes closed, Be brave. She could hear him muttering, 'Fuck you! Fucking bitch! Fucking whore!', his breath hot on her face. He kicked her ankles from under her and she crumpled beneath him, fell to the floor, her head twisted, squashed against the wall, the smell of paint in her nostrils, thick and acrid. Felt him fumbling at his trousers, then hard and dry between her thighs, forcing himself inside her. Think of nothing, she told herself, Imagine you're in bed asleep, Imagine it's a dream. But she couldn't. All she could think of was, He isn't wearing a condom, he's not even wearing a condom, oh God!

His release was sudden and brief and accompanied by a sort of pained, snarling yelp. A few seconds more and it was over, he left her, sticky and dripping from where he'd soiled her. Freed from his weight, she opened her mouth to take in air but instead what came out was a deep, ululating howl, expelling itself from deep within her lungs and wracking her body with a series of convulsive tremors. She wanted to move but was unable to do so, couldn't even open her eyes, paralysed by all the conflicting emotions – rage, self-pity, humiliation, shame – doing battle inside her. Why me? Why me? Why me? A door opened, admitting a blast of cold air, and she felt a foot nuzzling her in the small of the back. 'Come on, get up for Christ's sake.' The foot rolled her over once, twice – 'Get up, can't you?' – and she fell. Tumbling, turning, spreading her arms to brace herself against the unresistant air. Half-way down the staircase she came to a halt, skirt twisted round her waist, knickers round her ankles, coat and handbag following through the air in a graceful looping arc, slumping to the bottom of the stairs. 'Right fucking mess you look. Tidy yourself up before you go home.' She heard the door close above her.

It was over, then. Bruised, wheezing, sobbing, the taste of blood in her mouth, a sense of being torn inside, afraid to move for fear of ripping herself further, telling herself, It's over, He's finished, You're alive, It's all over now, He can't hurt you any more.

The door of the downstairs flat opened below her and a burly, bald-headed man emerged wearing a vest and pair of sagging trousers. He looked up at her briefly, shook his head a couple of times with a sort of weary sigh, then shut the door again. He'd seen it all before.

37

On the Saturday night, to his surprise, Daniel didn't dream of Ellie, he dreamt of Eddie.

They were together in his attic study, Daniel in his swivel-chair at the desk, Poe reclining in his shiny frock-coat on the couch, boots off, smoking a cheroot (something he hadn't known Poe went in for – perhaps he should include it in the book?). Daniel's manuscript lay heaped on the floor beside him.

'You liked it then, on the whole?'

'More than that, Daniel. It's the best book that's been written on me, the most honest, the most truthful. You've got to the very heart of me, laid my soul bare, captured my inmost essence. I was especially impressed with the way you demolished that charlatan Marie Bonaparte with her absurd psychoanalysing. Psycho anal-izing I believe you called it. Very witty, very elegant. Of course there's a few changes I'd like to see made, a few errors of fact, but, no, you've done an excellent job. My compliments. Why haven't you finished it?'

'Oh I don't know, these dreams I suppose. These other dreams, I mean, of Ellie. Can't seem to concentrate, they're taking up all my energy.'

Poe was nodding. 'Dreams,' he said. 'Tell me about them. Some of the dreams I had while I was alive, you wouldn't credit them. Shocking.' He stood up, assumed a theatrical pose, hand on hip, and began declaiming in a full-throated sonorous tenor:

Deep into the darkness peering, long I stood there, wondering,
fearing,
Doubting, dreaming dreams no mortal ever dared to dream
before.

'*The Raven,*' Daniel said. 'But what should I do about them? They're destroying my life.'

'Do? I'd have thought that was obvious. Get rid of her.' He returned to the couch, lit another cheroot. 'You've a lovely wife, Daniel, a fine, honest, God-fearing woman. Reminds me a little of my own darling Sissy. A more devoted and caring woman you couldn't wish to find. Don't risk losing her for the sake of that ... well, I won't tell you what I think of her. The love of a good woman's the most precious gift on earth, Daniel. Don't abuse it.'

'So you know Ellie then? You know who she is?'

'Know her? I immortalized her, didn't I? As if she needed immortalizing!'

'I don't follow. You mean – ?'

'Listen, Daniel. The woman you know as Ellie or Mary-Ellen, she visits all men at some point in their lives. Most fail to heed the call, which is as well for them. A few sensitive souls like us succumb. She is clever, Daniel, mightily clever. She takes different forms for different men, but always in essence the same. Always dark, always dressed in white. Shakespeare knew her well enough – she's the Dark Lady of the sonnets, as if you hadn't realized. For Keats she was the Belle Dame Sans Merci. Other men have called her the White Goddess. For me she was always Helen, my Hellenic Helen, the glory that was Greece, the grandeur that was Rome. I gave her other names in my fiction of course, but in my heart and in my dreams she was always Helen. For a time I thought I'd found her earthly incarnation in Helen Whitman – that monstrous woman! – but I was mistaken, a dupe of my own reckless passionate soul, my longing for physical requital. Be careful of her, Daniel, she doesn't like to be toyed with.'

160

'This is extraordinary,' Daniel said. 'I never realized.'

'There's much that people don't realize. My marriage to Virginia, for example, was one of the most misunderstood marriages in history.'

'You mean her being only thirteen? The Lolita syndrome?'

Poe flashed an angry look upon him. 'Don't mention that damned book to me! I was no Hubert Hubert or whatever his idiotic name is. A princedom by the sea, indeed! Why, some people take the most scandalous liberties when you're dead. No, I loved my Sissy for herself, not as a nympho, nymphet, whatever it is. You shouldn't believe everything you read, Daniel.'

'No arguing with that,' Daniel said.

They sat for a while in silence, the silence of two friends, Daniel liked to think, who can be eloquent without need of words. He offered his guest a glass of wine but the latter declined. 'I've finished with all that. Never could handle the stuff anyway.' He puffed on his cheroot. 'Apropos of your book. Maybe I can help.'

'Help – how?'

He sat up on the couch. 'I'd like to propose a bargain. Finish with this Ellie woman – once for all, mind, no half-measures! – finish with her and I'll give you your final chapter.'

Daniel bowed his head. 'I seem to remember you gave it to me once before and I let it slip away.'

Poe dusted the air with his hand in a gesture of dismissal. 'Why, you obviously weren't ready for it then. Now you're lucid, now you understand what's happening, now you have control and recall of your dreams. But I have to warn you, Daniel, this is your last chance. Fail me now and I'll be forced to find someone else for the job.'

'I won't let you down, Eddie,' Daniel said. 'You can rely on me.'

38

4.25 a.m. The saddest dream of my life. How can a dream make one so sad?

Walked to the park as usual to wait for Ellie at the bandstand. She arrives late, looking anxious; perhaps she's guessed what I'm about to tell her.

– I've something to tell you, I say.

– So do I. You go first.

– OK. Let's walk though.

Past the daffodil beds to the pond where the ducks gather to greet us, hoping for a hand-out. Ellie takes some bread from her pocket and scatters it on the surface of the water. Flurry of flapping wings. This park has become a part of us, eclipsing all former associations (picnics on summer Sundays, flying kites with the boys, warm beer and squashed sandwiches). I'll never be able to come here again, asleep or awake, without thinking of Ellie.

– I think it's time we parted, I say.

She doesn't respond, so I continue.

'I'm being torn apart, Ellie, I can't go on living like this. If this world was real – and don't object to my use of that word, we both know what it means – if it was real it might be different. But it isn't, it's a fantasy world. Every morning when I wake up alone after being with you I feel sick, physically sick, drained of all emotion, emptied of all will to enter the world outside my head. My work's suffering, my marriage is close to collapse, I'm coming apart. Unless we can be together in the real world – and that's impossible according to you, I know – well, I don't see anything for it but to stop seeing each other. It'll be hard, God knows, but what alternative is there? I have to choose the life over the dream, however imperfect that life may be, however seductive the dream. Well, that's what I wanted to tell you. Now it's your turn. But I warn you, nothing you can say will make any difference. My mind, what's left of it, is made up. What was it you wanted to say?

– I'm pregnant, she says.

How to describe the effect this simple statement has upon me, this statement that under normal circumstances would have made me the happiest man awake? A cloud of doubt and confusion descends upon me, literally, the park grows dark, swept by a chill winter wind, as if the physical surroundings of the dream are in subtle sympathy with my emotions. The dream as nineteenth-century novel.

– I don't believe it, I say. I simply don't believe it.

– Believe it or not, it's true.

– But how? When?

– In the cathedral, I suppose. That's the only time you didn't, you know, wear a condom.

– But this is a dream, you can't be pregnant. You can change it, make it go away. We can control things here, you said so yourself.

– There are some things I can't control and one of them is my body. My dream body. I thought you'd be pleased, I thought it was what you wanted. I should have guessed you'd react like this. Oh Daniel, you could be happy if you'd only let yourself. Why don't we go away together somewhere, just the two of us?

– What d'you mean? We're always going away together somewhere. That's what we do.

– No, I mean . . . somewhere else. Somewhere we'd be free.

There is a strangely solemn, bodeful tone to her voice.

– How free exactly?

– There is only one way.

– And that is?

– You know what it is, Daniel, you don't need me to tell you. Dreams don't end when life does, you must know that.

– I see. You're suggesting we enter into some kind of suicide pact, is that it?

– If that's what you want to call it. There is another world beyond this one, Daniel, I know, I've seen it, believe me.

– Please, don't start preaching to me. I didn't come here to be preached at. Look, in the first place I'm an atheist and a coward. In the second, I have responsibilities. To Emmy, to the boys –

– What about your responsibilities to me, to *our* child? 'In Dreams Begin Responsibilities.' Isn't there a poem called that?

– A story. Delmore Schwartz. Very witty, very apposite. But ridiculous. You want me to live in a dream?

– It isn't so ridiculous. Don't you live in a dream already? You get up, go to work, come home, watch TV, then you go to bed and sleep. Which is the dream, which the reality?

– Spare me the clichés, please. I'm a teacher of fiction, remember, I teach that stuff. Dream and reality, truth and illusion, fantasy and fact.

– Don't patronize me. I'm not one of your students.

– It might be different if you were.

– Meaning what?

– You know exactly what I mean. I can't throw my life away on a dream.

– But you can throw a dream away on your life, is that it?

– Look, this is getting us nowhere. I'm leaving now, I need to think this thing through. I'm going to wake myself up.

– So that's it, is it? You're just going to fuck off as if we'd never met?

The first time I've heard her swear and it shocks me.

– No, of course not. But I need some time. I'll come back to the park when I've got things clear in my mind.

– Don't expect me to wait for you. I have my own life too, you know.

164

– I'm aware of that. It's a risk I'll have to take.

– You seem willing to take any risks except the really important ones.

– Goodbye, Ellie.

I go to kiss her but she turns away.

– Take care of yourself. Who knows, perhaps it's for the best.

– Yes, who knows.

I turn and run, fighting back the tears. Out of the park, across the road, narrowly avoiding a passing motorcyclist. Into the house, upstairs to my study and into bed, burying my face in the pillow. No more of this! No more!

39

But there was more. It wasn't the end. She hadn't finished with him yet. She had other plans.

He wrote up the dream in his journal, then returned to bed and lay for a while staring at the shadowy cross cast on the far wall of his study by the full moon shining through the skylight. He was too upset, too distressed, too afraid, he didn't mind admitting it, to sleep. He felt sorry for his head. His poor head. All these dreams to contend with, these multiple lives crossing and tangling like one of those puzzles where you have to follow a thread of yarn through a snarl of loose ends. He'd lost the thread of his life, confused by all those loose ends. As if one life wasn't enough. Most people had just the one life, why should he be cursed with more?

At some point he must have dropped off again, because he found himself with Emmy in some kind of swish cocktail lounge or nightclub. Red carpets, plush velvet sofas, rotating mirrored spheres suspended from the ceiling, flashing spotlights, thudding disco music, crowded dance-floor, smell of sweat and booze, smoke like folds of blue drapery hanging in the air. Not the sort of place he normally visited. Too swank, too glitzy, too phoney, too loud. What was he doing here?

'Shall we have another drink?' Emmy was dressed in a short, low-cut, satiny dress that barely reached down to her crotch. Tits wobbling for all to see. Emerging from the hem, a set of lacy suspender straps bridged an expanse of naked thigh to clip on to a pair of black fishnet stockings. Lipstick, mascara and rouge like warpaint on her face. This was his

Emmy, his wife, the mother of his stepchildren. Modest, retiring Emmy, got up like some cheap tart from a Bangkok brothel. He wanted to wrap her in his jacket, cover all that bare flesh, shield her from all those prying X-ray eyes. This isn't how she normally is, he wanted to say, I don't know why she's dressed like this, I've never seen her like this before.

'Sure,' he said.

They made their way to the bar, sidling through the primped and preening crowds packed together in false intimacy like some flock of gaudy birds. All the bar staff, he now noticed, were topless and kitted out in leather, trousers for the men, skirts for the women, held up by thin leather braces. The barman who served them had pierced nipples, two gold rings in each. What kind of place was this? Emmy seemed fascinated by the barman's exotic taste in jewellery, couldn't keep her eyes off him. He noticed the direction of her gaze and grinned.

'Does it hurt?' she said. 'When they put them in?'

'Not really. Kind of enjoyed it actually. Why, thinking of having it done?'

She laughed. 'Oh no, don't have the guts.'

'Don't need guts. Just big nipples. Here, let's see,' he said and pushed back the front of her dress to expose both her breasts to his view. Emmy giggled again but made no attempt to stop him. 'Oh, those are lovely,' he said, perking her left nipple, tickling it, with his finger. It stiffened under his touch. 'Get three or four in there.'

'I don't think my husband would let me,' she said, gazing up provocatively at Daniel. Daniel felt like hitting her, or the barman, or both of them, slamming her in the face, tearing her away, dragging her home. But everyone around them was smiling, laughing, admiring Emmy's breasts, and he held his tongue, bit his lip, suffered in silence. He took a sip from the sweet-tasting paraffin-blue cocktail before him and turned away.

'Hello stranger,' he heard someone say.

It was Ellie, seated next to him on a barstool, a glass of

what looked like sherry in her hand. Lucidity, warm healing lucidity, washed over him like a wave. So it wasn't happening, it wasn't real. He was here again, where he always seemed to be, in a dream.

There was something odd about Ellie's appearance, he couldn't think what at first. Then he saw it was the clothes. A heavy, ankle-length tweed skirt and a ruched white blouse pinned at the throat by an ornate gold broach. He'd never seen her looking like this before, so chaste, so demure. Like a Victorian matron, like a spinster at a church tea-party or charity gala. She looked quite out of place.

'What are you doing here?' Daniel said.

'I could ask you the same question.'

'Aren't you going to introduce me?' Emmy said, returning her breasts to her dress.

I should go, Daniel thought, no good can come of this. It's a set-up. Nothing can come of this but woe. Yet something in him wanted to stay, to see what would unfold, to test the limits of Ellie's ingenuity, of his own tolerance of pain. It was only a dream, after all, he could leave whenever he wanted. Just one more damned dream.

'Ellie, this is my wife Emmy,' he said. 'Emmy, this is Ellie, my ... one of my students.' Was it really him speaking like this, delivering this formal introduction, making this show of urbanity? It was.

'Are you here on your own, Ellie?' Emmy asked.

'No, I'm with a friend. Someone you both know quite well, I believe. It's ... ah, here he is now.'

Daniel followed Ellie's gaze over the sea of bobbing heads behind them to a tall man in a blue blazer emerging from the gent's toilets and making his way towards the bar. Tod. What new trick was she about to pull?

Tod's face broke in a broad grin when he spotted Dan and Emmy. He threaded a path through the crowds towards them.

'Well well well, what brings you two here?'

'I did,' said Emmy. 'Daniel didn't want to come. He's

such an old fuddy-duddy, he thought everyone would be too young. He won't even dance with me. First disco we've been to in years and he just wants to sit at the bar the whole time.'

'You know I don't dance, Emmy. Besides, it's too crowded down there, hardly room to breathe. Tod'll dance with you, won't you, Tod?'

'Sure, love to,' Tod said, beaming. 'Come on, Emmy, let's teach those kids how to rock'n'roll.' He offered her his hand and they left, laughing, for the dance-floor.

'I thought we agreed not to see each other for a while,' Daniel said when they'd gone. 'Wasn't that what we agreed?'

'Was it?' Ellie said. 'You agreed. I didn't agree to anything. Anyway, I just popped in here for a drink with Tod before going home. Not my fault if we happen to visit the same bar. No one made you come here.'

'Oh no?' He drained his glass. 'Think I'll push off anyway. Say goodbye to Emmy and Tod for me. Nice seeing you again.' He impressed himself with the levelness of his tone, the coolness of his manner.

'OK. You'll miss all the fun though.'

'And what fun would that be?'

'Why don't you stick around and see? Never know, you might enjoy it.'

He fixed her with his eyes. 'Tell me, Ellie, why are you doing this?'

'What?'

'This. Involving other people in our dreams. People close to me. My wife, my friend. Why did you have to bring them into it?'

'Why do you have to automatically assume that I'm responsible for everything that happens in our dreams? Perhaps they came here of their own accord. Anyway, I thought it was what you wanted. It's what you said you wanted. Seeing other people, sharing our dreams with them. Isn't that what you wanted?'

'Not like this, Ellie, not like this.' He cast a glance behind him to make sure Emmy and Tod were still on the dance-floor, but the crowd was too dense, a squirming wasp's nest of colour and movement, impossible to differentiate. 'How do you know Tod, anyway? Do you know him? Is he really here? Is Emmy really here? Are they having this same dream too? Or are they pure invention? Whose invention, yours or mine?'

'Questions, always questions. Why don't you ask them? Here they come.'

'... bloody nightmare, 'scuse my French,' he heard Tod saying close behind him.

Daniel threw him a questioning look.

'Just saying, Dan,' he continued when they'd resumed their places at the bar, 'bloody murder down there, didn't think I'd make it back alive. Nearly raped three women just turning round.'

'And two of them were me,' Emmy said.

'Well, who's for another drink? Thirsty work, that dancing.'

'Here, I'll get them,' Daniel said. Why not? It was only dream money.

'Oh look,' Ellie said, 'the competition's about to start.'

Daniel turned towards the raised platform at the back of the dance-floor where the DJ or MC or compère or whoever he was – a thick-set, smarmy looking fellow in a glittery suit with slicked-back black hair and an oily smile to match – had stopped the music and stepped out from behind the disco equipment to the front of the podium. Beside him was a revolving wooden drum of the sort found on tombola stalls at fêtes and fairs. He raised his arms for silence and spoke into the mike.

'Ladies and gentlemen, a bit of hush please. Yes, it's the moment you've all been waiting for, the climax of tonight's show.' A ripple of laughter from the crowd gathered on the dance-floor below. 'God, you're a dirty lot, you are. Yes, the climax of tonight's show, the reason we all come here.' More laughter. 'Ladies and gentlemen, the Palace of Dreams is proud to present – wait for it! – Competition Time!' Cheers and clapping and foot-stomping from the crowd.

'Now, to get things underway, I need the services of someone from the audience to help me pick tonight's lucky finalists. How about you, my lovely?'

A girl in pink near the front of the stage stepped forward and was helped on to the podium by the compère.

'That's it, don't be shy. What's your name, my sweet?'

'Virginia,' the girl said.

'Virginia, eh? Not for long, I bet.' The girl blushed. 'Now, what I want you to do is to pick out one of my balls. No no no, the balls in the drum,' he said, clutching a hand to his genitals. This was really third-rate stuff, Daniel thought, before reminding himself that it was actually his own, or Ellie's, invention. 'Now, give it a good whirl and pick a ball.'

The girl span the drum feebly, then reached inside and pulled out a coloured ping-pong ball with a number on it, which she handed dutifully to the compère.

'Stay there, my darling, don't go yet. Balls always come in pairs, didn't you know that? Unless you're Hitler, of course.' More laughter from the crowd. 'And tonight's first finalist is: number one-four-seven!'

'Oh that's mine, I think,' said Ellie, rummaging in her handbag. 'Yes, here you are!' she called, waving her ticket in the air.

'The lady in white at the bar! Come on down!' the compère shouted. 'And bring your partner with you – takes two to tangle, you know.'

'Come on,' said Ellie, grabbing Tod by the hand. 'This is fun, you'll enjoy this.'

Tod turned upon them a face full of comic horror and mock panic as if to say, 'What am I letting myself in for?', then followed her meekly like a child.

'And your name is?' the compère asked when they reached the podium.

'Mary-Ellen,' she said.

'And your husband's name? Is he your husband? Well, we don't ask questions here.'

'Tod,' Tod said.

'Our first two contestants, ladies and gentlemen. Mary-Ellen and Tod. A big round of applause please.'

The crowd clapped appreciatively and edged closer to the stage.

'Now for our second couple. Another ball, my lovely.'

The girl in pink took another ball from the drum and passed it to the compère.

'And the number is: two-six-two!'

'What's our number?' Emmy said. 'Something like that, isn't it?'

'Didn't know we'd got one.'

'Yes, they gave us one when they took our coats, don't you remember? You put it in your pocket.'

Daniel delved into his jacket pocket and emerged with a crumpled cloakroom ticket folded in two. He unfolded it and looked at the number. Surprise, surprise.

'See, I told you. Here you are, bingo, house!' she called, holding her arm aloft.

'Well well well, looks like we struck lucky tonight, lads,' the compère whispered in a stagey aside. 'The lady at the bar in the red slip! Come on down!'

The crowd parted to let them through, applauding till they reached the podium. Emmy responded to the chorus of wolf whistles and bawdy comments elicited by her passage with an exaggerated swagger and wiggle of her hips.

'And your names are?'

'Emmy,' Emmy said.

'Daniel,' Daniel said, resignedly.

'Well, Emmy and Daniel, if you'll just stand on the other side of the stage over there, I'll explain what you have to do.'

He took a stopwatch and silver whistle from his jacket pocket. 'Now, tonight's game is called Suck-Sex. Yes, ladies and gentlemen, Suck-Sex is the name of the game, and nothing sucks seeds like Suck-Sex.' Hoots of laughter from the audience, mixed with a few groans. 'What happens is this. When I blow this whistle I hold in my hand' – and he raised it to the audience like a magician demonstrating his equipment – 'the game will commence. The girls will then have three minutes to blow their *partners'* whistles held in *their* hands. Girls, your aim is to bring your partner off as quickly as possible. Guys, your aim is to hold out as long as you can. As I usually say, whoever comes first comes last.' More laughter and groans. 'The girl who brings her partner off the quickest and the guy who holds out the longest will then go forward to the final in a race against the clock for tonight's star prize, a dream holiday for two in the Virgin Islands.' A theatrical ooo-oh from the audience. 'Should neither of the men come within the allotted time, or should they both come simultaneously, the game will be adjudged a draw and two new couples selected.' Self-interested cheering from certain sections of the crowd. The compère glanced across the stage rapidly in both directions. 'Teams, are you ready?' Emmy nodded vigorously, already on her knees, her lightly-clad rump exposed to the leers and lascivious grins of the upturned faces below her. Daniel managed to catch Ellie's eye briefly before she broke the contact; she seemed determined to go through with this. 'Ready?' the compère announced. 'Steady? Blow!' The whistle blew.

Daniel watched with a sense of being an observer of his own experience, of being literally elsewhere (where? In my study, on my sofa-bed asleep, he repeated to himself), as Emmy tore at his flies and fumbled for his recumbent member. 'Give her a magnifying glass, someone!' came the compère's cry. He felt nothing, certainly not sexual arousal, but not even embarrassment, anger or shame, only a sort of generalized disappointment that his dreams should have descended to this sordid, tacky level.

'You don't have to do this, Emmy, it's a dream,' he said. 'Only a dream. You don't need to do it.' But the noise around them was deafening – cheers, laughter, whistles, whooping, clapping, foot-stomping – and she appeared not to hear.

He turned to see how Ellie and Tod were getting on. Tod's

trousers and boxer shorts were already round his ankles, his surprisingly long, slightly bowed member stiff in Ellie's mouth. Absurdly, unexpectedly, despite everything he knew, Daniel felt jealous. Keep a grip, keep a grip. This is a dream, it's not happening, it's not real, he told himself yet again. But why then was his heart racing, his throat dry, his palms slick with sweat? Why did he want to rush across the stage and tear Ellie away, or worse, to take Tod's place, to supplant Tod's organ with his own? He gazed down and noticed himself hardening in Emmy's mouth.

'Please Emmy, stop it, don't, I'm sorry,' he tried to say. 'It wasn't my idea, honestly. We can go home, let's go home.' But a violent cheer suddenly erupted around them, drowning his words. He turned back to see Tod bucking and pumping into Ellie's mouth, holding her head in place as he emptied himself inside her, semen dripping in threads and gobbets from her lips.

The compère clicked his stopwatch and blew his whistle. 'We have a winner,' he shouted above the clamour. 'Mary-Ellen and Daniel, kindly join me for tonight's grand final.'

So that was her game. How obvious, how predictable; he'd somehow expected better of her than this. He replaced his penis inside his pants and zipped his flies. Ellie was still squeezing the last drops of pleasure from her victory, nuzzling Tod's dwindling organ. Daniel jumped off the stage and began elbowing his way through the crowd, scattering glasses and drinks as he went, not caring. 'He's shy, Mary-Ellen, he's shy,' he heard the compère screeching maniacally through the hail of jeers and abuse accompanying his exit from the dream. At the door he paused and turned for one final backward glance. Emmy was now standing, legs apart, in front of Tod, lifting her dress up high for him to fondle her breasts and paw at her crotch, a look of utter startlement and unhoped-for bliss on his pale, blotchy face. Daniel crashed through the door into darkness.

For a long time after he awoke he sat on the edge of the bed in his pyjamas, oblivious to the cold night air whistling through the window and door, trying to clear his head of the loathsome images it had spawned, hating this secret life of his. Once it had seemed a liberation to escape into his dreams, now it felt more like a prison. The worst kind of prison, one he had created for himself, one he carried inside his own head and could never leave behind.

In the silence he thought he heard the stairs creak, footfalls. Someone must be getting up, one of the boys perhaps. He left his room to investigate.

Emmy was hunched over the kitchen table, a cup of water undrunk before her, head in hands, sobbing. She started when he entered, began dabbing at her cheeks with the backs of her hands. As if she could disguise her feelings from him. As if she'd ever been able to disguise her feelings.

'What's the matter?' he said.

'Nothing. Bad dream, that's all.'

'Maybe it's catching.' She didn't smile. 'Want to tell me about it?'

'I can't, it's too . . . oh, I don't know. So horrible. And it seemed so real.'

'I know,' he said.

She glanced up at him uncertainly, then away again. Blew her nose on a tissue, replaced it in the sleeve of her nightdress, sniffed.

'It helps to talk about it, you know. Why don't you share it with me?'

Again that darting, bird-like glance. 'No, I'll be all right. I just need to be alone. Go back to bed.'

'Well, if you're sure.' He turned to leave. 'We should have a talk some time, Emmy. There's things we need to talk about.'

'Not now,' she said. 'Not tonight.'

'No, OK then. Well, goodnight. Try and get some sleep. It's only a dream, remember.'

'Only a dream,' she repeated. Quietly, distantly, as if already sinking back into private thoughts. 'Yes,' she said. 'Yes, goodnight.'

40

From *The Case of Gabriel Flowers*

For the conclusion to Gabriel's story, in so far as it has a conclusion, we must turn to the final entry in his dream journal, dated 16 December, two days after my last meeting with him. The reporting of the dream marks a return to the 'vignette' style of the earlier entries. As before, I have simplified the report considerably for the purposes of its presentation here:

> In the park across the road, waiting for Ellie at the bandstand. She arrives and we walk. Past the daffodil beds and the duck-pond. I tell her I have decided it is time to end our relationship. She tells me she is pregnant and wants us to go away together, to vanish into our dreams. I am tempted but resist. I run from the park, crossing the road and narrowly avoiding a passing motorcyclist, till I reach home.

The territory should by now be familiar: the vaginal or womb symbols of the bandstand and pond, and the phallic symbol of the daffodils (note also the 'bed' in which the flowers grow). The conflict, too, between guilt and desire, superego and id, has become more explicit, the two opposing camps neatly facing one another across the idealized dream landscape. The girl, embodiment of the libidinous id, tempts Gabriel with the prospect of fatherhood, appealing to his fantasies of paternity. However, in the interval between this dream and the sex-in-the-cathedral one, the superego has had time to regroup, to marshal its forces in preparation for this final confrontation. The change signalled in Gabriel by the onset of paranoia and his fear of 'mind-control' is reflected by his behaviour in the dream. Instead of succumbing to the blandishments of the girl, to her offer of paternity and unlimited sex, he resists, he flees, leaving behind him the open parkland with its phallic and vaginal symbols and crossing the road separating the park from 'home' (his wife). The id, disguised this time as a rampant motorcyclist, makes one last attempt to bar his passage to safety, but without success. The super-ego is triumphant, the id repelled, order and sanity restored; but at what cost?

PART FIVE

My days have crackled and gone up in smoke,
Have puffed and burst as sunstarts on a stream.
Yea, faileth now even dream
The dreamer . . .

Francis Thompson, *The Hound of Heaven*

41

At work on the Monday morning Daniel did what he ought to have done long ago.

'Hello, Doctor Calder? Yes, I don't know if you remember me, I came along to one of your workshops, your lucid-dream workshops, about a month ago. My name's Fowler, Daniel Fowler.'

'Ah yes, Daniel, hello. We've missed you.'

'Yes, I'm sorry I haven't been able to make it to any more meetings. I've been rather busy unfortunately.'

'I understand.'

'The thing is, I was wondering if you could help me. I'm trying to get in touch with one of the other people who was there that night. A girl by the name of Ellie or Mary-Ellen.'

'Mary-Ellen? Well, it's an unusual name but, no, I'm sorry, I don't seem to recall anyone by that name.'

'You must do. I'm sorry, it's just ... well, it's rather important, that's all.'

'I see. Do you know her last name?'

'No, I'm afraid I don't.' Stupid! Why had he never asked her that?

'Well, as I say, I don't seem to ... perhaps if you described her to me?'

'Yes, of course. Well, she was quite slim and had long, very straight black hair. I'm sure if you looked back over your notes for that night ... she was the one who talked about applying lucid dreaming to our daily lives.'

'Ah, you mean Marie.'

'Marie?'

'Yes, I believe that's what she said her name was. I'm afraid I don't know any more about her than you do. She only came to that one meeting. I seem to recall she phoned up shortly beforehand, said she'd heard about the group and was very interested in what we were doing, and could she come along? I'm afraid that's about all I can tell you. I don't take down people's particulars unless it appears they're seriously interested in attending on a regular basis.'

'I see. So you don't know her address then, or her last name?'

'I'm afraid not. Will we be seeing you again, Daniel?'

'No, sorry, busy, can't make it,' he said and hung up.

The discrepancy in names disturbed him and cast an even blacker shadow over his mind. What did it mean? Did it imply that she was, after all, merely a spectre of his unconscious as Eidel claimed, a figure plucked from the crowd and assigned a name and nature of his own invention? But in that case why 'Ellie', a name that meant nothing to him except in so far as it sounded like 'Emmy'? Or did it imply, on the contrary, that she'd lied to him about her name in order to preserve the secret of her identity, to prevent him from doing precisely what he'd tried to do, namely track her down in the real world? Or, again, perhaps Mary-Ellen or Ellie was her real name and she'd lied to Dr Calder for similar reasons. So many questions.

In search of answers he placed a notice in the small ads sections of the London *Evening Standard*, *City Limits* and *Time Out*. The notice read: 'Lucid dreamers – earn money dreaming at home. For details ring – ' followed by the university phone number and his own office extension. It was a long shot, but long shots were all he had.

42

She must keep a grip, keep things in perspective, not let them get her down. She'd had a bad experience, OK, but it wasn't the end of the world. Christmas was nearly upon them, there were the boys to think of, she mustn't let them suffer, let them see how she was feeling, must make it up to them, make it a good Christmas for them, they deserved it. Time to stop putting herself first.

Is that what she'd been doing, putting herself first? It didn't feel like that. It felt like everyone wanted a piece of her, like lions squabbling over a piece of meat, tearing her this way and that. Philip had wanted her body, the kids wanted her time and attention, Daniel wanted ... what did Daniel want? A housekeeper perhaps? A mother? A nursemaid? He was becoming unbearable. She felt herself stiffen every time he walked in the room, and always with that weary, burdened, I'm-so-troubled look about him. Did he think he was the only one in the world with problems?

Men were such animals. No, that was unfair to animals. What right did Philip have to treat her like that? She'd let him do anything and everything to her, things no one else had ever done, she'd degraded herself for him. And what did he do? Chew her up and spit her out. She ought to report him to the police, she knew – he was a menace, he should be locked up – but how could she, what would she say? At least the holidays had started, she wouldn't have to face him every day, she didn't know if she'd be able to control herself. The pig. And what would happen in the New Year? Would it be possible to carry on working at the school, forced to see him, speak to him, act as if nothing had happened? Perhaps it'd be best to look for another job, she'd get good references, there were other language schools, it wasn't the end of the world. But why should she be the one to change jobs?

Only now did she begin to feel guilty about what had happened, what she'd allowed to happen. Not on Daniel's account particularly – hadn't he driven her to it? – but on her own. She felt as if she'd betrayed herself, cheapened herself, forgotten who she was. Was sex really that important, worth losing yourself for? Such a fool I've been, like a school-girl with a crush.

That was the meaning of that horrible dream, she supposed, that disgusting performance in front of all those people, first with Daniel, then with Tod. Why Tod? He was the last person in the world she felt sexually attracted to. Perhaps it was a sort of transference – displacement, wasn't that what they called it? By turning Philip into Tod, the dream had been trying to show her how ghastly Philip really was, how misguided her choice had been, as well as how sluttishly she herself had behaved by moving from one to the other with such wanton ease.

Time and space, that was what she needed. Time on her own to re-examine her life, space to rebuild. Fat chance there was of that. All the preparations for Christmas still to do. Then Christmas Day at her mother's, pretending everything was rosy: 'How's work, dear? Sure you're not taking on too much? You do look a bit pale, I must say.' To think that a few months ago none of these problems had existed, or hadn't seemed to.

She dried her eyes on the corner of the pillow, worried with the point of her tongue the chipped incisor she'd explained to Daniel as the result of a fall on the squash court. Must get that seen to before Christmas, one more thing to add to the list. Reached across, switched off the table-lamp, drew the covers tightly around her, tried once again, hopelessly, to sleep.

43

Insomnia was a new experience for Daniel. The perils and pitfalls of sleep he was familiar with, but not the more subtle trials of sleeplessness. Falling asleep had always seemed to him the simplest and most natural thing in the world: you put your head on the pillow and closed your eyes and nature did the rest. So why was nature now refusing to co-operate, why was there only this impenetrable wall of wakefulness, this babble of voices circulating in his head, competing, debating, disputing, this jangling carousel? Of course, he knew the answer: to remain awake was not to dream, and not to dream was to be safe. Safe from what exactly, he wasn't sure. All he knew was that each time he managed to clear a space in his head, to calm the voices and lead his mind to the verge of surrender, each time he felt himself starting to slide, exhausted, down the languorous slope to forgetfulness, some alarmed instinct within him would spring to life, sounding klaxons and dragging him kicking from the vertiginous edge. Let me go, let me go, he wanted to cry and perhaps did so, I must sleep, I must sleep. But the words were just another voice swelling the colloquy in his throbbing brain, one more point of view demanding to be heard.

He tried all the conventional remedies. A hot bath and a mug of warm milk (so he was reduced to trying Glazier's advice after all!). Relaxation and visualization exercises: imagine a tiny black dot on a field of pure snow, watch the dot grow, expand, engulf you in its blackness ... A half-bottle of Scotch. He even found himself resorting to that most desperate and forlorn of expedients, sheep-counting, in a final pathetic bid for relief. But nothing helped. Still the voices chattered on. He regretted now that he'd made a point of high-mindedly throwing away the last of the sleeping pills remaining from his prescription. He didn't feel so high-minded now. If the price of deliverance was a drug, he was ready to devote himself to a life of hopeless addiction.

Then, on top of everything else, there was Christmas. All the preparations, the arrangements to be made. Not that he normally took much part in that side of things; that was Emmy's domain. Daniel would buy the tree and carry it home, he'd get some drink from the off-licence, he'd do a bit of shopping, make a cotton wool beard for his Santa costume, and then he'd expect to put his feet up for the festivities, to be fed and entertained. Well it was only fair, Emmy was home all day after all, he wasn't being unreasonable.

This year he seemed to do less than ever. Leading, as he now did, a more or less separate existence from Emmy and the boys in the seclusion of his attic study, he felt strangely detached from the day-to-day running of the house, a guest in his own home, the lodger upstairs. Besides, Christmas seemed so unimportant and unnecessary somehow. What was it all for?

As a token gesture he helped blow up a few balloons and hang some decorations while Emmy wrote out the last of their cards.

'Here, or here?'

'There, I think.'

'Sean, hold your end up higher. High as you can. It has to go all the way round.'

'I can't. My arm hurts.'

'What's the name of that chap you knew at university, still sends us a card? Lives in Bristol?'

'Stuart? Stuart and Sandra? Sean, it has to go higher than that.'

'What's their address?'

'I can't, I told you.'

'Don't remember, got it written down somewhere. Liam, don't touch that please.'

'But I want to help.'

'Would you sort it out for me? I want to post these today.'

'Liam, leave that alone. Sean's doing it, not you.'

'Liam, get off. Mummy, he's –'

'Look, if you're not careful the whole thing'll –'

'Mummy!'

'Liam!'

'Look out!'

'There!'

'This is hopeless,' Daniel said. 'Bloody hopeless. Why does it always have to end up like this?'

'Calm down, for Christ's sake,' Emmy said. 'We don't need that one up anyway, there's plenty of others. Look, go and sit down. I'll do the rest tomorrow.'

So he went.

These were the sorts of things that came back to him at night, lying tight-eyed on his sofa-bed trying not to think, trying not to try too hard to sleep. Snatches of conversation, echoes of phrases, his own and other people's, all mingled and mangled together, a confused, rowdy din. No wonder his head felt so heavy, with so many voices to support.

44

It came as something of a relief, after nights and evenings like these, to reach the sanctuary of his office each morning. Teaching had finished the week before, so the demands on his time and thought were minimal. True, he had a mountain of paperwork to get through before the official end of term on the Friday – late essays to mark, student reports to write, book lists to compile, a class test to set – but that could wait. For the moment he was free to sit looking out on to the corner of paved garden and single bare cherry tree visible from his ground-floor window. And this was mostly what he did.

On the Wednesday afternoon he went shopping for a present for Emmy. He wanted to buy her something symbolic, emblematic, something that would encapsulate his feelings for her and sum up his hopes for the future. Not in a trashy, sentimental way, not a heart-shaped ring or album of love-songs or anything of that sort, but something that would have meaning for the two of them alone as part of a shared code, a private alphabet of experience. He thought back to that day on Margate Beach in the summer of 1980 when he proposed to her, or she to him, he wasn't sure which. He'd been about to go in for a swim, and had given her his watch to look after. For some reason, instead of simply handing it to her, he strapped it to her wrist. As he snapped the clasp shut he said, half-playfully, 'With this watch I thee wed.' 'Do you?' she said. 'Do you mean it?' 'Yes,' he said. They were married a month later.

Back in his office, he sat down at his desk and carefully

unwrapped his purchase. It was more than he'd intended to pay, but he didn't regret it. It was a delicate, elegant piece of workmanship with a natural symbolism all its own: twenty-one jewels (because she was his jewel), shockproof and water-proof (because their love was proof against anything), gold (because that's how precious she was to him). He set the hands to the correct time and polished the crystal with his sleeve before returning it to its blue velvet case and placing it, lid open, on top of his chaotic desk. If one sat very still and concentrated hard, one could just make out the tiny tremor of its mechanical heart beating out the seconds. He sat and listened to the passage of time.

Yes, he was pleased with his gift. Love-token and peace-offering combined, it said the right things. What it said was, Remember Margate Beach 1980, how I pledged my love to you with a watch, now I pledge it a second time. It said, Forget the past, let's reset the clock, start again at year zero. It said, Time is ticking away, why not put aside our differences, get on with the business of making a life together now? It said, We have plenty of time, this is just a passing phase, things will be better in the future, I promise. It was a useful, ambiguous kind of symbol.

He looked up to find Tod gazing quizzically at him from across the room. How long he'd been standing there he had no idea. Perhaps he'd knocked and Daniel hadn't heard him.

'Counting the hours, eh, Dan? You and me too. Still, only two days left. God, what a mess,' he said, casting a disbelieving eye over Daniel's groaning desk.

'Oh, soon clear that lot up.'

'Rather you than me.' He picked his way delicately through the minefield of books and papers littering the floor. 'Nice watch. Who's it for?'

'Emmy. Think she'll like it?'

'Don't ask me, I'm hopeless at all that. I'm sure she will. What've you got for the boys?'

'Not sure. Think Emmy's taking care of that.'

Tod walked to the window and stood with his hands in

his pockets, gazing out. 'Must be fun at Christmas, with the boys I mean. Watching them unwrap their presents, helping them with their Meccano sets and Airfix kits and all that.'

'Don't think kids play with Meccano sets any more, Tod. All computerized now. Things that go wrong and have to be taken back to the shop. Things that don't come with batteries or need a transformer. Things that break on Boxing Day. Take my advice, you're well off out of it.'

'Maybe you're right.' It was the usual kind of idle inconsequential chat that passed for conversation between them. They talked about their plans for the holiday.

'... Christmas dinner at Emmy's mother's, I suppose, but that's about all. Why don't you come over on Boxing Day if you're not doing anything? Emmy always enjoys seeing you and the boys like it when you're there, they know they can get away with murder. You can help mend a few toys.'

Tod laughed. It was the last time the two men ever laughed together.

'Well, I'll let you get back to work. Reckon you'll need all the time you've got. Roll on Friday, eh?' he called as he left.

'Need all the time I've got, yes,' Daniel said, turning back to gaze on the face and hands of Time. But already he was no longer there.

45

Daniel's notice first appeared in late editions of the Wednesday *Evening Standard*. The response was better than he'd expected: between nine-thirty and twelve on the Thursday morning he took some fifteen or twenty calls. The majority of these, it must be said, were clearly from cranks and bluffers who had no idea what lucid dreaming was but merely sniffed the scent of easy money. If the caller was a man, he informed him that there had obviously been a mistake in the printing of the number, the number he had dialled was that of the university and please not to bother him further, he was in the middle of a class. If it was a woman, he explained how he represented a major research foundation who were interested in exploring the 'healing and humanitarian' possibilities of lucid dreaming. When they went on, as they invariably did, to ask for clarification of what this meant exactly, he told them he was not at liberty to discuss the question over the phone but if they would leave their name and address he would arrange for them to be sent full details free of charge. In this way he elicited the names and addresses of some half-dozen callers, none of whom, however, bore the name Mary-Ellen or Ellie or Marie. One of the inquiries, he was not altogether surprised to find, was from Isabel Calder, whose obvious frustration at the cageyness of his telephone manner – 'Look here, I'm one of the chief authorities on lucid dreaming this side of the Atlantic, I really think …' – Daniel interpreted as a kind of territorial display. Hands Off, it said, No Trespassing, Poachers Shot.

Later that afternoon Daniel's head of department, Harry

Thorncote, popped his head round the door and inquired in that over-genial tone he reserved for matters of a particularly grave nature whether he had time for a 'little chat'. Daniel traipsed grudgingly into Thorncote's office, cursing the fellow and thinking it would be typical if the call he was waiting for were to arrive at the very moment he was no longer manning the phone.

'Yes, what is it?' he demanded abruptly.

'Sit down, Daniel, sit down. Like a cigar?'

'No, I'm rather busy at the moment, can't this wait?'

'Actually, Daniel, it can't.' Thorncote lit one of the obnoxious panatellas whose odour gave the department a permanent stale-party smell, and blew a leisurely plume of blue smoke high into the air. 'Are you happy in the department, Daniel?'

Why did he have to pussyfoot around like this, why not get straight to the point? 'I suppose so. In so far as life admits the possibility of happiness in general.'

'Oh dear, that sounds rather depressing.'

'Look, Harry, I've got a pile of papers on my desk this high and only one more day to get through them. I don't want them spoiling my Christmas. Would you please get to the point?'

'Very well, since you express yourself so bluntly, I will. The switchboard informs me you've been receiving a large number of private phone calls today. Are you running some kind of business?'

'I'd prefer not to talk about it if you don't mind. It's a personal matter.'

'Oh but I do mind. The university is not the place to deal with such matters, that's what homes are for, surely I don't need to remind you of that. Of course I've nothing against you using the phone for the odd private call now and then, that's quite acceptable, but this is clearly rather more than that. I don't know what you're up to, Daniel – I confess I listened in on one of your calls and couldn't make head or tail of it. Frankly, I don't care. All I'm saying is that it has to stop at once. Otherwise I'll be forced to give some serious consideration to your position and future in the department.'

'I see. Is that what this is about then – spending too much time on the phone?'

'It's not just the phone calls, Daniel. It's this on top of everything else. I've received a number of reports from students complaining that your teaching this term has been, well, let's say not all it might have been.' He coughed apologetically, or perhaps it was the smoke. 'You've forgotten to set essays, you've failed to mark or return those you did receive, your lectures have been short and by all accounts rather, well, shall we say rather difficult to follow, you've missed just about every departmental seminar – shall I go on?'

'No, that'll do. Can I go now?'

'For heaven's sake, Daniel, why must you always be so aggressive? I understand you've been suffering from certain emotional or psychological problems lately?'

'Who told you that?' Finkel the fink!

'I don't wish to name names, you know the university grapevine. Have you considered putting in for a sabbatical, you must be due for one about now? It'd give you a chance to finish your book on Poe and the break might do you good.'

'Don't need a break, thanks.'

'There are those who think otherwise.' Daniel let this pass. 'How's the book coming along, by the way?'

'It isn't.'

'I see. What about the MLA conference in Washington, are you still planning to attend? I notice you haven't put in a claim for your travel expenses yet. I thought you were giving a paper?'

'No, not bothering. Can't think of anything to say.'

'It seems to me, Daniel, you're being deliberately provocative. I'm afraid if your attitude doesn't improve you may force me to consider some more drastic action.'

'Consider what you want. Can I go now?'

Thorncote returned him a gaze full of silent admonishment and pity, the gaze a headmaster turns on a once-promising but now wayward pupil. Daniel stared him down and left.

46

He hadn't been in his office long the following morning, after another wide-eyed, wakeful night chasing the receding tail of his own fatigue, when the call he'd been hoping for arrived.

'Oh hello, good morning. I'm phoning to inquire about the advert regarding lucid dreaming.'

He recognized the voice at once, or seemed to: the bright, confident, businesslike tone, the clipped vowels, the suggestion of an acquired mask of refinement overlaying a more common accent beneath. He launched into his spiel about the healing and humanitarian possibilities of lucid dreaming. 'If you'll just give me your name and address I'll arrange for our material to be sent to you.'

'Well, I don't know. Couldn't you tell me a bit more about what's actually involved?'

'I'm afraid, as I've said, that's not possible. All I can tell you is that the Everly Foundation is a highly reputable organization and a registered charity. I can also assure you there's no question of your being asked to part with any money. It's all explained in detail in the information package you'll receive. However, if you'd prefer not to be considered – '

'Well, I suppose it's all right. Yes, OK then.'

He breathed a silent sigh of relief. 'Good. The name?'

'It's Albin. Mrs M. Albin.'

'Could you spell that for me?'

She spelt it.

'And the address?'

'Yes, it's 121 ... Farringdon Way ... Hornchurch ... Havering ... Essex.'

'Thank you.' Scribbling the information on the back of a library recall slip, jabbing the pen to a triumphant full stop. 'You'll be hearing from us soon, Mrs Albin.'

Ten minutes later he was in a taxi on his way to the West Station, leaving behind him, for the last time, his desk buried beneath unmarked essays and unanswered letters, unwritten reports and unread memos, books, files, paperwork. One of the books, a volume of essays by Ralph Ellison, bore on its back cover a clear imprint of the name and address he'd jotted down.

He'd been counting on the 9.36 London train being late as usual, but for once it must have arrived on time and he missed it by a couple of minutes. It was an hour till the next one and starting to rain, thick heavy dabs of wetness like someone spitting from above. He went to the station buffet for a coffee. Probably he should eat something – he couldn't remember the last proper meal he'd had – but he seemed able to survive these days on air alone. It was funny: no food, no sleep, yet he felt driven by a sort of pure manic energy. This thing had to be seen through to the end. Then he would eat, then he would sleep.

Sipping his weak grainy coffee in the barbarous plastic surroundings of the buffet, he let his mind roam over the various scenarios that might be about to open up before him. One possibility, of course, was that he'd made a mistake, the woman on the phone might not have been Ellie at all but someone else entirely. He could have been wrong about the voice, and M. was a common enough initial (Mary, Martha, Maureen, Meg, Marilyn, Margaret, Marjorie, Millie). But such an idea was scarcely worth contemplating and he banished it from his mind at once. Another scenario rose mistily before him: perhaps she'd intended him to track her down like this, to play the knight errant to her trembling ice queen (his metaphors were becoming as mangled as his moods), perhaps it had all been part of the plan, a test of his

195

resoluteness, his ardour. Perhaps when she saw him there on her doorstep, realized the lengths he'd gone to to seek her out, perhaps she'd fall at his feet and declare her undying love in a fit of grateful tears, beg him to leave his wife and come live with her, give her the child she so desperately craved. Was that likely? Well, frankly, no. But then, was anything that had happened to him in the last few months likely, could it have been predicted in advance? Life itself, after all, wasn't likely, when one came to think about it, but a series of more or less improbable coincidences, a succession of one-in-a-million chances. Predictability was a fiction in some clumping statistician's brain. Contingency was all, randomness, chaos, the stumbling collision of blind atoms throwing up the occasional illusion of design.

A crackly nasal whine from the public address system informed him of the imminent arrival of his train, and he left the buffet for the platform. The engine trundled down the track towards him like some lumbering, malevolent giant. How easy it would be to throw oneself under, a matter of seconds and it could all be over. But then none of his questions would be answered, or perhaps they all would be.

He settled into a window-seat with his back to the engine and gazed out at the grimy, rain-spotted platform. A baggy-uniformed BR employee tramped the length of the train, slamming doors as he went. He signalled to the guard. A whistle blew. How many times had this routine been performed before, by different men, in different stations? The familiar rituals with which we regulate the world, struggle to keep chaos at bay. But the world didn't run according to railway timetables – not even imprecise BR timetables – and life wasn't a train running on well-worn tracks but a striking-out into the dark unknown, the tangled wilderness of human possibility. All these analogies, he must stop it. Neither was life a text to be read and criticized, with symbols and motifs and objective correlatives. Life was simply life. Period.

At the last moment, as the train was about to pull away, a denim-clad figure strapped to an oversize orange backpack came lolloping through the ticket barrier, threw open the door of Daniel's carriage and hauled himself, breathless, aboard. With a sinking heart Daniel recognized the youth as one of his students, a north-country lad by the name of Rick or Dick or Nick who thought D. H. Lawrence the greatest writer in the English language.

'Hello there, Doctor Fowler,' he said in his coarse lumpish accent (the title was one with which his students frequently honoured him – he saw no reason to disabuse them, diminishing himself in their eyes). 'Nearly didn't make it. Mind if I sit down?'

Daniel listlessly waved his consent as Rick heaved himself free of his backpack and wrestled it strenuously on to the facing seat, sinking down beside it with an effortful groan and wiping the sweat from his brow with the frayed cuff of his denim sleeve.

'Off to London are you, Doctor Fowler?'

'Mm,' Daniel murmured. 'You?'

'Back to Harrogate. See some real people for a change. Northern people.' He showed Daniel a mouthful of the sort of strong white teeth that real people possessed.

'Christmas shopping is it?' Dick inquired. 'In London?'

'What? Oh yes, something like that,' Daniel muttered.

After about ten minutes of awkward, stumbling conversation, to which he contributed little more than a series of curt monosyllables, Daniel decided he'd had enough.

'Excuse me, back in a minute,' he said and headed towards the toilet. He continued on through a number of intervening carriages till he reached the rear of the train, where the only available seat was opposite a large, harassed-looking woman trying unsuccessfully to bottle-feed a bawling and thrashing infant. He sidled on to the badly-sprung seat across from her, trying not to alarm the child further by his arrival, and turned his attention as best he could to the blurred, rain-sodden landscape sliding by with a susurrant swish outside.

At Ashford the overweight Madonna and Child left the

train and were replaced by a couple of pensioners cheerfully discussing their health.

'I don't worry about it any more,' the woman said. 'No point, is there? I mean you can get knocked down crossing the road, can't you?'

'Course you can,' the man said. 'Or you can slip over on the ice, break your bloody neck.'

'That's right,' the woman said. 'Or you can trip up on the kerb, fall into the road and get run over by a lorry.'

'Course you can,' the man said, 'Course you can.'

They got off at the next stop and to Daniel's relief nobody filled their seats. He allowed himself the luxury of closing his eyes. The clatter of the rails beneath him set up a rhythm in his brain – course-you-can, they said, course-you-can course-you-can – and for a while he drifted in and out of something resembling sleep, dozing, waking, dozing again. At one point he had the impression he was on a train to London while opposite him a denim-clad Poe shook his head wearily and berated him in a comic northern accent for the folly of his ways. 'By gum, lad, you disappoint me, you really do – blooming wild goose chase – you Southerners are all alike, no character – blooming nancy boys, every man jack of you – real man wouldn't go chasing after a bit of tail like that – chasing your own tail, that's what tha's doing, lad.' Daniel tried to explain that he had no choice in the matter, it was a loose end he had to tie up, a plot he had to resolve, a story, a tale, he had to complete before he could get on with the rest of his life. Besides, wasn't Poe himself a Southerner and hadn't he also chased after – ? But Poe continued to shake his head grimly and sigh, staring stolidly at the floor.

Daniel left the train at Waterloo East – an ominous sign, it struck him: was this to be the scene of his own Waterloo? Ahead of him he caught a glimpse of a stumping Nick, hunched beneath the burden of his backpack like some unfortunate natural impediment he'd been saddled with at birth and was forced to drag with him everywhere, disappearing into a coffee shop. He descended into the Tube and took a train to the Embankment to get on to the District line heading east. Everywhere signs of the approach of Christmas were at hand: people laden down with bags of shopping and bulky, gift-wrapped packages tucked uncomfortably under their arms; groups of office workers, ties askew, joking and laughing too loudly, already the worse for drink; a silver-haired man in overalls fixing a broken escalator with an oily spanner, whistling a tuneless 'White Christmas'. Everyone seemed either unusually genial or unusually morose.

Daniel's own mood was one of vague apprehension. What would he find at No. 121 Farringdon Way? Would he be granted an answer to his questions? What were his questions anyway? As he drew closer to his destination, he found himself preparing a mental script, in fact several mental scripts, of what he proposed to say. 'Look, I have no wish to interfere in your real life, I don't want to complicate things, all I'm asking for is confirmation that, that . . .' No, no. How about: 'I have one question – answer me that and I'll leave you alone'? No, again, no. It all sounded so stilted and false. How was he supposed to think straight, how make himself sound like a reasonable human being, when he hadn't slept properly in four days?

By following the instructions of the surprisingly helpful ticket-clerk at Hornchurch station, he found his way shortly after one o'clock to a small terraced house in a nondescript part of town close to a busy industrial estate. A street like any other. Dogshit on the pavement, small untidy gardens, overgrown privet hedges speckled with dust. He paused briefly outside the gate. It struck him as wildly inappropriate, yet somehow oddly fitting, that he should be about to come face to face with his dreams in this most ordinary, extra ordinary, of environments. Telling himself he'd know what to say when he said it, he walked up the short uneven path to the front door, breathed in deeply and rang the bell. No answer. Rang it again, keeping his finger pressed on the button. Still no answer. Damn! He stepped over the low wire fence into the weed-choked garden alongside and peered in through the window. An empty coffee cup on a table, newspaper spread open beside it. A fat black cat curled asleep on a chair. Shading his hands against the light, he further made out a looping string of Christmas cards tacked above the mantelpiece, a few balloons and decorations pinned to the wall, an undressed tree shedding needles on to the carpet. What did all this tell him? Nothing. It told him it was Christmas.

He walked disconsolately away. Wandered to the end of the road and stood for some minutes on the corner, stamping his feet and clutching the collar of his hopelessly inadequate raincoat against the bitter, swirling wind, trying not to look as if he was loitering without intent. A light snow was beginning to fall, blown in gusts so it seemed to be snowing upwards. Every few seconds the net curtains in the window of the house behind him would part and a scowling, hag-like face briefly occupy the cracked, grimy pane. To escape this unwanted attention and find some refuge from the shivering wind, he returned along the street in the direction he'd come from till he reached a small, unsanitary-looking baker's doubling as a café. He ordered a cup of strong coffee and took a seat at a window table from where he was just able, by squinting hard, to keep the house-front of No. 121 in view.

The street was almost devoid of activity. Daniel sat for a long time and watched nothing happen. Snow fell, the street clothed itself in a shawl of white. An alb for Mrs Albin.

He was on his third cup of coffee when a familiar figure passed in front of the window, startling him out of his torpor. She parked the buggy she pushed, containing a child of indeterminate age and sex heavily swaddled against the cold, and entered the shop. Dressed in a silk headscarf and duffel coat and without her mask of make-up to lend a false flush to her cheeks, she had a rather dowdy, used-up look about her. So this was the life she wished to conceal from him: a housewife and (single?) mother in some shabby nowhere town, spinning out her days in a round of routine errands and tedious household chores. Hard-up no doubt, frustrated, lonely, bored. No wonder she sought to escape in her dreams. She approached the counter, ordered two cream buns from the slovenly assistant with cold-sore lips, engaged in a brief exchange about the weather, and promptly left. Not once did she glance in his direction.

He allowed her ten minutes to get in and unpack her shopping and child, then walked back to her door. He rang the bell again and took a deep breath again. This time there could be no mistake.

'Yes?' She was wearing a loose-fitting smock and an expression of weary indifference, hair tied back in a rubber-banded ponytail, pair of soapy rubber gloves dripping in her hand. A cat could be heard mewing importunately down the hall.

He stood for some moments without speaking to see what her reaction would be.

'I'm sorry, can I help you?'

'You don't recognize me?'

'No. Should I?'

'Maybe. We've met.'

'Really,' she said without interest. 'I'm afraid I don't ... weren't you at that meeting of Isabel Calder's a while back?'

Daniel smiled. 'It's a good act. How long can you keep it up?'

'Look, I'm sorry, I don't know what you want but I haven't got time to stand out here in the cold being spoken to in riddles. If you ...' Her eyes narrowed suddenly. 'Are you anything to do with the Everly Foundation? If so, I told the man on the phone that ... It was you, wasn't it? You were the one I – '

'Forget the Everly Foundation, it doesn't exist. I just want some sign that you know who I am and what's been going on. Give me a sign, Ellie. A sign, that's all. A word, a nod. Then I'll leave you alone, if that's what you want, you'll never see me again. I don't want to interfere in your life, not if you don't want me to. But I must know the truth.'

'Really, this is quite ridiculous. In the first place my name's not Ellie, it's Marie, you've clearly got the wrong person. Furthermore, if you don't leave immediately I'll phone the police. You have no right to go around harassing people like this.'

That was rich, coming from her. 'And you have no right to go around entering people's dreams, destroying people's lives.'

'I don't believe this,' she said. 'Are you crazy or what?'

'Are you pregnant?' he replied. 'If you're pregnant, I'm not crazy.'

'Oh I've had enough of this. Piss off, you creep!' She tried to close the door on him but he had his foot in it.

'Just tell me, are you pregnant? Then I'll leave.'

'Look, go away!' she cried, pressing herself against the door and scouring the deserted street beyond with a look of mounting panic on her face.

'I'll take that to mean yes. Especially in view of the smock. Next question: are you married?'

'Yes, I am,' she said, seizing on the opportunity. 'And my husband's just popped out for a minute. He'll be back any second, so if you don't want a bloody nose I suggest you leave this instant.' She pressed her full weight against the door. A child began to cry close by. 'It's all right, darling,' she called behind her. 'Stay there. Mummy's just coming, it's all right.'

'OK, I'm going,' Daniel said, softening, and took his foot from the step. He laughed bitterly. 'Bye, Ellie, have a nice life, it was fun while it lasted. We shared a dream, didn't we? Pity we couldn't share a life. Perhaps life is harder to share than dreams, perhaps you're not capable of sharing your life, only your dreams, perhaps one day you'll discover they aren't the same.' But all this was addressed to a mute, still shuddering door.

47

He was still grieving over his parting from Ellie-Marie when he turned his key in the lock and returned to the only refuge he had left. Two things struck him at once: the unnatural quiet and the battered, leather-strapped suitcase standing in the hall. So she was leaving him, he thought with a kind of dispassionate interest. Well, who could blame her after the way he'd treated her recently? A wonder she hadn't done it before. On the other hand – clutching at straws – perhaps if he explained to her exactly what had happened, told her everything, who Ellie was, how he'd finished with her, would never see her again, by day or by night, how *she* was the only one he loved, would ever love, how life without her would be unbearable, unthinkable, well, perhaps there was still hope. He walked through to the kitchen. Emmy was standing at the sink, puffing nervously on a cigarette, something he hadn't seen her do in years. A look of understanding passed between them and he knew there was no hope.

'Where are the boys?'

'I took them to my mother's. I thought you might make a scene.'

'I see. You're going away then. Is there room at your mother's for all of you?'

She snorted. 'I'm not going anywhere. You're the one who's leaving.'

He rested his head against the door-jamb, giving her words time to filter through to his consciousness, to arrange themselves into a sense he could comprehend. So: he was being booted out, banished from his own home. Could she do that? Well, it made no difference. Either way it was all over. He considered making a scene, since she expected him to, but decided against it. What was the point?

'Is it too late to say I'm sorry?'

'Yes, Daniel, it's too late for that.'

'Emmy – '

'Don't say anything, please. I just want you to listen while I explain what's happened and why I'm doing this. Then I'd like you to take your case and leave, spend Christmas somewhere else. I've packed everything you'll need – I put the notes for your book in there as well, I know how protective you are about it. You can tell me if there's anything I've forgotten and pick it up tomorrow.'

He slumped into a chair. 'Go ahead.'

She took a series of rapid puffs from her cigarette, exhaled a thick cloud of choking blue smoke, coughed, and began.

'I had two phone calls this morning. First I got a call from Harry Thorncote, he thought you'd be here as you weren't at work. He asked me to tell you that your classes for next term have been reassigned and would you phone him or go and see him for a chat when you get the chance. He asked me if everything was all right, as if he knew some reason why it shouldn't be. That started me thinking. Then Doctor Eidel rang. He wanted to know how you were. He asked me if I knew you'd walked out during your appointment with him last week, abandoned the treatment, he said. He was hoping you'd change your mind and go back and see him this morning, but you didn't. He didn't say a lot but he implied there was more going on than I understood. Well, of course, I was curious. And worried. And angry that you'd given up the treatment. I then did something you'll probably think is unforgivable. I went to your study and looked for your dream journal. I found it. And I read it.'

'You read it.'

'Daniel, how could you say those things? I'd forgotten how it felt to really want someone. If you were real I'd leave my wife tomorrow. However unsatisfactory that life may be.

Shall I go on? Well if life with me is so unsatisfactory I think it's best you leave today. I know you have a lot of problems at the moment but I really don't think I can help you with them any more, I think you'll deal with them better on your own. Perhaps you'll regard this as hitting you when you're down, I don't know. But I have a life too, I need support too. I just don't think we're good for each other any more. Somewhere along the way we grew apart, without realizing it. It's just not working, is it? I don't feel I understand you any more, I can't reach you any more. All that sex in your dream book. Where do I fit into all this, where do I figure in your dreams? You don't need me any more, Daniel. Perhaps you think you do, but you don't. And I'm not sure I need you. That sounds hard, I know, but the truth sometimes is hard. Excuse the cliché – I know you don't like them.' She doused her cigarette under the tap. 'Well, that's all I wanted to say.'

He felt the silence between them like a solid, mineral presence, a wall built up over years of misunderstanding that words alone were powerless to surmount.

'I have to say I think you're over-reacting, Emmy. I mean for God's sake these are dreams. Dreams. Are you the same person in your dreams? Don't you sometimes do things, say things – ?'

'It's not just the dreams, is it, Daniel? It's everything else, everything I've been talking about.' She lit another cigarette. 'I'm sorry, but I don't think I can live in the same house with you any more. Not the way things are at the moment. I'm being stifled. By *your* problems, *your* needs, always *your* needs. I don't feel I can talk to you any more. I'm frightened in case I say something wrong, upset you in some way. And you never talk to me these days, not properly. Or the boys. It's as if any attention you pay us is a special favour, a privilege you grant us out of a grudging sense of duty. What happened to sharing, what happened to togetherness? The boys are different people when they're with you, they become – '

'OK, OK, you've made your point. Guilty as charged. So that's it then, is it? We shake hands and say goodbye forever?'

'Don't make it harder for me, please. I never wanted this to happen, I didn't plan it this way. And of course it's not goodbye forever. I can't say how I'll feel in the future when I've had time to think things through. But I know how I feel right how. I need time, time to be alone, time to – oh I don't know, time to find myself, I suppose, corny as I know that must sound.'

'You could have waited till after Christmas. You could have found yourself in the New Year.'

'I could have done, yes. And what sort of a Christmas do you think it would have been, with me carrying all this around with me and not saying anything? You don't even know what presents I've got for the boys, do you, you've been so wrapped up in yourself?' Even at this moment of humiliation and despair he couldn't help noticing the unintended pun.

He decided on one last gamble, one final change of tactics. 'You think I like the way I feel at the moment, the way I've been these last few months? You think I enjoy feeling like this?' It was meant to sound like anger but came out as self-pity.

'I'm sorry, Daniel, I'm not prepared to discuss it any more.' She stubbed out her cigarette on a plate as if squashing a life.

A prickly silence descended again.

'There is one other question I'd like to ask, if I may.'

She turned her cold blue gaze on him across the table. 'Well?'

'Well I'm not sure how to say this but, is there someone else? I mean – '

That derisive snort again, that tiny explosion of contempt. 'That's typical of you, that is, typical of a man. You can't comprehend that I should want to leave you for my own reasons, you assume there must be another man involved.'

'I don't assume anything, I'm just asking.'

206

'Hah!'

'You haven't answered my question. Is there anyone else?'

She looked away, through the window to the untidy garden with its knee-length grass and broken swing dangling from a tree. 'No, Daniel, there's no one. There's just me.'

'Promise?'

'For God's sake! Promise!'

'OK, OK.' He got to his feet and turned towards the door. So that was it, his marriage over, just like that. Blink and you missed it. He felt the need to say something further in his own defence before leaving, to put in a plea for extenuating circumstances, diminished responsibility, insanity, but found himself saying something quite different instead. 'I understand your reasons, Emmy. I can even admire them in a crazy sort of way. And I just want you to know that . . . well, I still love you. Corny as I know that must sound. Despite everything I've done, written, dreamt. Perhaps one day you'll let me explain what I've been going through, perhaps . . .' But here his words dried up. 'Well, say goodbye to the boys for me. I hope you'll let me see them sometime.'

'Of course. Any time, you know that. Where will you go?'

'Oh, don't worry about me, Tod'll put me up, I suppose. Or I'll find a room somewhere, don't worry about me.' He rested his hand on the doorknob. 'Well, bye then, Emmy. Have a nice Christmas.' It struck him that he'd never get a chance now to give her the watch he'd bought for her. Time had run out, beaten him to it.

'Goodbye, Daniel.'

It all seemed so amiable and polite and lacking in feeling somehow, like closing a business deal. Was this how marriages ended?

He clicked the final door shut behind him.

48

At the traffic lights by the End of the Road he came, appropriately, to a halt. There seemed no good reason for taking or not taking any one of the three roads that stretched unbeckoningly before him. The only road that was barred was the one he had come from. No going back. But apparently no going on either. He walked up to the kerbside railings and stopped. Planted his suitcase on the ground at his feet. Gripped the bars of the rusty iron railings in two tight fists and squeezed. Hard. The bars bit into his flesh like teeth, paint flaking under his frozen fingers. Squeeze harder.

He felt the slow, heavy welling of an enormous self-pity threatening to burst over him and knew he must not succumb. Don't think! Don't think! But thought was all there was.

So this is what it's come to, he thought. Immobility, paralysis, stasis. The end-game of his love-match. He felt no bitterness, only regret that it wasn't otherwise, that life had not lived up to his dreams, that his dreams had not lived up to his dreams, that the world was more pain than pleasure, that happiness was not the norm but a lucky chance-in-a-million accident, a bright secret shared by a fortunate few. Or was it just *his* life, *his* world, that was so blighted? Perhaps certain individuals were singled out at birth and the woes of humanity distributed among them, heaped upon them, so the majority could lead their comfortable lives secure in the knowledge that others, at least, suffered worse than they. Perhaps I'm a martyr, he thought, a human black hole whose function it is to gather to myself all the miseries of the world, to suck up all the dust and debris of interpersonal space, leaving the air fit to breathe. An emotional vacuum-cleaner.

He made a mental list of all he'd lost. His wife, his family, his home. His job, his career, his prospects. His love, his hopes, his dreams. His self-respect, dignity, pride. Should he go on? How much can one person lose and still manage to survive? There comes a point when what you've lost is greater than what you're left with, when what remains isn't worth hanging on to. We think we have so much, we never imagine it can all be snatched away, so easily, so quickly, like a bone from a toothless, slack-jawed old dog.

It started to snow. White confetti from the dark heavens as if in ironic celebration of his marriage to misery. He half-emerged from his reverie and gazed forlornly about him. Look at all these people, in groups or couples or alone, out shopping, driving home. Home! Home! They all had somewhere to go to, all had a home. Only he, he alone among the crowd, had no direction or meaning to his life. Only he had no home. Take this fat man with the pipe in his mouth in the Range Rover coming towards him, he looked happy enough, content with his lot, why couldn't I be him? Or this guy on the motorbike with his girlfriend riding pillion, arms strapped tight to his chest as if not even death should prise them apart. Or take this fellow in the car behind, the one with – but as the car approached across the lights, the face behind the wheel grew for a moment eerily distinct. The two men's eyes briefly locked in recognition before the motorist turned abruptly away, crouching hunchbacked over the wheel, receding into the gloom. Daniel watched with the sense of a long-shrouded mystery finally being unveiled as Tod Finkel's red hatchback sped away down the road towards Daniel's former home.

Red hatchback, Emmy. Emmy, red hatchback. Tod.

So now he was a cuckold as well. The final indignity: cuckolded by his best friend. How apt, how Chaucerian, how wonderfully fucking Chaucerian! Hadn't taken her long to summon him over, had it? You can come round now, Tod,

I've kicked him out, the coast's clear, we can be together at last. His mind fled back over the events of the past few weeks, making sense of what till now had needed no explanation. All those nights at the health club, those visits to the cinema, that mysterious dark hatchback dropping her at the lights. No, Daniel, of course there's no one else. Bitch! Liar! Whore! That elaborate charade of telling him how awkward and boring she thought Tod was, how unattractive to women. And what of Tod? Claiming he'd 'bumped into' Emmy in the supermarket and how worried she was about him. And that invitation he'd wangled for himself for Boxing Day. And the babysitting. Anything to steal a few precious minutes together. God, what a fool they'd made of him. How they must be laughing! Images of love-making – no, fucking! Let's not mince words – flashed across his mental screen, fragmentary and plotless, like a montage of every blue movie he'd ever seen or imagined. How could they do this to him? How long had it been going on? Weeks, months, years? Had no one given a thought to how *he* might feel? Had no one thought to say, Hey, wait a minute, won't Daniel be terribly hurt if we go ahead with this? So much for marriage. So much for friendship. So much for loyalty. So much for fucking everything. It wouldn't have been so bad if she'd been swept off her feet by some young dickhead in a Porsche – that at least would have been understandable. But Tod! Dull, boring, sexless Tod! God, she must have been desperate. Or perhaps she did it to spite me, he thought, to wound me, to insult me. The memory of his nightmare at the Palace of Dreams swept back unwilled before him. Was that the meaning of that whole ghastly episode, was that why Ellie painted him that picture of a sluttish Emmy and lecherous Tod, to alert him to what was going on between them? Tod! Tod! The name continued to resound in his brain, as if repetition might diminish the shock.

A juggernaut shuddered past, inches from where he stood, spraying him with slush. He looked about him. It was snowing more heavily now, thick wet flakes falling in clumps, sparkling in the iridescent shimmer of the traffic lights. The pavements, the rooftops, the cars, the railings, his suitcase, raincoat, shoes, hands, everything was coating itself in a greasy grey–white film. He picked up his case and propelled himself forward. Walk! Move! It doesn't matter where. Just walk, you bastard, walk!

49

Did he recognize me? Don't think so. God, he looked terrible, as if he hadn't slept for a week, like an old dosser. Thought it was a dosser at first. Those eyes. What am I doing, why didn't I stop? She said she wanted me to help look for him, didn't she, find him and bring him back? Well, there he is. So why didn't I stop?

But he continued to drive. After all, he could always go back and pick him up after he'd seen Emmy. She sounded so distressed, he'd never heard her sounding so distressed before. She needed him as much now, perhaps more, than Daniel did.

He re-ran the phone call in his mind, wanting to get things straight before he saw her, to know what was expected of him. What had she said exactly? That she and Daniel had had a row, that she'd thrown him out, that she wondered whether he'd called because, if not, well, she was afraid he might do something silly, and would Tod help her look for him in the car, she couldn't let him wander the streets like that in the snow. So she wanted him back because she was scared of what he might do, out of pity and a sense of guilt, for no other reason. Of course, it would be tragic if she and Daniel were to split up – though, from what he could see, it had been on the cards for a long time, think of the way he treated her at that dinner party a couple of months back. But what was remarkable, what was – he couldn't help forming the word in his mind – exciting, was that he, Tod, should have been the first person she thought to call on in her hour of need. I must be careful not to read too much into it, he told himself, I must be careful, but still he was excited.

He parked his car a short way round the corner and sat for a moment composing himself. Leant towards the rear-view mirror and ran a comb through his lank shiny hair (pity he hadn't had time to wash it – would she notice?). Brushed a few spots of dandruff – or was it snow? Hard to tell – from the shoulder of his brown acrylic overcoat, flushed his mouth with two puffs of breath freshener, restarted the engine and puttered up to the house.

'Oh Tod, thank God you're here, I thought you were never going to come,' she said as she opened the door.

She burst into tears and he took her quickly in his arms, kicking the door shut behind them.

'There there, Emmy, come on, don't cry, tell me all about it.'

'Can't we just get in the car?' she asked between sobs.

'We're not going anywhere till you've told me exactly what's happened. Come on now, let's go and sit down.'

He led her into the lounge and sat her on the sofa. Removed his coat and shook it free of snow, a tiny shower of glittering silver scales trembling to the floor. Folded it neatly and draped it over the back of an armchair. Sat down beside her. 'Now, dry your eyes and tell me what happened, it can't be as bad as all that.'

'I blew up,' she said. 'I've been under a lot of pressure lately and I just blew up, packed his case, told him to leave.'

'What, just like that? Out of the blue?'

'Oh does it matter? What does it matter? Can't we just go and look for him?'

'I'm only trying to help, Emmy,' he said, somewhat miffed at the aggressive attitude she seemed to be adopting. 'And I can't help unless I know what's happened.'

She blew her nose noisily on the large linen handkerchief he'd produced for her and tucked it up her sleeve. 'I know, I'm sorry, I suppose you're right.'

'Well then?'

'Oh, it was a small thing, a trivial thing. You remember I told you he'd been having these, well, this recurring dream? Well I know I shouldn't have done it, but I found the diary where he wrote down all his dreams and I read it.' She looked away. 'It was full of . . . of sex. With another woman. The dirtiest, filthiest sort of sex you could imagine.'

'Poor Emmy,' he said.

'Well I know it's not his fault what he dreams about, but it just sort of brought it home to me that, well, how far apart we've grown, how little I seem to mean to him these days.'

'I can't say I'm surprised. You and him falling out like this.'

'You're not?'

'No, I thought it had been on the cards for a long time as a matter of fact.'

'Well anyway, then I regretted what I'd done. I mean it's nearly Christmas, what's he going to do all by himself over Christmas? I'm afraid he'll, you know, do something silly, he's been under such a lot of pressure recently, what with these dreams and work and everything. So that's when I phoned you. I thought, if he'd called or if he was there, may- be I could speak to him, tell him I was sorry, was willing to have another try, and if not, well, you could drive me into town, we could have a look for him.'

He thought of the ravaged, wild-eyed figure he'd seen standing at the side of the road in the snow with his cardboard suitcase at his feet, like some Orwellian down-and-out. No, no, it wasn't cardboard, that was overdoing it. 'How long ago did this happen, Emmy?'

'Oh I don't know. An hour maybe, I don't know.'

'Well, he's probably booked into a room somewhere by now. He's hardly likely to stay out long on a night like this, it's bitter outside.'

'Well that's why I wanted –'

'Listen, I'll tell you what we'll do. Leave it for tonight. It'll give you both a chance to cool off a bit, you'll see things more clearly in the morning. Then, if you still want me to,

I'll drive you round town tomorrow and we can check out all the hotels and guest houses to see if he's booked in somewhere. How does that sound?'

'Well, I don't know.'

'Yes you do. Look, you stay there and I'll make you a nice cup of tea, How about that?'

'I don't want any tea.'

'Come on. You'll feel better for it.'

In the kitchen he again thought of Daniel, out there on the street in the snow, those mad, blazing eyes. Surely he wouldn't still be there. Besides, it was dark, they'd never find him now. Or was it, he wondered, simply that he didn't want to forgo this moment of intimacy with Emmy, to jeopardize whatever it might lead to? What might it lead to?

'Where are the boys?' he called through the open door, spooning tea into the pot.

'At my mother's,' a shaky voice returned. 'She's bringing them back tomorrow.'

Was it wrong, Tod asked himself, to feel happy in the face of others' misfortunes? Because that was how he felt right now: happy. Here he was, alone with Emmy in her house, making tea for her, comforting her, consoling her, offering her his support. And he could make her happy too, if only she'd let him.

'Here,' he said, returning with two mugs of dishwater-brown tea and placing one on the arm of the sofa beside her. 'I found a drop of Scotch in the kitchen and put a little nip in yours. It'll do you good.'

She smiled weakly.

'I just wish I knew what had gone wrong,' she said, as if continuing her thoughts aloud. 'We used to be happy together, not delirious but, you know, contented. But these last few months ... well, we haven't even been sleeping together as a matter of fact.'

Tod blushed and sipped his tea. He hadn't expected her to be this forthright.

'Then, oh, about a month ago, well, I met someone else,

215

someone at work. It didn't mean anything, it was just a stupid childish fling, and Daniel never knew about it, I'm pretty sure of that. I just felt I'd been starved of affection for so long, I wanted someone to be nice to me, to appreciate me.'

He couldn't believe what he was hearing. Here she was, telling him she'd been unfaithful before, she wanted affection and love. What was she saying?

She began sobbing again quietly and he put his arm round her shoulder, drew her towards him, stroked her hair. 'It's all right Emmy, don't cry please, everything's all right now, I'm here, shh.' Hesitantly he reached down and wiped a tear from her cheek with his finger. 'You know, it's funny, talking about dreams, I dreamt about you the other night.'

'Did you?' she said, still gulping back short, choking sobs. 'Yes, I – I dreamt about you too.'

His heart lifted, took flight, soared. Oh my darling! He buried his face in her fragrant, luxuriant hair, began pecking at her crown in a series of light, swooping kisses. It seemed to him she offered no resistance. Emboldened, intoxicated by the subtle perfume that enveloped him, he lowered his head and sought out her lips.

'No!' she screamed. Pushed him away, jerked violently back, sending her mug of tea sloshing and clattering to the floor. 'Get out! Get out of here! Out of my house!'

'Emmy, please, I'm sorry, I can explain, it won't happen again, I promise, I thought it was what you wanted, I'm sorry, I'm sorry.'

'Get out! Out! Out!' Ranting, hysterically, pummelling his chest with her tiny, bunched fists.

He grabbed his coat and fled.

50

For what seemed like weeks but could only have been hours he wandered the streets of the town centre, suitcase in hand, in a daze. Jostled by late-night shoppers, mocked by festive display. Tinsel and fairy lights and plastic nativity scenes made in Taiwan. Glutinous carols and every pap singer's Christmas jingle dripping from endless shop doorways: God wrest ye married gentlemen, No-el No-el, Fuck the world. Muttering to himself, one of the outcast now, friend of the friendless, at home among the homeless, trying unconvincingly to convince himself like some latter-day Candide that all was for the best in this bastard impossible world. Who could say, maybe his present trials would prove a secret blessing, a necessary sacrifice whose true redemptive meaning would only become apparent with time, a crucifixion from which he would eventually rise, reborn and transformed into ... but here his imagination failed him. Try as he might, he could conceive of no possible theodicy, no system of deferred rewards on heaven or earth that would justify so much as a single splinter of the crosses he had had to bear. Christ, what a fairy tale! Christmas, kiss my ass!

The snow continued to fall, soundlessly, inexorably, drawing a curtain over the world, softening its edges, masking its blackness. It piled itself on walls, heaped itself in corners, lodged itself in crevices and cracks, cancelling differences, homogenizing the landscape. He found himself in the cathedral precincts. It would have been tempting to go inside for a while, if only to escape the cold, but there was nothing for him there, that avenue had been closed long ago.

He continued on, round and round, up and down, on a pilgrimage to nowhere.

Shivering, footsore, soaked to the skin, he came to rest on the steps of a small hotel on the outskirts of town called, of all things, Paradise House. Booked a room under the name of Mr Fowlup. Collapsed fully-clothed, sopping raincoat and all, on the bed. Took out a handkerchief to blow his nose and crumpled, convulsed, beneath a wave of wet grief.

Emmy – Ellie – Emmy – Ellie – Emmy – Ellie. All gone. His life snuffed out like a candle. For thirty-two years he had worked at building a life for himself, like a ladder, adding rungs as he went. A job, a wife, children, a home. But the wood was rotten, it couldn't support his weight, and in a single day all his labour had collapsed, sending him hurtling back to earth.

Alive to the dangers of solitude, he left his spartan room (bed, sink, wardrobe, cabinet, tassle-fringed table-lamp) and stumbled in and out of a number of pubs in search of forgetfulness. Attracted some good-humoured attention in a smog-choked den near the East Station when he fell off his bar stool and was unable to get up. Continued on. Bumped into a group of students, who greeted him with embarrassed smiles and much rapid exchanging of glances. Continued on. Bought a bottle of Scotch and twenty Bensons at closing time in a pub called the Jolly Something-or-Other where he found himself in an argument with a man at the bar over a packet of crisps which had or had not been paid for by him or someone else. Continued on. Nearly got run down in Northgate when he lurched off the pavement into the middle of the road and the path of a furiously cursing motorcyclist. Returned to his room and applied himself in earnest to the task of anaesthetizing his brain, his pain. Make it all go away, make me a child again. I want to be rocked on my mother's knee, not all at sea where strange things happen. Take me back to Ole Virginny where the deer and the anteloplay. Meaningless jingle bells, jingle bells, jangling in his brain.

Lying there half-unconscious on his lumpy, sagging bed in the grip of a drunken delirium, he felt the darkness pressing in on him and congealing into familiar shapes. Presences blossomed from clumps of shadow, faces bred in corners, as if he was on his deathbed and the past was gathering to bid him farewell. Everyone he knew seemed to be there and everyone was somehow his family: Uncle Leonard, Auntie Isabel, Cousin Ellie, Brother Tod. Emmy was there with Sean and Liam. His mother and father were there too, though his father's face was all chewed up so he couldn't see what he looked like, yet still he knew it was him. He thought the walls would burst, so many people seemed packed in the confined space of his room. He could hear them all talking about him, but he couldn't answer. Not long to go now, someone said, it's nearly over. Poor sod, he's suffered. Perhaps it's for the best, he couldn't go on like this. Should we call a priest, d'you think? No, he wouldn't want that. Just so long as he knows we're all here and we care. I think he knows, don't you? Hard to say. Voices, voices, humming and buzzing, circling and spinning, merging and meshing and melding and mingling, wrapping him round in words. And he tried to tell them it was all all right, everything was all right, he wasn't afraid of dying, he welcomed it, let him go peacefully, don't try to detain him, he was a stranger here anyway, he didn't belong, he was going home, to a better world, a friendlier world, because anywhere was better than here. But he couldn't get the words out, they refused to pass his lips, or perhaps they were just drowned by all the other voices. And when he did finally manage to whisper the single word, 'Okay' – shh, he's trying to speak, someone said, he wants to tell us something; no, he's just delirious, another said – when he finally succeeded in packing all the meaning and wisdom he'd achieved into those simple, all-encapsulating two syllables, well, it must have come out wrong because, Bouquet, someone said, he wants a bouquet, go and pick some flowers, and he sank back on the bed with the effort and futility of it all, and a hand reached up across his face – don't bother, it's too late, it's all over now – and drew itself down like a veil over his eyes, curtaining the light.

Some time later – cigarette in one hand, bottle in the other, waste-paper basket strategically placed by the side of the bed to collect the contents of his stomach, which experience had taught him would rise during the night – he must have fallen into a deeper and more settled sleep because he found himself back at his old school. It was deserted now, everyone gone home, everything locked up. At the edge of his consciousness, dull but insistent like a throbbing toothache, was the knowledge that he had to get out, he had an appointment somewhere, in a park, he didn't know who with or why. He tried the main door but it was locked. Tried the windows but they too were firmly bolted shut – curiously enough, from the outside. He wandered off in search of another exit, but all the doors led inwards, to other rooms with other doors leading further inwards still. He appeared to be trapped in some kind of diabolical maze, cleverly constructed to conduct the innocent traveller to its inescapable heart. At length, exhausted and disoriented, he came upon an open door with a flight of stone steps leading down into darkness. Perhaps it would take him to the kitchens, the cellar, the boiler-room. Perhaps there would be a ventilation shaft big enough for him to crawl through or some other passage to the outside world. Perhaps escape was still possible. He followed the steps down in a winding, spiralling descent, groping his way in the blackness, slipping on the damp stone, clawing invisible cobwebs from his face, till the walls grew dank and chill, the atmosphere thick with the odour of confinement and decay. Something brushed against his leg, squealed and slid past. Was that dripping water he could hear or was it the sound of his own perspiration breaking on his skin, his blood drumming in his ears? Surely the kitchens couldn't be this far down? At last he rounded a corner and found his way blocked by yet another door. He felt for the handle and turned it, dismayed as to what he should do if it proved to be locked. But with a click it opened, blinding him with a sudden burst of light. He entered a small, brightly illuminated room, quite empty except for a gas cooker standing, incongruously, in the middle of the floor. Perhaps these were the kitchens after all. He walked round the cooker, trying to fathom its purpose. What was it doing here, what did it mean? He opened the oven door and looked inside. Nothing. Empty, cold and gleaming, as if it had never been lit. Then he saw its meaning. So this was the escape that had been prepared for him, this was his way out. It wasn't the one he'd expected. But why not, after all? Was there not an aptness to such an end? Was he not also an exile, a wanderer, a Jew of sorts? He lowered himself to his knees and pressed and turned the knob marked 'oven'. Bowed his head and placed it inside. Began breathing in deeply, counting, deeply.

Foup! A jet of blue flames burst into sudden life at the back of the oven, almost singeing his hair. He withdrew with a start, banging his head and cursing the instrument of this, his final, humiliation: a self-lighting oven.

For some moments he remained on his knees, red-faced in the oven's jaws, unwilling to admit defeat. The heat was quite intense now and appeared to be growing, sending beads of fresh perspiration rushing to the surface of his skin, but still he didn't move. He began to cough and felt a sharp, searing pain in his lungs as he struggled for breath. He crawled away but the heat seemed to follow him, reaching out to engulf him from behind. Another fit of coughing overtook him, and in what was almost literally a last-gasp effort to clear his lungs he let out a suffocating bellow and awoke.

The room was in flames around him, reds and yellows and violets and blues dancing through a lurid swirl of smoke. For a second he lay without moving, thinking himself still in the dream, fascinated by the play of colours and forms. Then the pain in his lungs dealt him another sharp reminder and, as a window smashed and the sudden inrush of air whipped the blaze to an even more spectacular frenzy, he scrambled across the rumpled bed and groped his way blindly towards the door. At first he thought he'd never reach it, so far away did it seem, and perhaps he wouldn't have done so had the room been less economically furnished. But some instinctual force appeared to be guiding his movements. And dodging the burning drapes, now stretched like pennants in the fanning wind, and raising his arms to protect his head from the fragments of incandescent fabric raining down from above, he beat a stumbling path to safety.

Outside the alarm had already been raised and the other guests were being evacuated from their rooms by a young and panicky desk-clerk. In the general confusion no one seemed to notice Daniel as he emerged, blackened and spluttering, on the landing. Still coughing and wiping his soot-streaked eyes, he followed the rush of shadowy figures down the stairs and into the street.

By the time the fire brigade arrived, splitting the night with their bright red scream, the blaze had taken a firm hold. Standing watching it among the huddle of guests and onlookers that had gathered outside, some in dressing gowns, others with topcoats draped over their pyjamas, he wondered why he hadn't allowed himself to die, to end his life here in this small provincial hotel, registered under an assumed name, the chance victim of a pointless death. Was it not curious and remarkable that, with nothing to live for any more, he should have fought so hard to survive? Did it not imply that the nightmare of his life, for all its frazzled horror, remained in some sense worth living, was preferable at least to the dreamless sleep of death?

He gazed about him at the red and silver machines, the falling masonry, the scurrying helmeted men, the descending curtain of snow, the writhing snake-like hosepipes, the festive orange glow turning night into day. He looked down. He was missing something: his suitcase with his box-file inside, the manuscript of his book. He remembered his recent dream of Poe, and for a moment was tempted to rush back inside the burning building in a mad bid to recover what had doubtless already been consumed. 'Eddie!' he appeared to cry (or it may have been 'Emmy' or 'Ellie', there was some kind of obstruction in his throat), and burst into sudden tears.

A church clock struck from the direction of St Dunstan's. Mechanically, he bared his wrist and glanced at his watch, its glass aflame with lambent reflections, as the digits announced the new hour. 24:00. The symbolism was so crude as to be almost a mockery. The eleventh hour had come and gone, and he had failed to heed the warning, failed to avert the disaster. Time had come full circle. A sudden thought occurred to him as he pressed the tiny silver button on the side of the watch that summoned the digital calendar with its new configuration of ciphers. Yes, 12.22 – 22 December, the winter solstice, the day the sun stood still. He turned his back on the noise and the people and the leaping exultant flames, and set his face to the frozen night. The darkest day had yet to begin, then, the soul's dark night had not been reached. But afterwards would come – surely there had to be! How could one survive otherwise? – a new dawn, a new spring. He turned up his collar against the icy fingers caressing his throat and offered himself to the darkness.

Postscript

For over four years nothing was heard of Daniel. No letters, no phone calls, not even a Christmas card or birthday card to the children. To all intents and purposes he simply vanished into thin air. Life went on without him.

Emmy took a new job at a language school in Broadstairs, and at the end of the statutory two years obtained a divorce from Daniel on the grounds of desertion. At her new workplace she struck up a friendship with the Director of Studies, a divorced man fifteen years older than herself, which eventually blossomed into romance. They were married in the spring of 1988. To my surprise I received an invitation to the wedding. I had seen little of Emmy over the previous four years, and always as it were by accident. It was a source of considerable satisfaction to me to be invited to resume our friendship, albeit with a certain unavoidable coolness between us. I myself had remained unmarried and continued to teach at the university, where I was appointed head of department in 1987 following the sudden death of Harry Thorncote from a heart attack while attending a conference in Spain. In August 1988 Emmy Grant, to accord her her new married name, gave birth to a baby daughter, called Lucy.

Early in 1989 a letter arrived at the Grant household in Broadstairs, addressed to Emily Fowler and forwarded from the house in Canterbury which she'd sold a year before. The letter was postmarked Glasgow but bore no sender's address. This is what it said:

Dear Emmy,

It's taken me four years to write this letter. In my head I've written it a thousand times and now that I finally come to put my thoughts on paper I find it almost impossible to separate them from the echoes of all those unwritten letters, composed in despair or self-pity or tenderness or regret. I'll try to write plainly and clearly. What I want to say is very simple and at the same time almost beyond my powers of expression.

I want to explain why I acted as I did, why I vanished so suddenly, without even a proper goodbye, and why I've kept silent for so long. This was not an angry or resentful silence, Emmy. Whatever you may think of me, I never intended to cause you pain. I was silent because only in silence did I believe myself, do I still believe myself, to be safe.

I've understood, and failed to understand, many things over these last few years. One of the things I've understood is that only by living in complete isolation and anonymity can I guarantee the integrity of my dream-life and with it my sanity. I don't know why this should be so. Sometimes I wonder whether I wasn't perhaps the subject of some bizarre, elaborate experiment – in thought-control, dream-control, call it what you like – whether I wasn't set up, whether Glazier and Eidel and Calder and that woman whose true name I never discovered (you know who I mean), whether they weren't all in on it from the start. Who knows what sort of research in psychological warfare may be going on behind our backs? Think of the possibilities from a political point of view if the minds of individuals could be entered while they slept, ideas implanted, suggestions sown, intentions undermined. Maybe Orwell wasn't so far from the truth with his thought police. What if world leaders could be driven mad or suicidal through an assault on their dreams? This sounds crazy, I know, even to me. Yet sometimes I think it's the only explanation

that makes any sense. How else account for all that happened to me? How else account for the fact that the
moment I arrived here, the moment I escaped the clutches
of doctors and psychiatrists and dream-therapists, my
dreams instantly lost all trace of menace, returned to
what I can only call normal. You can't understand,
Emmy, no one can understand, the sense of freedom
and release that goes with an untroubled dream-life. I
barely even recall my dreams these days, they vanish
like the mist that lifts from the slopes of the three
broad-backed hills that greet me each morning when I
rise.

I lead a simple life here (don't ask me where, I can't tell
you). My needs are few and easily satisifed. I live on a diet
of seafood and gulls' eggs, with potatoes and turnips from
the vegetable garden I've planted and, if I'm lucky, the
odd rabbit or trout (imagine me as a trapper and
fisherman!). Fresh water is plentiful. For fuel I burn peat
that I dig from the bogs. I sleep in an abandoned
shepherd's hut, on a bed of dried bracken that's as soft as
any mattress. I never dreamt (hah!) that my life would
come to this, but it's not such a bad life, all things
considered. My own little Walden, New Walden. Reading
all that stuff came in handy after all.

I've strayed from my point. Four years is a long time,
Emmy. I don't know if this letter will find you. Perhaps
you've sold up, moved away, started afresh with someone
else (I still have trouble imagining you and him together –
yes, I know about him – but that's your business, I have
no wish to drag up the past). Perhaps you'd prefer not to
be reminded of your life with me, perhaps it seems like a
bad dream to you now. Was I a bad dream in your life?
I don't know how you feel about me any more. But if you
have any affection left for me at all, then I ask you, please,
not to think too badly of me, to know that I wish you only
good things in life, and to be happy for me, Emmy, be
happy for me, because I've found a kind of peace at last.

229

I hope you have too. Kiss the boys for me. May all their dreams be sweet ones.

Love,
Daniel

PS I leave it to you to decide whether or not to tell the boys about this letter. But I beg you, please, not to show it to anyone else. However much you may doubt it, I assure you that my sanity, maybe even my life, is at stake here.

A few days after receiving this rather mystifying communication, Emmy paid me a visit at which she apprised me of its contents. In fact she allowed me to read the entire letter. She did so, she said, in the full knowledge that she was acting against Daniel's wishes as expressed in his postscript. However, it was obvious to her that, whatever he might claim to the contrary, he was clearly not happy or at peace, and was in fact in dire need of help (take that crackpot theory about thought-control, for example – did that not prove how confused he was?). She wished me to see the letter, she said, in the hope that I might be able to offer some suggestion as to his likely whereabouts. Unfortunately, I had to disappoint her. While I agreed that the letter did not seem the product of a happy and healthy mind, I was unable to hazard any guess as to the precise location of the area it described. Clearly it sounded like Scotland – the Glasgow postmark suggested the west coast or one of the Hebridean islands – but that was about as much as I could say.

Neither of us, incidentally, chose to say anything about the accusation of infidelity contained in Daniel's letter. Emmy, I imagine, must have assumed that it referred to the short-lived affair she told me about on the night of Daniel's disappearance. I of course had reason to believe otherwise, but like him I had no wish to 'drag up the past'.

Something about Daniel's letter continued to niggle at me, however, like an itch or a toothache that wouldn't go away. It was his reference to the abandoned shepherd's hut where he said he lived. I had the distinct sense that I'd encountered that shepherd's hut before, though I couldn't for the life of me think where. Then, a week or so later, in the middle of the night, I suddenly woke and remembered. I rushed to my study and took down Bernard Crick's biography of Orwell and there, in the chapter headed 'Jura days', I found what I was looking for. In a letter to Sonia Brownell written from Jura, Orwell makes mention of 'the completely uninhabited bays on the west side of the island, where ... [a]t one of them ... there is a shepherd's hut which is disused but quite livable where one could even picnic for a day or two.' Later in the chapter I was reminded of how Orwell once had a near-fatal accident while returning from a trip to this hut. I also recalled – how could it have slipped my mind! – a conversation I had with Daniel in 1984, following a TV programme about Orwell and Jura, in which he remarked on how he'd always been fascinated by that period of Orwell's life. It wasn't until I'd returned to bed and was lying awake pondering the chances of my hunch being correct, that it struck me as at all ironic that the connection between Daniel's and Orwell's letters should have occurred to me while I slept.

The following morning in the university library I garnered what information I could – which wasn't, to be honest, a great deal – about the island of Jura. The picture I built up certainly seemed to fit with the brief account of his surroundings Daniel gave in his letter. But, then, countless other areas of Scotland would no doubt also have fitted the bill. There probably existed any number of disused shepherd's huts scattered throughout the islands and coastal regions of that under-populated land, and who was to say that Daniel's hut and Orwell's were the same? Of course, there was the aside about Orwell's thought police in the letter. But it was only when I came across a reference (in a book called *The Islands and Highlands of Scotland*) to the so-called 'three paps of Jura' – a group of hills rising to a height of around 2500 feet in the southern part of the island – and recalled Daniel's own reference to the three hills he could see from his hut, that I felt the bounds of coincidence had been reached. I phoned Emmy at once, and later that day took her an ordnance survey map of Jura that I bought in town and on which I marked the likely and approximate location, on the south-west coast, of Daniel's dwelling.

Emmy set off, alone, for Jura in the first week of April 1989, entrusting baby Lucy to the care of her husband. A few days later she returned with a man I would have had difficulty recognizing, had I not known who it was. The change that had taken place in Daniel during the four years since I'd last seen him was dramatic and depressing. Emaciated and stoop-shouldered with a pronounced limp and gnarled, sun-weathered hands, he looked to have aged fifteen or twenty years rather than four. What little hair remained on his head had turned grey, supplemented by a grizzled, unkempt beard. A sickly pallor extended over his features, giving his sunken cheeks and mottled, sallow skin the appearance of someone in the final stages of tuberculosis. A dry, hacking cough and festering sore on his lower lip completed the sorry picture.

As Emmy and I had agreed prior to her departure, I offered to provide Daniel with lodgings till he was well enough to look for accommodation of his own, an offer he accepted with frank indifference, as if he was the one doing me the favour. There followed a period of nearly four months during which we shared the same home – in principle at least, for in practice we scarcely shared anything more substantial than air. Indeed, we might almost have been inhabiting different planets. Daniel led a virtually anchoritic existence, eating in his room and rarely venturing outdoors. How he spent his time – whether he read or watched the portable TV I'd supplied him with or, as I suspect, merely sat and brooded on his problems – I have no idea. On the few occasions we spent time together, we spoke only of casual, superficial matters, avoiding the past by common consent, and this despite the fact that I quickly disabused him of his mistaken notion that Emmy and I had ever conducted an *affaire*. I felt I was living with a total stranger, an empty husk of a man, someone trying to impersonate, not very successfully, the friend I once used to know. This was brought home to me with special force one morning when Emmy paid us a visit and, thinking it might do Daniel good, inquired whether he'd like to see Sean and Liam – now bustling young lads approaching teenage years – to which he replied matter-of-factly, 'I don't think so.' His physical condition, at least, showed signs of improvement, even though he staunchly refused to see a doctor: he began putting on weight, his limp no longer seemed to inconvenience him, a trace of colour even returned to his cheeks. But as for the inner man, well that was an entirely different matter.

On Friday 11 August 1989 I returned as usual from my weekly shopping trip to Sainsbury's at around 6 p.m. and knocked gently on Daniel's door to see if he'd like a cup of tea. Receiving no answer, I assumed he was asleep or did not wish to be disturbed, and returned downstairs. Knocking again around 8 p.m. and again receiving no response, I tried the door. It was unlocked. Inside, the drawers to his dresser hung open and empty. On the table was a note, scrawled in an erratic hand. It read simply, 'Please let me go.'

It has not been easy writing this account of Daniel's life. Many times I have been tempted to abandon it altogether, conscious of the pain I might be causing Emmy and her family and unsure of the benefits to be gained from opening old wounds. But something within me compelled me to continue, as if only by opening and cleaning those wounds could the infection finally be removed and the injuries given a chance to heal. As if only by resurrecting the past could it finally be laid to rest. I felt I owed a debt of friendship to Daniel, or to his memory.

And have I succeeded, have I made amends, have I brought Daniel back to life again, if only in the imagination or memory? I don't know, how could I? I have tried to give him a voice, to take his part in the tragic dream-play that was his life, to see things as he might have seen them, as I've tried also to take Emmy's part, and Eidel's, and my own. Whether I've succeeded is not for me to say. Only one person is qualified to be the judge of that, and he is not here to offer his verdict.

At least, not in the flesh. The other night I dreamt of Daniel. I returned home and found him sitting where I sit now, at this desk in this silent, too big house, with these pages open before him. Is it OK? I said. Is it fair, is it accurate, is it faithful to your experience of events? But he didn't answer, didn't speak, just stared back at me from hollow black orbits, vacant and sightless as the night. And in that hollow stare I received an answer of sorts. He didn't know, any more than I did, what was true and what was not. There was no truth, he seemed to say, there was only this cavernous absence, this blind vision, this blank page, where the truth ought to have been.